Destiny Drop

Book 1

The Diana Diaries Series

Other Books by Cindi R. Maciolek

Destiny Dollars – Book 2: The Diana Diaries Series

Divatiel: Reflections of a bird's companion

How to Screw Up a Good Idea

Tame Those Pesky Details

Java Jems: 5 Minute Inspirations for Busy People

Destiny Drop

Book 1

The Diana Diaries Series

Cindi R. Maciolek

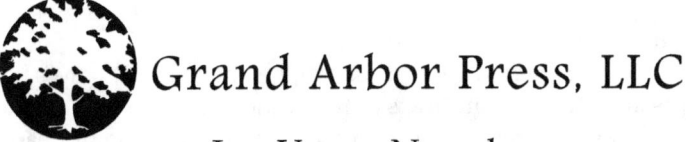 Grand Arbor Press, LLC

Las Vegas, Nevada
www.grandarborpress.com

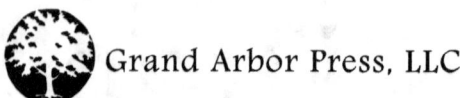 Grand Arbor Press, LLC

Grand Arbor Press, LLC
1930 Village Center Circle #3-388
Las Vegas, NV 89134

Visit our website for current contact information:
www.grandarborpress.com.

Grand Arbor Press, LLC books may be purchased for educational, business or sales promotional use. Please contact the company for more information.

Grand Arbor Press, LLC and the Grand Arbor Press logo are trademarks of Grand Arbor Press, LLC. All other trademarks are the property of their respective owners.

Printed in the United States of America.

First Print Release: February 2017

Credits:
Cover design: Charles H. Small

Print Edition:
ISBN13: 978-0-9647911-5-2
ISBN10: 0-9647911-5-3
Electronic Edition:
ISBN13: 978-0-9647911-6-9
ISBN10: 0-9647911-6-1

To those searching for your future – you are not alone

Table of Contents

Dear Diary,

I can't believe it's been over three years since I started working in retail. For better or worse, it's what I now do as I struggle to define my future and pay the rent. I've been working my way up the sales ladder with each job, but I still don't feel fulfilled. I spend my days dealing with haughty customers and even haughtier sales clerks. I knew the fashion industry was tough, but I had no idea how much bullshit I'd have to put up with at this level.

I'm tired, my feet ache, and I'm not using any of the skills that I developed all those years as a marketing manager and consultant in high tech. I'm intelligent, I have a college degree and I'm very personable. I'm amazed that the best work I can find in this town, Las Vegas, is retail! Las Vegas is the entertainment capital of the world, with millions of worldwide visitors annually. Sure, shopping is a huge part of the Las Vegas experience, but I want to be part of so much more! The creativity and ingenuity in this town is incredible, yet here I am.

No one has any idea what really goes on behind the scenes in retail until you've actually been there, as I have. When I tell my friends true stories of customer antics – and attitudes – and colleague and management atrocities, they just don't believe me. They think that because I've worked at some of the most prominent companies in the world, that these things just couldn't happen or else the organizations couldn't survive with their reputations intact.

But, they do! Sex in the fitting rooms, bitches with Birkins, intolerable cruelty from the staff, the Drama.

Sometimes I just want to shove a stiletto up someone's ass.

I thought of writing a letter to Dear Abby – no, several letters – but no one ever recognizes themselves even when it's in print. They read, they laugh and always but always think it's someone else.

Still, I feel the need to share. Some of these stories are just too good, too juicy to keep to myself.

Maybe I'll write a book…

More tomorrow!

All my heart,

Diana

High Tech

Dear Diary,

It's wonderful to be in love! I am so lucky to have found Chris. He is the first guy I've ever dated who actually wanted to talk business with me. He loves me not just for my body but for my mind as well. What a pleasant change.

It's hard for us to spend a lot of time with each other since we both travel a lot. At least we make every attempt to connect in cities where our paths cross. Sometimes it's London, at times Paris, occasionally Austin. It just depends on our schedules. It really doesn't matter to me, as long as we get quality time together on a regular basis.

Chris does have one really odd quirk, however. Seems he can't make love in a hotel room! I mean, what guy in this entire world has problems with that? When we're traveling we'll get together, have a nice dinner, go up to the room and really start getting into it when he just stops. He says he feels uncomfortable, that people in the room next door will hear us. I keep telling him that's what hotels are for, but he just stops then goes to sleep. He rarely has this problem at home, only on the road. Maybe it's all the stress from travel. It's a shame but, oh well, at least I don't have to worry about him cheating on me!

More tomorrow!

All my heart,

Diana

Love & Marriage

{ ONE }

I was sucked in by the accent.

Chris Christensen and I first met when we worked together at a high tech company in Silicon Valley. My heart leapt when I saw him from across the room during an E-team meeting. Immediately, we had a connection I just can't explain. Tall and blonde, with the bluest eyes I'd ever seen, I needed to know right then, right now, who he was and how I could make him mine.

Turned out, he was fresh out of business school, in his early 30s, handsome as ever, hired into a mid-level management position. He was from Sweden, supposedly a distant relative of royalty. Once he spoke, with his lilting accent, I didn't care who he was, where he came from or who he was related to, for that matter. I wanted him and that was the end of that.

Chris was married at the time, but things weren't going so well at home. I was his rock during the break-up and divorce, and the more time we spent together I knew that a future with me would be all he ever needed.

Once the divorce was final, it was heaven. We were always together – snuggling, canoodling – we couldn't keep our hands off each other. Even the people at work were a little sick of us, but we only had eyes for each other.

We stayed up late nights talking about all those stupid things you talk about at three in the morning after a couple bottles of wine. He told me about his family, and how close he was to them. He intimated that he had worked for the Swedish equivalent of the CIA but it must have been a desk job. He was good-looking but definitely not a martial arts master or a gun-slinger. And, he dreamt of opening a restaurant. Not sure when, not sure where, or even what kind, but that was definitely on his list.

We had great management positions with the company, but as time went on, we realized we needed to chase our dreams. Things were booming in Silicon Valley, so we both opted to step away from our full-time jobs – and regular paychecks – and join the ranks of consultants where we could make significantly more money. I had a good reputation in town and I found clients for my marketing consultancy almost immediately. Chris left shortly thereafter and became a management consultant. With our complementary skills we thought about going into business together but my boss at the time advised against it.

"Your relationship is too new," he said. "It could get messy. You're so fiercely independent, Diana, I'm surprised you would even consider commingling your life with someone else so strongly, even someone like Chris. Play it safe and run your own show. In the end, you'll be glad you did."

Once we started consulting, Chris and I both traveled a lot, but we managed to meet in some of the most romantic places: my favorite chocolate shop in Paris; London's Heathrow Airport; the snack bar at a trade show in Austin. OK, so they weren't all romantic, but these little moments helped to hold our relationship together.

When we were in town we usually got together at my apartment. It was small – 550 square feet – but meticulously decorated, comfy and cozy, and always spotless – I had a great cleaning lady – a sanctuary in the midst of Silicon Valley. Chris had a much larger home but he could never claim to be an interior designer, nor could his ex-wife. He had only what he needed. I had what made me happy.

I'd cook dinner for him – out of habit, out of love or just because I liked to cook. He never helped. We chatted or he'd watch television or text. Sometimes he would stare out the patio door, wine glass in hand and say, "I'm certainly spoiled now aren't I."

He was, and I was a big part of that. I don't know if he felt I was more his lover, his mother, his valet or his maid servant. He felt pampered and that was what I was trying to accomplish. I may be fiercely independent in business but when it came to personal relationships, I was all about nurture. Yes, it was a departure from the way most people saw me, but when I love someone, I can't help but treat them the best. I never thought about how he would view things.

Whenever he spoke, I was entranced. That accent was music to my ears. I always thought I had my feet on the ground, but I was lifted to another plane when words came out of his mouth. I knew it. I was smitten. Chris was the one.

Chris loved the fact that I was working and I had ambition. He loved my intelligence and my kindness. He didn't always know how to reciprocate, but, after all, he is a guy, so I cut him some slack. He did his best and that was what counted. He valued and respected my opinions about work, and I appreciated that. We had what you might call a personal business connection, with more of a focus on business and less personal. I didn't know it could go deeper than what we had. Chris was, by far, my first serious romantic relationship.

He finally asked me to move in with him, hoping that we'd see enough of each other to make sense of our situation. One day he came home and announced that he had landed a big client. Yippee! We would live the good life, both of us in control of our incomes, the people we work with, our schedules. Life couldn't get any better.

Chris was hell-bent on fulfilling his dream of opening a restaurant, so we lived somewhat frugally while he put the majority of his income into savings. He had access to family money but he really wanted to build the restaurant business on his own. Any splurges came from my revenues even though he made three times as much as I did. Still, I felt we needed to have a little fun now and then and we were both accustomed to a higher standard. If he wouldn't pay for these little extras, I did. You only live once, right?

One day after Chris returned from a long trip back home to Sweden, he insisted we go out to dinner. I was certain he was going to propose. I mean, he must have discussed our relationship with his family during the visit, right? We'd been together long enough that it seemed the logical next step.

He took me to one of our favorite restaurants, and he reserved the table in the middle of the room – what better place for all the other diners to see him drop to one knee and ask me to become the new Mrs. Christensen!

Instead, right before dessert, he hit me with a bombshell. Although he felt we had a good relationship and a unique connection, the timing just wasn't right. Instead of a proposal, he said he needed a break. HE NEEDED A BREAK! What kind of fool tells the love of his life he needs a break?

There was nothing I could do, no changing his mind. It was over, for the time being. Of course, he still wanted to remain friends. Asshole. He said he chose the center table in the restaurant because he knew I would refrain from throwing my glass of wine in his face and cause a spectacle. Chris knew me too well, but I obviously didn't know him.

I cried during the entire car ride home. When we got to his place, he said he understood that it would take me a day or two to arrange to remove my belongings. What a jerk! I packed some clothes and drove to my dear friend, Gizzi's, place where I would stay until I leased an apartment. Oh, and I had a moving truck at his house the following morning to pack my belongings and put it all in storage.

"I should have seen it coming, Gizzi," I sobbed through my wine, tears streaming down my face. Gizzi handed me a box of tissues I was sure to empty before night's end. It wasn't the first time I cried my heart out at Gizzi's. She was prepared for tonight's sob story.

Giselle "Gizzi" Boudrot is my martini swirling, cigarette smoking, semiconductor sales friend whom I've known for years. She's my go-to person for all business affairs, and sometimes affairs of the heart. I can always count on Gizzi to tell me the truth when I need it, whether or not I want to hear it.

Tonight, she just sat there, sipping her martini and taking long, meaningful drags from her cigarette. She did exactly what a good friend should – she listened to me blathering about my heartbreak – until it was time to slap me back to reality, so to speak. Gizzi was always so strong when it came to relationships with men. She loved 'em and left 'em. She didn't put up with any crap like I did.

"I don't know why I would have thought he was going to propose," I continued, trying to calm my sobs. "Besides, any time we had a problem in our relationship it was right after Chris spent time with his little brother, Magnus. Chris just got back from a three-week vacation with him so I should have known something big was about to drop. A phone call with him could cause us to argue. Three weeks should have sent us to the opposite ends of the Earth! I can't believe someone I never met could have such a big impact on my relationship."

"Well, there certainly must be a good reason for Chris to drop you like a hot potato, sweetie," Gizzi said. "No royal bloodline, I suppose."

Gizzi snickered while I snorted a half-laugh.

"I thought the fact that his family was so far away would be good for your relationship. No constant interference. But, even I can be wrong on occasion," she opined.

Gizzi looked at me with her big brown eyes, a look that fell somewhere between sympathy and pity. I'd seen that look before. Gizzi used it on me more frequently than I appreciated, but she had a hard time hiding her thoughts when it came to my love life. I hope she has a better poker face for sales.

"I know you don't want to hear this, but your relationship was destined for doom from the start. Have you forgotten you were born on Princess Diana's birthday and Chris was born on Prince Charles's birthday? If they couldn't make it work, how could the two of you?"

Of course, of all the things I shared with Gizzi about my relationship with Chris, she had to remember our birthday connection to the former royal couple. It should have been a warning sign of what was to come. Instead, it was just one of those little relationship red flags I chose to ignore.

Gizzi could see that her comments were not necessarily making me feel better, so she decided to take a different approach to help me get over my broken heart.

"I'm sorry, sweetie. It's just a bit of trivia I can't forget. So, how did your sister take the news?"

"Oh, you know Helen. She said he was a jerk and didn't deserve me and I shouldn't shed a tear for such slime."

"Hmm...I tend to agree with her," Gizzi said. "He is a jerk. You deserve better. If he can be so easily influenced by his little brother, he doesn't have the balls to be a man – your man. Is that what happened to his first marriage? Did little brother stick his nose where it didn't belong?"

I hadn't really shared why his first marriage broke up, but there was no reason to hide from the truth. It had nothing to do with Chris's little brother and everything to do with his ex-wife. At least that's what Chris told me.

"No, Chris's family didn't influence that break-up at all," I relayed. "It was all about Elsa. She hated living in California and wanted to move back to Stockholm to be near her family. And, she wanted children but that wasn't in the cards."

"Why, does Chris have problems with his little swimmers?"

Gizzi did that one-eyebrow raise that only people who don't use Botox are capable of.

"No, nothing as simple as that. It's more psychological. Chris was born on the same day as his father and grandfather and he feared breaking the tradition. He thinks his family would disown him."

"Are you kidding me? What grandparent wouldn't love their grandchild regardless of its birth date? I think you're lucky Chris broke up with you. Sounds like he has a lot of issues. After all, you do want kids, right Diana?"

Honestly, I had never really thought about having them so when Chris informed me children were off the list, I was relieved I didn't have to make that decision. But, that's not an answer that would satisfy Gizzi.

"Kids aren't a top priority for me right now," I said, tempering my true thoughts. Gizzi could be brutally honest, but I just wasn't that sort of person, except when it came to business. "I'm traveling a lot and still building my career, so it wouldn't be a good time to bring kids into the mix. But, if my husband wanted them and I felt he would be a good father, I'd definitely consider it."

"OK, that makes sense," Gizzi concurred. "Get all that travel out of your system so you can stay near home and be a mom."

Gizzi may be strong when it comes to men, but she feels very strongly about being a stay-at-home mom, at least until the kids are in school. As she says, "I can always work from my home office, sweetie. CEO of the crib."

"Well, that's also the problem. With me traveling so much, guys aren't interested in relationships. Trying to match calendars with a man of my standards reduces my options. Most men at the executive level want their women around or at least near the house. Look how difficult it was to connect with Chris with both of us on the road all the time.

"That's why we were so perfect for each other," I tried to justify. "We were independent but yet a couple. And we made an effort to connect when we were away on business. Not many guys will put up with that. I can't tell you how many wonderful men passed me up, knowing I could be away for long stretches at a time. But, Chris was different. He supported my work. He wanted me to be successful."

"And he also expected you to take care of him, cook for him and satisfy him...in other ways. He wanted it all. But, have you thought about what you want? Being in a great relationship is not about settling. Just because your travel schedules occasionally merge does not mean he's the man for you."

As I said, Gizzi doesn't hold back. Although, she's not married either, so is she really the one to give me advice about the best way to handle a relationship?

"Well, it wasn't always like this. When we worked for the same company, we spent a lot of time together. We didn't travel very much. It was great! It was a very different relationship than what we had now. As consultants, we hardly saw each other even though we lived together. I didn't have as much time to nurture him."

"But did he nurture you? Honey, relationships are a two-way street. You can't just give. You have to be able to receive as well."

Figures. Gizzi would give me food for thought. If she didn't, Helen certainly would. But I've often heard, you can't help who you fall in love with. Are Chris and I the perfect couple? Probably not, but when we're together, it somehow works and it works beautifully. Unless, of course, he's been in contact with Magnus.

I wiped the tears from my eyes, leaned back on the sofa and took a deep breath. Life without Chris would not be easy but certainly there was no turning back. Chris needed a break, and women around the world know that's a coward's way of breaking up with someone. Hell, he should have just sent me a text and a moving van. Why treat me to a nice dinner? Guilt? Whatever. Time to move on.

"C'mon, Diana. Get some sleep. It won't necessarily be better in the morning, but it will be the start of a new day in your new life sans Chris. And, unfortunately, I have some work to do."

"You're right. Sleep. Sounds good. Night, Gizzi."

"Night, Diana."

Staying with Gizzi was always an adventure, but in no time at all I had moved into a fabulous apartment in downtown San Jose. Slightly larger than my previous place, it was on the top floor of a recently renovated building, with great views of downtown and airplane traffic at the airport. It wasn't much but it was mine, and with its proximity to shops and dining, I was certain to eventually pull out of my funk.

Getting over Chris would not be easy, but each day I put one foot in front of the other and gave a good show to my clients. Once I got home, I'd pour a glass of wine, sit on my balcony and try to figure out what went wrong. There were so many warning signs I couldn't believe I was so blindly in love.

For instance, although I had never met or spoken with any member of his family, not one of them felt I was good enough for Chris. At least, that's what he told me. Why he would share that with a woman he supposedly loved is now beyond my comprehension. And why wouldn't they love me? I'm a great person. I know I am. Any man would be lucky to have me. Why wouldn't his family appreciate that?

Then there was the whole baby brother issue. Whenever he spent time on the phone or in person with Magnus, trouble brewed between us. Life with Chris was not always easy, regardless of his brother's interference. If Magnus and I had met and didn't hit it off, I could understand his distaste for me, but quite the contrary, we had never spoken. I never formed a negative image of any member of Chris's family, in spite of all my negative reviews. I could only imagine Chris and Magnus must play some little mind games with each other to sabotage their relationships. Sickos.

Chris had so many hang-ups, many of them sexual. (I'm not bitter, am I?) He couldn't always perform in the bedroom – at such a young age! I thought that was just because he was tired from traveling so much. Could it be he wasn't attracted to me as fully as I was to him? Or, was it because he thought he might create a baby Christensen born on the wrong day of the year? Fear like that could ruin sex for him – and me! I couldn't imagine that any 30-year-old man would need artificial help in getting it up, and Chris didn't use anything, but considering the amount of times he had trouble, he should have at least seen a doctor.

And, it seemed that he would only have sex when he was drunk. Well, actually, he needed a drink to do anything outside of work. I thought it was due to his Scandinavian upbringing, because he always drank a lot with dinner. Without dinner. During lunch. A glass here or a glass there, it seemed as if he always had a drink in hand. Yet, I wouldn't classify him as an alcoholic although he had more bottles in his wine collection than I had shoes in my closet. I ignored it all – I had to – and went on with my life.

And what a life I led. I was making gobs of money, although it costs gobs of money just to survive in California. I spent like I had just won the lottery – everyday. Designer clothing, a new BMW, more shoes than one woman can imagine. The money kept coming in, and I certainly looked and lived the part of a successful businesswoman. I had a good reputation, and my client list grew simply by recommendation. I never had to advertise or solicit work. In fact, I had clients I never met! Ah, the wonders of the Internet.

When it came to business, I was an opinionated high-tech slut, working for the almighty dollar. Oh, and I had some brains to back it up. As they called us in Silicon Valley, we were whores for the electronics industry. There was no other work we could do in the Bay Area and make as much money as we did and receive all the perks that we got. It was just too good to pass up.

Life without Chris was nearly unbearable when I was alone in my apartment. On so many levels, we were perfect for each other. But, work was a good distraction and I took advantage of every opportunity to keep myself busy with the best clients in town, and to attend as many key networking events as I could fit into my schedule. In fact, I already had my eye on my next conquest. I was just waiting for our schedules to mesh.

About six months later, I heard a knock on my apartment door. It was a delivery man. In his hands were a dozen long stemmed red roses, a box of my favorite Neuhaus chocolates, a little blue box from every woman's favorite jewelry store and a prenuptial agreement. Not the most romantic proposal, I grant you, but a proposal nonetheless. My cell phone rang with the Swedish National Anthem so I knew it was Chris. I should have deleted his number after all we'd been through, but I just couldn't do it. And, boy am I glad I didn't!

"Well???" he asked, not even bothering to say hello.

Chris was in Stockholm visiting his family. Don't ask me how I knew. I just did. However, I didn't know then and I don't know till this day what conversations took place during his visit. Something, somehow convinced him to ask me to marry him.

"Yes! Yes of course! What took you so long?" I gushed. I shouldn't have had to wait six months in the first place, but that was all behind us now. We were getting married!!!

"I had to have a talk with my little brother."

He had to go there, didn't he. He couldn't leave well enough alone. We were having such a happy, memorable moment and he had to bring up Magnus.

"So, little Magnus finally approves of me?"

I had to know although I wasn't really sure I wanted to.

Chris laughed.

"No, of course not. No one will ever be good enough for me in my family's eyes. Except Elsa."

Well, nothing like making a girl feel wanted.

I cleared my throat, holding back tears of both joy and anger.

"So, why the change of heart?"

I held my breath, waiting for his response.

"Six months ago I said I needed a break. Well, I've had one and in spite of the number of women I've seen during that time, you and I still seem to be the best match."

I told you that, you idiot, but you didn't listen to me.

"And just how large is that number of women?"

Chris laughed again. I'm glad he finds all of this funny. He was able to find time for someone else but he and I had trouble matching schedules.

"Nothing for you to worry about. As for the wedding, I think it should be small. This is my second, after all, and none of my family will be able to make it."

"What? We haven't even set a date yet. How do they know? Don't they want to meet me? Or, celebrate your special day?"

"None of my family will be able to make it, so let's just keep it small, OK?"

I get it. He doesn't want to spend any money. With all the money he has, he sure has a hard time spending it.

"OK, got it. When are you coming home?"

"Saturday. It will be great to see you."

"Hmm...Saturday I'll be in Boston. Back on Wednesday."

"Tuesday I leave for Singapore. I'll be gone for two weeks."

Here we go again. The infamous scheduling challenge.

"Well, let's just text each other and find a day when we can celebrate. Love you!"

"Sounds good, Diana. Text soon."

Life with Chris was back to normal. The only difference was now I had a wedding to plan, regardless of how small it will be.

"Are you nuts?"

OK, so my sister isn't too keen on my engagement. Maybe I should have waited to call her.

"Helen, it was so Chris. The delivery man, the flowers, the chocolates. Everything!"

"Sounds more like a guilt gift to me than a proposal. Didn't you say it included a prenup?"

"Yes, I told him long ago I would sign one. I'm not worried."

"If he truly loved you, he wouldn't even bring it up, let alone present it during the proposal."

"I'm actually the one who brought it up. I know he has a lot of family money, so I didn't want him to think that's why I wanted to marry him."

"But, a prenup during the proposal? And, what a coward! He couldn't even propose in person. He was probably afraid you'd finally fling that glass of wine at him so he didn't want to risk it. I think you just need to walk away from Chris for good, Sis. Everything is about him and what he wants. What do you want, Diana?"

"I want to marry Chris, Helen. I know things have been a little strained lately ---"

"A little strained? He dumped you over dinner!"

"Well, technically he didn't dump me. He needed a break, remember?"

"And what happens the next time he needs a break?"

"Helen, don't you remember all the wonderful times Chris and I had when we first met and he was going through the divorce?"

"I know you seemed happy, Diana, but, really, weren't you just a good listener and a convenient lay? I don't mean to insult you, but everything is always about him and what he wants. It was then and it still is. The prenup. A small wedding. His family not attending. I'd like to support you but I think it's all a mistake, Diana. Really, I do."

OK, so Helen is as enthused about my marriage to Chris as Magnus. Maybe I'll share the news with Gizzi.

"Diana, you're a smart woman. Why must you rush things? Can't you just date again for a while? It's been six months. What's the hurry?"

Gizzi is just as excited as Helen about my impending nuptials. Why is everyone questioning my judgment?

"Gizzi, you know how much I've loved Chris. It's been my dream all along to marry him. And, how often does a man get to the point where he actually proposes? If I suggest we wait, he may never ask again and I can't bear the thought of losing Chris a second time."

Gizzi just looked at me with wonderment, then turned her attention back to her Chinese chicken salad.

"You've finally gotten your life together, Diana. Your business is going great! You're traveling the world. Throwing a serious relationship into the picture is fine, but not with Chris! I'm not sure how that will make your life better right now."

I dove into my crab cakes, a little frustrated at the lack of support I was getting from my best friend. Gizzi tried again.

"How do your parents feel about it?"

"Well, you know how parents are. My Mom is thrilled I'm finally getting married. She had hoped to have more grandkids by now. Helen only has two children and that's just not enough for my Mom."

"And Daddy?"

"As far as Dad's concerned, if the man has a good job and can put a roof over my head and food on the table, he's perfect."

"So, they never ask you about sexual compatibility and satisfaction?"

I just stared at Gizzi, and we both burst out laughing.

"Sweetie, if Chris is what you truly want, then go for it. Just be careful and watch him like a hawk. At least if the two of you split you'll be entitled to half of what he makes once you get married, and he's making pretty good money right now. So, I guess it can't be all bad."

Hmm…did I fail to tell Gizzi the details in the prenup?

Gizzi looked down at her phone.

"Gotta go, doll. I'm working on a big sale and I need to get back to the office. Call if you need me. Have fun in Boston."

Gizzi got up and air-kissed a good-bye as she went flying out the door.

"No worries, Giz," I yelled after her. "Lunch is on me today!"

"Sorry, Diana, but I can't in good conscience advise you to sign this."

Brian Garcia, my attorney, practically threw the prenup across the desk.

"It's a sham. Who does Chris think he is?"

"Well, he is related to royalty."

"We're probably all related to royalty at some point in our lineage. It doesn't give us the right to screw the people we supposedly love."

Brian reached across the desk, grabbed the prenup and started leafing through the document again.

"Have you read this? You're pretty good with contracts, Diana, so you should understand. It's an ironclad agreement, all in his favor."

"No, it's in our favor. It's everything Chris and I discussed. We'll maintain separate finances and separate businesses. His is his and mine is mine and never the twain shall meet. We'll leave the marriage with whatever we brought into it. And, I keep my maiden name."

Well, technically, Chris and I hadn't discussed this particular prenup as it regards our relationship. When I was helping Chris go through his divorce, he mentioned that if he ever got married again, he'd insist on a prenup. He wouldn't marry without one. Everything would have to remain separate – finances, business-es – everything, including names. His new wife would keep her maiden name so, should they divorce, there would be no residual issues.

I saw how much Chris was hurting and I couldn't imagine him going through that again, nor would I want to. What he said made sense. If you have two people who are making a good in-come and are able to uphold their end of the financial burden of marriage, why not keep everything separate? I wasn't thinking I'd ever divorce once I got married, but I also know how skilled I am from a business standpoint, and I'm perfectly capable of standing strong on my own two feet. I told Chris I agreed with everything he said about the prenup, and he must have remem-bered because this agreement I was about to sign was exactly as he had described.

"Diana, I'm sure by now you've seen the amount of money he has and how much he's making, but everything is tied up in trusts, LLCs and family limited partnerships. You'll never get ac-cess to anything."

I let out a deep sigh. I had no idea what Chris's finances were but what did that matter? Why do people not understand me lately?

"Brian, are you listening to me? I don't want it. Any of it! If we divorce I'm certain just to get him out of the house would be enough for me. I wouldn't want a penny from him. Absolutely nothing! I'm successful in my own right. There's no need for us to rely on each other financially. And, he's making more than I am so he certainly wouldn't get a dime from me in a divorce."

Brian sensed that I was a little too enthusiastic.

"What if you decide not to work anymore?"

"I highly doubt that will happen. I love to work and I love to make money."

"But what if you have children and decide to be a stay-at-home mom?"

Brian just wouldn't give up. I guess that's what attorneys do. But, I thought I was paying him to be on my side.

"First of all, I doubt that we'll ever have children. And if we do, and we divorce, the children will be taken care of by law. As for myself, I wouldn't want a penny from him. That just keeps him in my life. If we split, that's it. I want it over and done with."

"Well then, Ms. MacKenzie, it sounds like you've already made up your mind. All I can do is advise you. I can't pull the pen from your hand."

I smiled wide like a Cheshire cat, picked up the prenup, shook Brian's hand and practically skipped back to my car. Against Brian's better judgment and professional advice, I signed the agreement. Soon, and very soon, I would become Mrs. Chris Christensen.

"Why don't we just go to Vegas?" Chris asked one Thursday evening.

"You mean for the weekend?"

Chris and I were having one of our rare moments when we were both actually in town at the same time, so we decided to play hooky from our clients for the day. As usual, he was at my place where I had just finished cooking him a wonderful late afternoon lunch. We were now reviewing my ideas for our wedding over a bottle of wine.

"No, I mean for the wedding. We could just elope. That's what people do in Vegas, right?"

I thought they went to gamble and have fun but sure, I guess they go there to get married as well.

"It's not exactly my dream wedding, Chris."

"But you're not going to have your dream wedding anyway, Diana. It's going to be small. Neither your family nor mine is attending. Why don't we make it even smaller, save the money and just do it?"

Ouch. Nothing like bursting a girl's bubble. But, I knew it was a money issue with Chris, right from the proposal.

Still, it was a thought. Did I want to spend gobs of money to have my clients attend our reception? Probably not. Just a few close friends, but that wouldn't make my dream wedding come true. Helen and my parents said they wouldn't be able to make it, even with a few months' notice. Just too costly for them, although I'm sure there were other reasons like the fact they didn't want me to marry Chris. And we know Chris's family wasn't coming out for our big day. Maybe Chris did have a point.

"When were you thinking about going?"

"I think there's an eight o'clock out of SJC."

"Tonight!?! Like, in a couple of hours? I won't have any time to shop."

"Shop for what? You have two closets full of clothes."

"For a dress. For our wedding. What do you intend to wear?"

"I don't know. Maybe khakis and a button down? I hadn't really thought about it."

Oy, the Silicon Valley uniform. That's why we need plans, mister.

"Well, maybe I have something that will work."

I put down my wine and my wedding notes and glanced up at Chris. He was smiling. No, maybe smirking. Either way, he seemed happy. That was all I needed. I got up, grabbed my favorite new cocktail dress, some fresh undies and off we went to the airport.

Upon arrival in Las Vegas, Chris rented a convertible – his first splurge in years aside from my engagement ring – and off we went to get our marriage license. Who knew the bureau was open till midnight? We headed to a wedding chapel with a drive-thru on the Strip, and before we hit the slots, we were proclaimed mister and missus. By Elvis. Chris opted for the single-ring ceremony which meant he wore no ring, and he "regifted" my engagement ring to me as my wedding ring.

He's so much more frugal than I remember. OK, cheap.

No gown, no flowers, no reception. Not even a cake. What's a wedding without the cake? Photos. I do have photos. Well, one photo. With my cell phone. It's a little blurry. Chris drove away from that chapel pretty quickly. But, we went to a nice hotel room where we, um, slept. I guess that means we're officially married.

Chris was happy. I was happy. My family and friends weren't thrilled. They thought Chris was trouble, but I told them not to worry, I had signed the prenup.

Dear Diary,

Just call me Mrs. Chris Christensen!

Well, I guess you'd have to do that privately because legally I retain my maiden name. But, I still love the fact that Chris and I are married!

I thought having a drive-thru ceremony in Vegas would be hard to accept but I have to admit, it was kind of nice, just the two of us. Elvis as our officiant made it all that more memorable.

I told a colleague of mine about our wedding and he said it was every man's dream, that once a man decides to propose he feels like he's done his part and he's already married – on to the next priority. Dragging a man through a long engagement and a big wedding planning process just confuses him. Best to take care of it right away while it's top of mind and elope. How lucky I am that I did the right thing!

On the flight back to San Jose, Chris just happened to mention that he wanted to move to Vegas to pursue his dream of owning a restaurant.

Quelle surprise!

He said he was finishing up some projects he'd already been paid for, and he saved the bulk of his earnings since he started consulting. He would live off his savings and search for the perfect location and concept for his restaurant. And he felt Las Vegas was the perfect city.

Well, now, I'm not exactly keen on moving to the desert. California is God's country. There is no better place for me. But, as a woman – a wife – you go where your man goes, right? And, it's close enough to California that it shouldn't impact my consulting business one bit. After all, I hardly even see my clients and we basically live in the same town. We work by phone, text, email, video calls or I see them at trade shows and conferences. So, easy peasy!

I don't know Chris's timing on the move just yet, but it goes to show you that a life with Chris will be full of surprises.

More tomorrow!

All my heart,

Diana

The Divorce

{ TWO }

The limo pulled up in front of our house, well…Chris's house but as Mrs. Christensen, er, Ms. MacKenzie married to Mr. Christensen, I now lived there, too…bringing me home after a business trip to Seattle. I traveled so much I took advantage of whatever luxuries I could get, and the limo worked out nicely. If I drove to the airport and left the car in long term parking, it was nearly two-thirds the cost of a limo for my longer trips. Sometimes, it was even cheaper to take the limo. It was a cost my clients were willing to bear. And, my beautiful BMW didn't have to sit out in the elements while I was out of town.

I paid the driver, got out of the car, grabbed my luggage and looked up to see a "For Sale" sign on the front lawn! I knew Chris was interested in moving to Vegas, but I didn't realize he planned to move so quickly. He hadn't even mentioned to me that he had listed the house for sale. Aren't married couples supposed to discuss this sort of thing?

As I made my way up the walkway, Chris and an unknown male, presumably the realtor, stepped onto the porch, shook hands and parted ways. The realtor smiled and nodded his acknowledgment to me as he walked past. Chris caught a glimpse of me and waited for me to reach the front door. A little help with my luggage would have been nice.

"What's all this?" I asked. I was furious, but as we were newly married I controlled my words.

"What's all what?" Chris asked as he bent down to give me a quick kiss.

"The 'for sale' sign."

I pointed my arm in the direction of the lawn. Chris chuckled and rolled his eyes.

"Diana, have you forgotten already? We're moving to Vegas!"

He's a blonde, too, so why is he being so condescending.

"I know we're moving to Vegas, but I didn't realize you wanted to move today. It's only been a few weeks since you brought it up. We haven't discussed a timeline."

Chris opened the door for me so we could continue this discussion inside. Chris had lived in the house for quite some time and he didn't want the neighbors privy to our exchange. I plopped down on the sofa and he handed me a glass of champagne.

"Dear Diana, don't you remember how I work? When I have a plan in my head, I just start moving forward."

True, true. That's why people liked working with Chris. He put together a plan and began a swift and effective implementation. That's also why he garnered the big bucks. A smart man when it came to business, but I'm not so sure he gets five stars for personal relationships.

"Yes, yes, I understand that, Chris, but a little heads up on your end wouldn't hurt. I mean, I am half of the relationship here."

"But the house isn't in your name. It doesn't really affect you."

What? Selling the house doesn't affect me? Just how much champagne did he drink today?

"Uh, my life is being uprooted, too. I have packing to do. And I'd like to notify my clients and make any travel adjustments to Las Vegas. Plus, I'd like to help find our new home. We haven't even discussed it. Are we going to rent for a while in Vegas? Do you even know what part of town you want to live in? We haven't explored that at all. What exactly is your timeline?"

I was so frustrated at this point I just wanted to kick off my shoes – directly in his face. I used to love to listen to him speak, his accent music to my ears. Now I just wanted him to shut up. I couldn't even fathom what other surprises would come from his mouth.

"Babe, I just put the house on the market. I have no idea how quickly it will sell. Tomorrow morning I'm flying to Vegas to meet with a realtor and hopefully buy a new house. Once those details are in place, you can pack and we can move. It's not difficult."

Ooh, I hate when he calls me babe! He must have been talking to Magnus.

"Wait a minute – you're flying to Vegas tomorrow without me to choose a house we're going to live in as a married couple? Shouldn't I be going with you?"

"Well, you can if you want. I thought you might be tired from your trip. The house stays in the family partnership so you can offer an opinion but it really is my final decision."

So, that's the way it works, does it Chris? I knew we had promised to keep everything separate, but a little respect goes a long way. In his mind, that's it. Decision made. He put his house on the market and was shopping for a new one in Sin City.

"No, no, I'm not too tired. Let me switch out my carry-on. I'll take a hot bath and book a ticket. What flight are you on?"

"6:30 a.m."

Of course.

"OK, no worries. What do you want to do for dinner tonight?"

"You're on your own tonight, babe. I'm having dinner with some restaurateurs to get insight into the business."

"Want some company?"

"It's all business. No one is bringing a plus one. You can just stay home and relax. I shouldn't be too late."

Chris looked down at his watch.

"And, on that note, I'm off. Good night, Diana."

"Night, Chris."

Chris bent down to give me a kiss, put his champagne flute on the entry table, picked up his keys and he was gone.

I wonder if this is how Chris's first marriage functioned, I asked myself as I soaked in a deep, hot bath. *Maybe that's why Elsa was so frustrated living in California. Chris basically ran his own show and his wife was simply there in name only. And in my case, not even that!*

I can't bitch to anyone about this. Helen and Gizzi both told me not to marry him. Mom would never understand. Maybe I should call Magnus?

I'm sure there's an adjustment period when two people first get married and we just have to work through that. Our finances might be separate but our hearts are joined – aren't they? I'll have to do some research on the Internet. Someone must have advice for me. Is there a forum for women whose husbands are having a mid-life crisis about 20 years too early?

I turned to more positive thoughts. What can I control? Silicon Valley was booming, and as long as that continued, so would my business. I had great clients. I was making more bank than I ever imagined. And, I was married to a man with dreams he intended to manifest – in Las Vegas!

Sin City had its ups and downs, but it had long been experiencing major growth both in residents and tourism. What better place in the world to investigate restaurant opportunities than the bustling metropolis of Las Vegas? Honestly, when Chris said he wanted to open a restaurant, I thought he'd wait until retirement and run a little bistro in some small coastal town in northern California. I had no idea he was seriously considering entering such a competitive market as Las Vegas so quickly! What did he know about operating a restaurant anyway?

Well, Vegas wasn't exactly my cup of tea, but if that's what Chris wanted, if that would help him to attain his dream, then I was all for it. I'm sure he would support me if the situation were reversed.

I could still consult easily from there. It's just a short one hour flight to California. Yep, if that's what he wants then by golly, that's what we'll do. There didn't seem to be any roadblocks.

Although…I'm a bit curious, well, maybe, impressed that he saved enough money during the last year to be able to quit the lucrative world of management consulting and live off his savings. How much, exactly, did he have? I hardly saved anything over the last year. Life in California is expensive!

Did he have ample savings to invest in his dream restaurant, too? His bank account couldn't possibly be adequate to open and operate a quality establishment, so certainly there must be investors. Why was he keeping me out of all these decisions? We used to spend hours talking about business. Now, we talked about the most mundane things. Maybe I need another glass of champagne…

"This is a great house, honey. For what you could sell your house in California, you can get this mini-mansion here. And, in an exclusive guard-gated community! This is every home buyers dream."

It was now 4 p.m. and we'd already seen a number of amazing properties in the million dollar range, from single family homes to penthouse condominiums with private elevators. I was more impressed with Las Vegas real estate than I had expected. Chris's house in San Jose was somewhat modest, but with housing prices through the roof in Silicon Valley, it was enviable to many homeowners.

Here, in this desert town, his realtor was taking us through some of the most exquisite homes I'd ever seen, yet I could almost afford one on my own income. And, they were new! Not 40-year-old remodeled houses that had character but also character flaws. I was sold on the city. When do we move?

"I see your wife has fallen in love with one of the houses," Rosa the realtor said, her words pushing through mile-high lipstick. "You know the saying. Happy wife. Happy life!"

Rosa touched Chris's arm as she spoke.

Is she flirting with my husband? In front of me?

Chris smiled and looked at me with his piercing blue eyes.

"Agreed, Rosa, but I'll be making the final decision here."

"Ooh, such a macho man, taking charge."

Rosa flipped back her long brunette locks and adjusted her skin-tight dress around her recently enhanced bosom.

She is flirting with my husband!

"But, of course, I'd like your opinion, Diana. I much prefer the penthouse."

Oh my god, he's asking my opinion! He hasn't done that since we got married. I'd better get it right.

"The penthouse is nice, I agree, darling," I said, putting my arm through his and making sure my wedding ring shone brightly in Rosa's face. "But this one is much more impressive and has that fabulous view of the Strip from the terrace. The penthouse view is of the mountains and golf course."

"I do like the mountains, babe."

"But it's the Strip view that will be best for resale, I'm sure."

"Your wife makes a good point, Chris. Strip views always trump mountain views in this market."

Aha! I don't even live here and I can assess the situation and provide a worthwhile opinion. Why has he forgotten to believe in me?

Chris took a deep breath, looked at me, looked at Rosa, looked around the house and said, "OK, let's do it. I'll take this one."

I tried to hug Chris, but he first reached for Rosa then turned to hug me.

"Great! I'll get the paperwork ready. I'll fax it to your office for signature as I know you're heading back home in a couple of hours. Congratulations and welcome to Las Vegas!"

"Thank you, Rosa. You've been a great help. By the way, you know I'm interested in opening a restaurant in town. Can you connect me with someone to scout locations?"

"Absolutely! I have a colleague who specializes in that. I'll send along her info with the purchase contract. I know the two of you will get along splendidly."

"Perfect. Shall we head back to the airport?"

The next few weeks were a whirlwind of work, packing and moving. Chris's house in San Jose sold much more quickly than we anticipated. Within a week he was under contract with a solid cash offer. The deal in Las Vegas was completed as well, so in between business trips, I had to organize the move.

Chris was keeping right on top of the financial situation, making sure our finances remained ever more separate. As part of the moving contract, his belongings would be loaded onto the truck first, then weighed. My items would be loaded next, and the truck weighed again. He paid for his part of the move and I was required to pay for mine. Honestly, it was more like having a roommate than a husband.

In the midst of the chaos, I realized I hadn't called Gizzi who had been on a worldwide business trip, so I grabbed my cell phone and rang her up while I stuffed another box with my clothes.

"You're what?"

I could hear Gizzi searching through her purse for her lighter. After the way this conversation opened, she'd probably need a martini as well. She seemed somewhat in a state of shock.

Helen, on the other hand, was keen on Las Vegas. As a school teacher, she felt it was a great place for her to find work and she and her husband, Gabe, were actually considering a move to

Vegas themselves. At least that conversation was easy. Explaining all of this to Gizzi would be tougher.

"You heard me. We're moving to Las Vegas."

"I don't understand. The two of you are seasoned high tech professionals. Why would you move to a town that focuses on the hospitality industry?"

"Well, it's always been Chris's dream to own a restaurant, and he feels he can do that in Vegas. As for consulting, we're not that far away, just a quick plane ride. I know a lot of people who live in SoCal and jet up to Silicon Valley to consult. I'll just be a little bit east of them."

I'm sure it's a lot harder and more inconvenient than it sounds, but it's what I had to do in order to be with Chris.

"So when does all this take place?"

"Actually, Chris has already sold his house and we flew down a couple of weeks ago to buy one in Nevada. I'm just wrapping up things at home and we'll be on our way next weekend."

"Well, the good thing is you'll be buying a house together, a new one as husband and wife. No bad memories in there."

If only that were true.

"Umm...not exactly. Chris's house is in a family limited partnership, so the sale and purchase are out of my hands. But it will be a new house for the happy couple."

"You're telling me your name won't be on the title?"

"That's correct, girlfriend."

"So, if the two of you divorce..."

"No worries, we worked it all out in the prenup."

"Prenup! What prenup?"

Gizzi nearly jumped through the phone.

"The one I signed before we got married. Everything is spelled out. I'm fine with the details. Don't worry. I just wanted you to know I'm moving. I've set up a private mailbox for my business so I'll make sure you have that address."

"And the home as well."

"OK, but Chris doesn't want any of my mail coming to the house, so if you do want to send me something, just send it to my business address."

"Sweetie, I don't like the sounds of this. Why is Chris being so separatist? You're married but he's acting like he's single."

Lying, I said, "I'm sure it's emotional fallout from his first marriage. He'll warm up to things as time goes on. Right now, everything has been an absolute whirlwind. I wish I had more time to chat, but I really must go. So much to do before the move, and one of my clients is doing a major product launch in two weeks!"

Gizzi took a long drag off her cigarette. She must have found her lighter.

"OK, sweetie. But be careful. Don't get yourself into a situation that will come back to haunt you."

Gizzi's words sent a chill up my spine.

"I'm fine. Everything is fine. Don't worry. I'll keep you posted on my whereabouts."

Thankfully, the move went extremely well. It should have. Chris was known for spartan living and I mostly had clothes and shoes and a bedroom set. I didn't have a lot to move because I sold the bulk of my apartment furnishings after we got married. I didn't feel they fit the (lack of) décor of his house. However, once we moved to Las Vegas I realized just how empty 4,200 square feet can be. Oh, plus the outdoor living space.

I knew once my client's product launch was over, I had a bit of a breather before the next rush of trade shows and press tours. I took a long look around the house and approached Chris about a decorating budget over pizza on our lone sofa – his sofa – his neon green leather sofa – and beer.

"Chris, now that you have such a great house, an executive house, it really needs to be decorated appropriately."

"My other house was fine. I'll pick up a few things here and there."

It's always a money thing with him. I took a different approach.

"But, honey, you want to be perceived as a player in this town, don't you? If you have investors or business partners over, rest assured, they are going to judge you on your personal surroundings. I think you need to be serious about your house to be taken seriously in business."

Chris finished chewing, swallowed and gulped down some beer.

"So what are you suggesting?"

"Well, the landscaping has to be done within three months, for sure. It's in your contract. That's what Rosa said."

"That shouldn't be too much. What, a few thousand?"

"You have nearly half an acre! I would expect more in the neighborhood of $100,000 to $250,000 to create a nice entertaining space."

I thought Chris would choke on his veggie delight.

"Is there more?"

"Well, there's the whole interior! We have your bedroom set in the master, mine in one of the guest bedrooms, your office furniture – which could probably be updated, by the way – and this green leather sofa which certainly has seen better days."

"Hey, I like my green leather sofa! I wanted one for years, and when Elsa and I married, it was the first piece of furniture I bought. It holds a lot of memories."

I knew I shouldn't have brought it up, but I had to go there. The green leather sofa didn't match any décor that would be appropriate for this house.

"What else are you thinking?"

"Oh, the list is so long! Window coverings, the media room, dining room, living room, the spare bedrooms, the wine cellar, all the little touches like new dishes and glassware and even art for the walls. If you're going to entertain, this needs to be an entertainer's paradise! And, don't forget the patio furniture."

Chris took a long swig of his beer, leaned back and let out a belch down to his belly. We laughed! Here was mister "I'm a distant relative of royalty" throwing one down like a good ol' boy.

"I guess I hadn't considered the full ramifications of owning a home this size in this community. How about I make a deal with you? I'll take care of the landscaping, outdoor kitchen, media room, wine cellar, any electronics and shutters for the windows."

"Ooh, shutters! I love those plantation shutters!"

"And you handle the interior furnishings – sofas, tables, dishes, glassware and so on."

Wow! Chris was actually handling this like a partnership – a marriage partnership! That was the first inkling of solidifying our relationship since he proposed.

"Love it! You're serious, right?"

"Yes, I'm serious, babe."

Cringe.

"Do you have a preferred style? I mean, you've always been very, how shall I say, minimalistic in your interior design. I don't want to overwhelm you. I want this to be something that reflects the two of us."

"Nope, no preference. You have free rein to do as you please. It's your money so make it count!"

"Alrighty, then. Thank you, honey! You just made my day."

I leaned over to kiss Chris who quickly returned my affection. He got up and carried me to our bedroom where we celebrated this new phase in our relationship.

I immediately set out to hatch an interior design plan while Chris got to work on the exterior. Neither one of us had much in the way of furniture, so this house was like a blank canvas. I had never decorated on such a grand scale before, but I'd watched enough shows on HGTV that I was certain I could create a showpiece of this house.

I love, love, love Paris, so I chose to decorate in a modern Parisian style, with exquisite everything. Elaborate bookshelves, leather sofas, elegant accessories. You name it, I ordered it. Everything I bought was expensive, to match the character and value of the house. I was like a kid in a candy store and enjoyed every minute of the process. Seeing my plan come to fruition was one of the most satisfying projects I'd ever done in my life.

As amazing as Las Vegas was, I couldn't find everything I wanted in town. I did manage to connect with a number of furniture and accessories dealers, including those at the Las Vegas Design Center, but on my many business trips, I wandered through local shops or spent long nights online. I'd get an image in my head and search for hours to find something similar.

I furnished the house with an eclectic mix of new and old. I knew I was creative but even I was impressed with the results! Room by room, the house was coming together. Maybe I had a future in interior decorating!

The house was so big even I had a hard time imagining how much of everything it would take to make the house just right. Chris never really commented. He was used to frugal living and I had far more accessories in the house than he probably saw his entire life! Or, perhaps he was a bit peeved at me for relegating his neon green sofa to his office and out of public view.

While I was busy taking care of things on the home front, Chris kept his restaurant dream alive and started putting together some solid plans. He began working with a new realtor to find the perfect location for his restaurant. The city was growing fast, and it was difficult to find a location because good space was snapped up quickly. I supported him as a good wife should, and went about my own business.

I was hoping Chris would be impressed with my handiwork. On those days when I had moments to dream, I thought, perhaps we could be a team. Chris would build and operate the restaurants and I could do the interior design. Of course, I hadn't discussed this with him but it sounded like a viable future from my perspective.

"Have you been watching the markets?" Chris asked one morning on his way out the door.

Hmm...honestly, no I hadn't. Not too closely. I'd been tied up with clients, travel and home decorating. I was having my best year ever. I had clients I never even met! There was so much demand for my type of service that I began working with a client immediately following our telephone interview. It was an amazing time. I was really grateful for the business because it was costing me a mint to decorate this place. I'd been so exhausted I wasn't following my usual routine of checking all my favorite news and financial sites. I lied.

"Sorta kinda. Why?"

I took a sip of hot tea and a bite of chocolate chip cookie.

"It just looks like the economy is heading for a major slowdown. You need to make sure you're prepared, that's all."

Ah, isn't that cute! Chris is concerned for his little wifey.

"Thanks for the heads up, but my clients are rockin' and rollin'. I've never been so busy!"

"That's great for now. I'm just saying, it looks like it might get bad so be sure you're setting aside something for the downturn."

Setting aside something for the downturn? Who has money for that? Chris was implementing a plan to open his restaurant, but I had a plan of my own. I was furnishing my dream home. Never in my life could I even conceive of living in such a magnificent house! I had to stay focused and finish every last detail. Once I was done with that, then I could save some money. My expenses would be significantly less, but I didn't want to stop the process right in the middle.

"I'll keep that in mind, dear."

Summer was a scorcher, but between shopping in wonderfully air conditioned stores and flights out of town for business, I was able to survive. As Chris had forewarned, all the news programs were reporting a cautionary note about the economy. I expected it might hit certain sectors, but Silicon Valley was still going gangbusters, and I was busier than ever.

Toward the end of the summer, I started to hear about layoffs in various industries, including hospitality in Las Vegas. Tourism was down, construction was nearly at a standstill but as other areas of the world were feeling the effects of a looming recession, I continued to work my plan. I still hadn't seen any signs of it affecting my business in the least. My clients hadn't mentioned a word to me about cutting budgets or postponing projects. The good life for me was still on-going. I expected to finish the house just in time for Thanksgiving when Chris and I planned to host a big business dinner. Then I could become diligent about my finances once again. Or, as diligent as I personally could be.

Then mid-September hit. The economy nearly came to a halt. The stock market dropped and dropped to its lowest level in 10 years. Everyone, and I mean everyone, was rethinking budgets. Within three weeks, I had lost all my client work. I was devastated. I was hit, and hit hard. I had absolutely no income! And, I had developed a lifestyle that required one. A big one!

My clients appeared to be very forthcoming, that things were just put on hold until January. In spite of the economy, they had to launch new products to keep their own businesses going. I felt I could hang on that long without any problems, so I just enjoyed all the free time I had. After all, I had a beautiful roof over my head, a handsome husband in the bed next to me, and *some* money in savings. It was rare to have a long break to smell the roses, and I felt it was well deserved. I'd been working like a maniac since I began consulting, so some down time was pleasantly received. While Chris was often out of the house working on his dream, I spent the days exploring my new home town and completing my own plan.

Chris was quickly getting indoctrinated into Las Vegas with all his contacts. I, on the other hand, only knew people who wanted money from me like the furniture dealers and my personal shoppers at the local boutiques. I'd been so busy and traveling that I didn't have time to go out and make new friends. So, when Thanksgiving dinner came, I had no one to invite.

Our Thanksgiving business dinner was a big hit. The house was finally done and it looked fabulous! Chris received numerous compliments and I took them all to heart. I don't know how I had time to work *and* do the decorating for all those months, but I did. It was so much fun! I was nearly going through withdrawal from visiting all my favorite stores.

Chris, on the other hand, had made several friends in the development process for the restaurant, some of whom were sharing Thanksgiving with us. Many people in Las Vegas are transplants and have no family in town to visit for the holiday. Chris thought it was the perfect way to solidify relationships and build rapport with potential investors and business associates. I concurred. And, perhaps, I might be able to snag a business contract out of the evening. It might be fun to work locally for a change.

I looked around and felt a bit envious. Chris had connected with so many great people. I didn't know a soul in the room except for my husband who treated me more like a caterer or a house manager than a wife on this occasion. Following his lead, someone actually started a tip jar for me on the wet bar! I made $452 that night.

Chris went back to Stockholm for Christmas and I popped into Detroit to visit family for a few days. Chris didn't feel the holidays were the best time for me to go home with him and meet his family. When I returned to an empty house, I spent my quiet time researching client opportunities online. I knew my clients would come roaring back at the start of the New Year – business always does – so I didn't want to overload my schedule with new contracts. However, it didn't hurt to look.

When the New Year came, I decided to join the local country club. It was so inexpensive, compared to California, that I was thrilled! It was another dream come true. I thought I would make some business contacts there – you have to spend money to make money, right? And maybe pick up a friend or two.

As it turned out, I had little in common with most of the other members. When Chris and I went together, the men would go off and talk business in the locker room, playing poker and smoking cigars, and I was stuck with the trophy wives who knew nothing more than how to spend their husband's money. Many of them had children, and since Chris and I didn't have any, I couldn't relate. Chris was utilizing my membership to seek out investors for his restaurant business while I ended up sitting by myself on the patio overlooking the greens. So, I played tennis occasionally, but I used the club mostly for my workouts.

I contacted my clients to get an update on their budget status and to find out when we could start working together again. The news was dire. Budgets were still cut and projects were postponed until March. When March came, they were moved out again to an unknown date.

I was now an official wreck! I had had no income for several months. I had used up my emergency funds, thinking more money was on the way soon, and I had no other savings. I spent everything furnishing the house. I asked Chris for some help to sustain me during this down time, but that was a lost cause.

Chris was not interested in helping me out. He said our agreement was very clear, that we would keep our finances separate. He had no legal obligation to support me financially because that would cause problems in maintaining the integrity of the prenup. He said I had breached the contract, and immediately filed for divorce.

Oh, and one other thing. He was having an affair with his realtor.

Dear Diary,

Divorce is so hard. The split with Chris was such a shocker, but today it was just so final. Today was moving day. I'm so exhausted I can't believe I even have the energy to write. But, in order to keep my sanity, I must.

I truly had no idea how much *stuff* I had. When the movers arrived this morning, they brought one 24-foot truck. Well, I needed three of them! Chris didn't want to keep any of the furnishings. I had selected and paid for them, and now he had some new woman to decorate *his* house. I spent hours decorating his house, and loved every piece! Unfortunately, I moved to a rental about one-third the size, and now my garage is stuffed to the rafters with *stuff*! I'll figure it all out tomorrow. Right now I need to rest and find some income – fast!

It tore my heart out to drive down that hillside through the gate for the last time. I was crying so badly I could barely see Chad, the security guard, in the guardhouse. I couldn't even muster the strength to wave to him, although his job was more the comings than the goings. He didn't care who or what left, just who or what got in.

I led the caravan of three trucks to my new place. Even with my help, it took over 12 hours to get it all moved. I had them set up my bed, paid them with cash and a hefty tip for the overtime, and they were gone. My new life has begun, but I still don't know what that is.

More tomorrow!

All my heart,

Diana

Moving On

{ THREE }

Divorce? Breach of contract? An affair? My head was reeling. This couldn't be happening. Everything I did for him and he was kicking me out of his life? In retrospect, maybe I should have made him wash the dishes or clean the toilets to get his head out of the clouds.

I had signed the prenup but we hadn't been married for very long. I didn't even have an income at the moment! I couldn't be left without anything, could I? It didn't seem possible that my marriage to Chris was worthless. I wanted to march my Manolos down to my attorney, Brian's, office hoping he'd say it isn't so, but I had to settle for a long distance phone call.

"I'm sorry, Diana, but this is exactly the scenario I was worried about. Something catastrophic happens, and you're SOL."

Brian wasn't very forgiving. He had warned me but still, he was my attorney. Couldn't he do anything for me?

"But, he had an affair! Isn't that worth something?"

"We could have written in a clause regarding affairs, but you were too eager to sign the agreement as it was."

Aaarrrggghhh! Why does Brian have to be so cut and dry?

"Couldn't I fight it?"

"Well, you could attempt to do that, but you'd have a hard time since you were not under duress at the time you signed the prenup. Plus, quite frankly, you don't have any money to fight with."

"But, just like that, I get nothing?"

"Well, not necessarily. Did you contribute financially to any part of the marriage?"

"Yes, I bought all the furniture."

"Then, you'll get the furniture."

And, just like that, I was a divorcee with 4,200 square feet of furniture and no place to put it.

I managed to procure some funds from my family to help me get re-established. I thought about moving back to California but I really didn't have enough money to do so, and it was less expensive to live in Las Vegas. Since I didn't know how long it would take before my income was flowing smoothly again, I thought it best to stay put. I was just a one hour flight away if an opportunity in California sprung up.

Besides, my skills must be transferable, right? I mean, all those years of business experience must certainly amount to something. I was a highly paid marketing consultant and I would be once again. I just needed to do a little bit of marketing of my own. No problem.

Chris and I did have a chat about what went wrong, and I was astonished to find out that he no longer found me attractive once I had no income. He felt I was too needy. He only knew how to deal with a woman in more factual terms, and when I wasn't working, I appeared to lack ambition and motivation. To him, he was simply cleaning house, firing his business partner, not divorcing his wife.

The only good thing I had on my side – per the prenup – is that I never took Chris's last name. So, people I met in town would never know that we were married unless he brought it up. I wasn't about to. Let the scumbag, unfeeling bastard build his new life. I wasn't going to be part of his past or his future. My life would go on and I'd show him what an idiot he was. I had success once, and I'll have it again.

I found a realtor of my own, a rather handsome, lanky Italian who not only wore Boss, he was the boss. But I digress. We went looking for a new place for me. I loved the area where Chris lived, so I didn't want to move too far away. I rented a darling little townhouse in an upscale development, directly across the street from the site of a new designer shopping mall. As a self-employed consultant, they only needed to see last year's tax returns to verify income, so I qualified easily.

Moving day was a nightmare. I really had no idea just how much furniture I bought. Not only that, some of my favorite pieces couldn't even squeeze through the door of the townhouse. They were purchased for Chris's home, and just didn't fit, in more ways than one. The furniture claimed prime real estate in the garage while my Beemer was left to sit in the driveway, absorbing the desert sun.

I wasn't too worried. I had spent really good money on my furniture, so I was certain that I would recoup most of that by selling what I didn't want. I set about deciding what to keep and what to sell, and promptly placed an ad online. That was another reality check. In a transient town like Vegas, furniture can be had for cheap. I was offered $50 for my $4,000 sofa. As one buyer lamented, "a sofa is a sofa, don't matter what it cost. Your ass still sits in it the same."

I was really hoping to live off the money from the furniture sale for a while, but I didn't know how to make that happen. After all, I had spent over $200,000 furnishing Chris's house! I always believed if you bought quality items, you could sell them if you needed money. Well, you can sell them all right, but you won't get anything substantial for them, particularly in a down economy when everyone else is desperate and trying to offload their goods, too.

I finally found a consignment store that carried better quality furniture. They would even pick up the items. Yippee! Well, that was a short-lived celebration. They would price each item at 40 percent or less than original cost, then split the proceeds with me 50-50. So, if I paid $1,000 for something, they would sell it for $400 and I would receive $200. Heart wrenching. But, if there's something I learned from marketing, an item is only worth what someone will pay for it.

I shipped off part of the contents of my garage and vowed to take whatever I could get. After all, business would pick up soon. My clients had promised me it would. It was now June, and I proposed over $60,000 worth of projects for my clients, at their request. The work would begin in September, a year since the economy took a downturn and I last had any designer-boutique-worthy income. I just had to hang on a few more months.

September turned to January and January to March, with no significant client commitments. I did some small project work here and there, so I wasn't totally destitute. However, my overhead was a bit higher now. I had rent to pay, as well as utilities, insurance and association dues. Since Chris owned the house, he used to pay for all of that. I was only responsible for my own expenses. Most women would look at that as a blessing. Now I see what a curse it can be.

I had hope. I had faith. I had trust. The only thing I didn't have was money.

Dear Diary,

Consulting is both a blessing and a curse. When things
are going well, you feel like you own the world. But,
when things are bad like they are now, everything is so
frustrating. To paraphrase Robert Kiyosaki, when you're
self-employed, you don't own a business you own a job.
Or, perhaps, the job owns you.

In the last month, I've contacted over 300 technology
companies to inquire if they needed any marketing consulting. Three hundred companies! And no one needs
any help. I find that so hard to believe.

Of course, not everyone replied. Out of the 300, only
25 companies answered my inquiries. The ones where
I directly knew the management didn't even respond!
Surprisingly, I received the best responses from companies where I didn't even know a soul. Of course, their answer was that they didn't need any help, they were doing
it in-house or it would be three more months before they
could use someone with my expertise. Just what I needed, more empty promises. I missed the days when people
knocked down my door for my skills.

Some even questioned my commitment to technology.
"You live in Vegas, now, right? How serious are you
about working in high tech? And, why should we pay to
fly you in when we could probably find a perfectly good
consultant down the street?"

I'm stumped. It's like I'm between a rock and a hard
place. Companies in Silicon Valley don't want me and

people here in town don't seem to consider my skills reputable. How dare they! I'm great at what I do.

But, I have to face reality once again. As much as I'm fighting it, as much as I can't stand to be an employee – not the boss – I have to get a job. A job! There was a time in my life when I was excited about getting a job. When I was a teenager. When I was in college. When I graduated from college. When I moved to California. At each of those times in my life, I was excited about getting a job. But, not any more. Now, it seems like prison. Dealing with traffic, schedules, rules, alarm clocks, lack of sunshine, catering to your boss's whims – none of that sounds like fun.

Fun. That's it! I'll look for a job that's fun! Retail always seems like fun, and there's certainly a multitude of retail in this town. All the designer boutiques, the major stores, the excitement of the Strip. I'll be fine. It'll also be good for me to get out of the house. I know the economy will pick up soon, and I can leave my retail servitude behind. In the meantime, just think of the discounts!

More tomorrow!

All my heart,

Diana

The Job Hunt

{ FOUR }

"You have to do something, sweetie. How much did you get for your furniture?"

Gizzi was worried about me, which was comforting after all I'd been through.

"Just a little over $6,000. That should hold me for two or three months. Client work should pick up by then."

Six thousand dollars was not very much. I was used to spending a lot more than that on a monthly basis. But, I took a look at my expenses and if I really watched my spending for the next couple of months, I could survive.

"Just $6,000? For everything?"

"No, but for most of what I had in the garage. I kept some of the furniture. I mean, I need a bed and a table and a sofa, after all."

"You should just sell everything. You don't need such elaborate furnishings now that you're not in Chris's house, and you don't need any more reminders of him hanging around. Sell everything and buy something more practical."

"But I love these pieces! I'm not sure I can part with everything, especially since I see how little I'm getting in return. Besides, once business picks up, I'll buy a house just like Chris has, but with my own money."

"Are you sure you want to stay in Vegas? Come back to California. I'm positive you can find a corporate or agency position here with your skills."

"You know, Giz, I have to say, now that I live in Las Vegas, I actually love it. Besides, Helen and Gabe and the kids are seriously looking at moving here. She's been applying for teaching positions and Gabe can hopefully find a job as an electrician. It would be great to live near family again. As much as I love California, being near my family, watching Helen's kids grow, nothing beats that."

"I applaud your sense of loyalty to your family, Diana, but you have to look out for yourself. If you can't make a living, it doesn't matter how much you love to be near them. Even family will push you out the door if you can't pay the rent. No one likes a freeloader. It's time to view yourself as an employee again and not as a consultant and find a full time job."

Ouch! Gizzi had never spoken to me so harshly before. She didn't have to physically strike. Her words did it for her. I loved her for her honesty but reality was not something I was prepared to accept just yet.

Helen had echoed Gizzi's sentiments during a recent phone conversation, adding comments that spewed out of her mouth, mimicking words Dad would say. "You're still young but you'll hit 70 before you know it. You have to think about retirement. Work for a company that will give you a good pension plan."

I wasn't as worried about benefits from my future employer so much as finding a job that would pay my bills until my business built up again, without having to dip into my own retirement fund.

"What's it really like in Silicon Valley now, Giz? Do you think I could find a job?"

"It's a bit harried, I'll admit, but certainly better than Vegas. At least the jobs are far more professional. I'm grateful I was promoted into a director of sales position last year. I'm not so reliant on my own commissions but I know my team is worried. There are budget cuts all across the valley. A lot of companies are under a hiring freeze, too, so I know my team won't stray but there are so many new startups that, with your expertise, someone should welcome you with open arms."

"Doesn't the marketing budget get cut before sales? Why would they hire me?"

"You could go straight into a director position. That seldom gets cut. Companies still need a marketing guru. You'll just have to do all the work yourself. Long hours but certainly stock options and definitely a regular paycheck."

Well, something to think about, but I still wasn't sure I would make the trek back to Silicon Valley. I love California, but I really want to be near my family. If I can hang on until Helen finds out if she's moving to town, then my decision will be easy.

"As always, Gizzi, food for thought. I'm already here so I'll explore a little more fully before I check into relocating."

"You'd better hurry, doll. Companies are digging in their heels. They expect this to be a deep and long recession. If you don't get hired in the near term, you may be on the streets. Now, go get some sleep and get a fresh start tomorrow."

"Thanks, Giz. You're the best!"

Lies, lies and more lies.

For years I've heard human resources experts tout the beauty of transferable skills. What a bunch of crap. While the skills may transfer, just try to convince someone to hire you. Not everyone is willing to take on that challenge.

With dwindling funds and increasing false promises from technology clients, I started to scout out local opportunities. The fastest growing city in the country was also the kindest to new businesses. With an amazing number of folks opening their neon doors, I would be there to help them tell the world.

I pounded the pavement, emailed, telephoned, networked, pressed the flesh, whatever, to no avail. The reason? I didn't have *their* type of experience. The biggest industries besides gaming were hospitality, entertainment, construction and retail. Yep, they were right. I had absolutely no experience in those industries. This is a town where applying for a marketing position can mean auditioning to become a Jägermeister girl.

As for consulting, there were other issues. Many companies were small and had minimal or no budget for my level of experience. Or, they were multinational chains who had their marketing departments located at their headquarters, somewhere outside of Vegas.

I even tried the local PR and marketing agencies, looking for a full-time job (shudder). But, alas, they wanted someone with consumer experience, no matter what they said at the initial interview. They were willing to take me on and train me but at a salary nearly 85 percent less than what I previously earned, for a 60 or 70 hour workweek. I think not. If the economy was a bit better, I might have been able to negotiate a higher salary, as many agencies turn 'em and burn 'em, but I didn't have the economy on my side at the moment.

Once you've worked for yourself, and had control over your time, it's very difficult to give that up. I'd been spoiled. I admit it. But I also had to admit that I had bills to pay. I sucked up my pride, printed a resume, and set out about town filling out job applications.

Besides salaried positions like those I had looked for at agencies, there seem to be three levels of jobs in Vegas. The first is a straight commission position, the second is minimum wage plus tips, and the third is an hourly position that pays minimum wage or just slightly more per hour, while performing a list of duties as long as your arm. I knew I was too clumsy to be a waitress and I didn't have the chest for cocktailing so I eliminated level two from the start. I could easily get a full commissioned position, but since I didn't currently have an income, I didn't think that was an intelligent option. So, I opted for the hourly rate. The most logical place to start? Retail.

I went to the local mall just a mile away and wrote till my hands were blue. Two weeks later, no response. Do you think I scared people away when I listed myself as president of my own company on the applications? I decided to tone it down and simply list my previous occupation as consultant. Most people think that consultants are folks that are out of work looking for a job. That would be me.

It was now March. Eighteen months had passed since the bottom fell out of the stock market. Things seemed to be getting worse instead of better, at least in the tech industry. I knew the economy would eventually pick up, and I knew my consulting business would be a success once again. There was not a doubt in my mind. However, in the meantime, I would find the perfect job – for me. And, it was right around the corner.

Well, actually right around the corner and about 15 miles down the freeway to the Strip. The Strip is where everything happens in Vegas, so I was certain someone with my qualifications could find a job somewhere down there. I hated the thought of commuting. I hated the thought of clocking in and being at someone else's beck and call, especially for the mere pittance they would pay me.

However, it was my reality and I would embrace it. Who knows who I might meet down there? Maybe a business owner will come into the store and need marketing help. Or, a celebrity will meet me, love me and take me on as a personal assistant. The possibilities are endless. I started to live the fantasy the minute my foot hit the accelerator and I sped down the US-95 freeway to my future.

I was living in a town that I hardly knew. I'd been here near-ly three years, but I hadn't really made any friends. And while the town was growing, there was still a small town feel to it, recognizing that a core group of people really made things hap-pen. The group was hard to break into, but I had to find a way in. They must certainly shop, n'est-ce pas? I felt empowered. I wasn't abandoning my existing business; I was creating a brand new world in a new place for me. I'm just dropping into my own destiny. At least until technology picks up again and I could kiss the sorry retail bastards good-bye.

Dear Diary,

Is image everything? Am I totally materialistic? I would think I've more soul than that.

The reason I ask is that today they took away my BMW. Who they? The repo boys. My, what a life they must lead, always being on the run, doing their work in the dark. I heard some noise outside in the early morning hours, but I couldn't bear to look. I just turned over, shed a tear, and went back to sleep. I knew they would come one day, so I just continued to park my car in the driveway.

Without a steady income, it was just impossible to maintain my high lease payment. I tried, but I had to make some choices. I could either continue to pay for my car, or continue to take care of myself. I calculated that my nails, eyebrows, hair, wax and massage on a monthly basis cost $500 or more, depending on how often I go and what I have done. And, I have to be realistic. I actually don't drive that much on an annual basis, so do I really need such a beautiful car? Will it absolutely make that much difference when I approach potential clients? I think not.

With much apprehension, I decided to take a chance. This is Vegas, you know, a gambling town. I don't really have an income right now, so buying a new car is pretty much out of the question. But, I've always had such bad luck with used cars, I was leery of going that route, too. And driving an inexpensive import was a little hard for me to stomach, in spite of the fact that people do buy them. My neighbor, Jeff, said that he had a co-worker who was selling a car that I could get at a good price, and I took the bait.

"Great!" I said. "What type of car is it?"

"A Buick, I think," he said. "It's a really good transportation car."

Hmm, OK, it's an American car, so that's a good thing. Jeff said that his friend would be willing to take a deposit, and I could pay the balance monthly until it was paid off. He was willing to accept $100 per month, and he'd give me the title right from the start.

It sounded like a good deal, but I was still concerned, both about the quality of the car and how I'd feel driving it. I hope that I won't need to use it for very long, but I have to have some sort of transportation. I was afraid to ask for pictures. Jeff has been a great neighbor since I moved in, so I decided to trust him. He took my $500 deposit, and in a few hours he was back with the car.

Oh, the devil is in the details. Lo, that I should have asked questions, even looked at a photo. Jeff knocked on my door and handed me the keys to my new car, a 1985 Buick LeSabre. Yep, Jeff's my hero.

More tomorrow!

All my heart,

Diana

The Perfect Job

{ FIVE }

Ah, shopping in Las Vegas. What a pleasure. Within a two-mile span on the Strip, you can visit nearly every world-class designer boutique, along with major department and specialty stores, and just about anything else your little heart desires. When I first moved to Vegas, I discovered that the best shopping was at Runway Fashion Mall, The Alexandria Shops and The Italian Romance Shoppes, but as time goes on, fashion retail is ever evolving.

My first stop was Runway Fashion Mall because Sherborne was there. This was their first store in Nevada, and people were excited. They had opened in November, but the first time I stepped foot in the place was to submit an application.

Sherborne is best known nationwide for their customer service. Sales associates have gone above and beyond the call of duty to service their clientele, and to my knowledge, are aptly compensated. I had some friends in California who decided to make a career of it with Sherborne, and if I recall correctly, were making about $50,000-$60,000 per year. Not a dollar figure that I was used to, but certainly a respectable salary for retail.

It was an absolute pleasure just to walk in the store. I had frequented multiple locations nationwide, and it really felt beautiful and peaceful to step foot on those marble floors. The pianist was playing, as any faithful shopper would expect, and I felt right at home. The company was known for hiring people from all walks of life, not just career retail salespeople, so I was quite confident that I would be hired quickly. I completed my application, shook hands with the gal at the HR counter and pranced away with a jump in my step, perhaps a bit too overconfident. I waited by the phone but no call came.

The next target for my job hunt was The Alexandria Shops. With all the amazing designer boutiques and major name brand stores, I was certain I could find temporary employment that would supplement my income until the tech industry took off again.

I went to all my favorite stores and chatted with my personal shoppers. Every conversation went basically the same way.

"It's so great to see you again, Diana! What can I help you with today? We just received a number of new items from the spring and summer collection."

Air kisses.

"Uh, hi, (insert name). Good to see you, too. I'm not actually shopping today. I'm looking for employment. Is (insert store name) hiring?"

Look of dismay and disgust, turning the conversation uncomfortable.

"I thought business was good, Diana. What happened?"

"Well, you know, the economy has been a little crazy these last few months. My clients are holding onto their wallets a little tighter so I'm looking for something to do in the meantime."

"You know, business has been really slow here, too. Luxury shoppers aren't purchasing as much, or they're doing it very discreetly. Everyone is looking for a bargain without any logos on it. They don't want to seem ostentatious."

"I have been reading about that. But, are you looking to add any staff?"

"Actually, no. Everyone's hours got cut. We're now only working about 20 hours a week, which means we lost many benefits as well. I wish I could help, Diana, but even if you had years of experience selling in luxury retail, we wouldn't hire you. The company would never invest in someone they know will leave once the economy picks up."

Why must people be so cruel? Does she think I'll come back and buy from her once my bank account is flush again after talking to me like this?

"No worries. I appreciate your honesty. I'm sure things will improve soon. I'll pass your name around to my friends. Hopefully, you'll get some business from that."

I really knew no one in town to pass her name to. So, there. You've just been touched by the Mistress of False Hope.

"Thanks, Diana. We sure could use it."

Air kisses.

I decided to walk the mall but I was a bit disappointed as very few stores were accepting applications, and the higher-end stores required several years' experience in luxury retail. Or, as I came to find out, you needed to know someone to get in, and I don't mean your personal shopper.

My last stop was the fabulously popular lingerie store, Isabella's Intimates. Isabella's started out as a lowly catalog company, but through genius marketing and planning, had blossomed into the brand for sexy everyday lingerie. Any article of clothing with the Isabella logo or name is snatched up by throngs of tourists and locals alike. I looked around and liked what I saw, and I felt it would be a fun and interesting place to work, fun being the operative word here. I completed my application and turned it in to the manager on duty.

"We're only looking for part-time right now. Would that work for you?"

"Yes, that would be fine. Would the shift be during the day or at night?"

"At night, most likely. If you're interested, I'll have you come for an interview on Thursday afternoon at 2:30 p.m."

"Sounds great to me. I'll be there."

Yippee! That was the first positive moment I'd had in a long time. I decided to celebrate and treated myself to lunch at the Palm. How I love their lemon chicken.

I went to the interview appointment as requested, and I was led into the back office area. Retail is all about sales per square foot, so office space is at a minimum. The office and stockroom are typically crowded closet-sized spaces that have to perform a multitude of functions.

When I arrived, I was surprised to find that there were five girls sitting in a circle in front of the employee lockers. This was to be a group interview. I'd experienced that before as a consultant, but it was usually the CEO and other members of the executive staff who wanted to gang up on me at once to see how I handled pressure from senior management. Not a problem. Still, I thought this was unusual, but what choice did I have. I took a seat and sized up the competition.

And size is an understatement. The girls were young, either seniors in high school or fresh graduates, all a size 0 or 2, with implants the size of grapefruits. Not that I'm old or big, but I felt that way next to these youngsters. That's OK. I'm head and shoulders above them in brains.

I hadn't met Mila, the store manager who conducted the interview. She was from Australia which added to the mystique of Isabella's. The company marketing was creative, compelling shoppers to believe Isabella's was a British institution, but the Australian accent was close enough. I never quite understood why they would embrace being a British company when Isabella's is all about sex and sensuality and the Brits are known for neither.

Mila ran through a prepared list of questions, and we responded individually when selected.

"Why do you want to work at Isabella's?"

"Because I think you guys have the sexiest stuff ever." "Because it's the only place I shop." "My boyfriend told me to get a job here so I could get a discount."

"What is our number one priority?"

"Making sure the store is stocked so customers can find what they want to buy." "Having everything in stock that's online." "Keeping an eye on the customers so no one steals anything."

"What is the image of Isabella's?"

"British." "Slutty." "Tall, super thin models with big fake boobs."

"What products do we sell?"

"Padded bras and thongs." "Bras and underwear." "Everything today's working girl needs, and y'all know what I mean by working girl!"

"How does your past work experience qualify you to work at Isabella's?"

"I've never worked before. This is my first job." "I can run the cash register as long as it tells me how much change to give back." "If I can work in fast food, I can work anywhere."

And on and on. I was the only one of the bunch who had no retail background, but I crossed my fingers that would not deter them from hiring me. At this point, I would accept any work I could get.

"OK, thank you very much for coming. I'll review your applications with the other managers, check references and we'll contact those that we feel are appropriate for our company."

I left the interview not feeling very confident. It looked like they really wanted to have a much younger image, considering the type of gals they were interviewing. However, two days later I received a phone call with a job offer.

"Can you start next Thursday?"
"Absolutely!"
And, just like that, I joined the ranks of the employed.

Isabella's Intimates

Dear Diary,

I finally got a job! This afternoon the phone rang and Mila, the store manager at Isabella's Intimates, called to offer me a position with the company. You'd think it was a day to rejoice, but I've been offered the princely sum of one dollar over minimum wage, per hour. Do you believe that! It's a long way from the $200 an hour that I make in high tech, but at least it could be some play money until my own business picks up again. I've been told that I'm at the top of the pay scale for Isabella's, so I guess I should be impressed with myself. I'm rich!

Cha-ching! Time to go shopping for new work clothes. Everything I have is either too professional (read: expensive) or too casual. Mila told me the dress code requirements and I have only two days before I start. So, I set my alarm for early tomorrow morning to hit the mall. I'm so excited! This is truly going to be a positive turning point in my life.

I was surprised to hear from Isabella's because during the interview I was told they would check references, and my references hadn't heard anything. I gave them Gizzi and Helen's info. There's no way I could actually have them talk to one of my clients. Besides, this job is just for fun, right? Anyway, I'm in touch with Giz and Helen on a regular basis, and neither has heard from Isabella's. Maybe they have some other way of screening candidates, but checking references isn't one of them.

One of the reasons I'm so excited about Isabella's is that the shift works perfectly for me. I don't start until 8 p.m., so that gives me all day to contact potential clients and work on marketing projects. The store closes no later than midnight on weekends, so I can't think of a better schedule for me right now. It's amazing how you look for something and it just drops in your lap – like destiny. This truly is a blessing.

More tomorrow!

All my heart,

Diana

Retail Is Not for Sissies

{ SIX }

I was so excited to get out of the house and be earning money again that I arrived at the store early for my first shift. I dressed per the dress code Mila gave me over the phone, and as budget-conscious as I tried to be, I was certain I was better dressed than any of my co-workers.

I had gone shopping for a work wardrobe that could double as business casual once I left Isabella's. I didn't expect to be there very long. Once the economy picked up, I was outta there, so I made sure that anything I purchased fit my style and would have a life beyond this store.

I wasn't required to wear a uniform, but the dress code called for black dress slacks, a black jacket or blazer without any identifiable logos and a blouse or top. The top could be as low-cut as we wanted – the lower the better – because we were supposed to portray that sexy Isabella's image.

It wasn't the way I would normally dress, but hey, this is Las Vegas where sexy reigns supreme. Besides, who am I going to run into in this store that I know from my high tech life? I think the low cut tops were also a way for management to confirm that we were actually wearing their product. Not a problem, since I absolutely loved Isabella's bras. And, I hear, we get free ones every now and then.

The blouse could be as colorful as we liked, but it couldn't have any specific writing or logos. We also wore black shoes, any style or heel height except for athletic shoes or sandals. Seemed very basic, but it made dressing all that much easier.

I found a beautiful blazer and matching slacks to wear for my shifts. I opted for a white shirt today, but purchased a few in colors. I'd mostly been dressing casually during my consulting days, so I took it up a notch without going all out. I knew how the Cupids, Isabella's world-famous models, dressed in the catalog and commercials, and although I wasn't quite Cupid material, I could surely portray their essence. I only wish someone had told me to buy the cheapest clothes I could find because when you work retail, your clothes get totally trashed very quickly. Don't ever wear something you love because it will get snagged, stained, stuck in something or simply worn out. But, that was the least of what I would learn about retail as time went on.

I walked the store to get a lay of the land before my shift, although I was certain management would give me a tour. The majority of the store was filled with bras of every style and size, with matching panties in an assortment of styles. There were the basic nudes – honestly, is that all women wear anymore? – but also the fashion colors for the season.

One section of the store displayed mostly clothing, workout and sleepwear. You really had to be tiny to wear this stuff. Anyone over a size 12 would be hard-pressed to be able to fit into anything in the store. Isabella's was strict about their image, and they didn't dare promote cellulite or obesity. If you wanted to be an Isabella's customer, you worked hard to find your body somewhere on their size charts.

One lone corner of the store housed their beauty line. Isabella's was well-known for fragrances and body products such as sprays, splashes and body wash. They also dabbled in makeup, but it never seemed to be a hot seller.

I finally made my way to the office to check in. My first day was also the first for two other girls. We began our shift by watching videos. So far so good. We learned about the history of the company, the bevy of Cupid supermodels that help to spread their image, and what to do in the event of a shoplifter. When the videos concluded, Mila gave us our keys to the dressing rooms, and sent us out onto the floor to work. No product training, no floor tour, no nothing.

I was left to the guidance of Penelope, the night manager, with whom I would work every shift for all my employ at Isabella's. I don't think she ever took a night off. Penny was a typical Las Vegas stereotype, although I don't believe she hailed from these parts. She seemed to have a lot of Texas in her and if you looked hard enough, Penny was probably packing a pink pistol somewhere.

Penny was diminutive, with long blond hair. She could be the perfect Cupid if she were 10 inches taller, 20 years younger and stayed out of the sun. And those ever-present stilettos! How she was able to walk – no run – the entire shift, I have no idea. She had perfect posture in spite of her 32F bra size. She was a bundle of energy like I'd never seen before, and although she appeared to have had a hard life, she always had a positive outlook.

Penny could tell I had a good head on my shoulders and that I was eager to learn as much as I could about the products I was selling, the hallmark of a good salesperson and something rarely seen in these environs. She took me under her wing with the hope that, long term, I could become management material. While I applauded her efforts, my sights were set elsewhere.

Penny had several years' background in selling bras, so she was able to guide me as to how to properly fit one. She handed me a tape measure which I was expected to always hang around my neck, like a prized and expensive lariat necklace that chaffed in all the wrong places. Before the lesson began, one of the girls who had just watched the introductory videos with me went whizzing by, first from the front of the store to the back office, then back to the front.

"What was that?" I asked.

"Another newbie quit," Penny calmly replied.

"Quit! She just started like 15 minutes ago."

"Trust me. I've seen it before. She quit."

Penny looked up at the shocked expression on my face and tried to make me feel better.

"Don't worry. You'll make it. You're strong, a lot stronger than she is."

I shook the image of Quitting Girl out of my system and gave my focus back to Penny.

"OK, now, have you ever done a bra fitting before?" she inquired.

I shook my head, "No."

"That's fine. It's not that hard to do. The instructions are printed on the back of the tape measure."

Sure enough, I flipped over the tape measure hanging around my neck and there they were, instructions on how to do a bra fitting the Isabella way. Penny pretended I was a customer while she taught me the three main steps of measurement.

"OK, first you measure below the breasts. That should be your approximate band size. Then, measure above the breasts and directly across the breasts. The difference here is your cup size. Every inch different in the measurement is one cup. So, in your case, there's a three inch difference. That means you wear a C cup. You should be wearing a 32C."

"What! I'm a 34B! I can't imagine I'm a C cup!"

"And, that's exactly the reaction nearly every customer will have. What you're wearing is a sister size. Down in the cup, up in the band. Down in the band, up in the cup. So a 34B is relatively equivalent to a 32C, although the 32C should fit you just slightly better. Got it?"

"Uh, sure. Got it. But what if the customer argues with me about their size?"

"First of all, measuring isn't an exact science, particularly when it comes to breast implants and larger cup sizes. So, give it your best shot, pull five bras and have the customer try them on. If they don't fit like she wants, pull some more until she finds the size that makes her happy. Your goal is to sell an entire bra wardrobe – five bras – to each customer: t-shirt, strapless, work-out, push-up and lace.

"Second, approximately 80 percent of women are wearing the wrong bra size either because they've never been fitted, been poorly fitted or they don't want to face reality. Our goal here is to satisfy customers by selling bras. If the customer is happy wearing the wrong size, fill up her credit card with them. We don't care. If they leave here with a smile on their face wearing our product, what more could we ask for?"

And with that, my lesson was complete. Penny had been eying the growing lines at the front registers while she was teaching me the ins and outs of bra fittings, so once she finished her comments, she sprinted to the checkout to help those happy customers purchase more ill-fitting bras. While 80 percent of all women are wearing the wrong size, I would discover that most women don't really want to know their correct one. They'd rather live in a fantasy world, no matter how much the bra pinched, pulled and hurt.

Isabella's Intimates at The Alexandria Shops was always incredibly busy. I'd shopped here before but never really paid attention. If the line was long, I just texted while I waited. Now that this store was a part of my life, I viewed it differently. The place was hopping, and it was 9 p.m. on a Thursday night! This location was the number one volume store in the country, but I really had no idea they could do such brisk business.

We pulled in numbers that were overwhelming. It's amazing how quickly $50 bras can add up. A typical Saturday night brought in $32,000 with a $50 ADS and 650 transactions. Weekdays were just slightly less volume. And, regardless of how much we sold, the store never looked empty. I would think that selling tens of thousands of dollars every day, a store this size would seem sparse. Still, it always looked as fresh as could be. I can't even imagine the total dollar value of the inventory on that floor.

There were two classifications of girls during a shift – floor girls and cashiers. The cashiers spent their hours ringing customers and answering phone calls from behind the front counter, occasionally straying to help straighten the merchandise near the front of the store during the few slow times.

The sales floor was divided into four distinct selling quadrants, and the floor girls, once assigned, were not to leave their post for the shift. It was a way to help prevent theft by always having floor coverage, but I think it was bad service to hand off the customer you'd been helping as they crossed into someone else's zone. Still, since we only got paid by the hour, and not by commission, I guess the company determined that this was the right way to organize the staff. If you needed to leave for any reason, you had to get someone else to cover your area.

I was generally in the back part of the store where their most popular bra styles were displayed. And the dressing rooms were in my territory, so I was helping to actually fit customers as they tried on their bras.

Being part of a casino shopping mall, Isabella's had a sort of party atmosphere. People from all over the world came to our store with shopping lists from family and friends so they could stock up until another of their relatives made a trip the following year. Many walked in with drinks, and if they didn't have alcohol in hand, it was obvious they had already imbibed.

There were certain key times when hordes of people would descend upon the store. We were situated near the roving magic act, so when those shows ended (usually every 30 minutes), hundreds of people would make their way into Isabella's, mostly just for a walk-thru. The other popular shopping time was late at night after the headliner show let out. Folks always came to Isabella's with their programs and drinks, to top off the night with a new intimate ensemble. It was an absolute madhouse.

There was also an atmosphere of sex. Not raunchy, porn star sex, but even the everyday lingerie the store sold was intended to be taken off – by someone else. You just assumed everyone who shopped at Isabella's was gorgeous, had a statuesque figure like the Cupids, and was having really good sex every day. That's the image they portrayed. Then there's reality…

"Is it always like this?" I asked Penny as I cleaned out another disgusting fitting room.

"Like what?" Penny replied.

"Well, you know. Do we have to clean up someone's bodily fluids on every shift? I can't believe the company doesn't supply us with rubber gloves."

"You'll get used to it. At least they used a condom."

Yes, sex in the fitting room occurred on nearly a daily basis. There were about 30 fitting rooms, and when all of them were occupied, it was impossible to keep tabs on each and every customer. Unlike many stores, Isabella's allowed men into the fitting room, explaining that it was common practice in Europe so it fit their image. I think the health department would have been interested to know what actually took place when drunk men and women went behind a locked door to "try on" sexy lingerie.

But, sex isn't the only smelly thing happening at this Isabella's.

"What's that odor?" I asked, my eyes watering from the acrid smell.

"It's the sewers," Melody, one of the veteran sales girls, answered. "This mall was built on top of a sewer. Sometimes it gets so bad customers won't even try stuff on."

Melody had exotic good looks that perfectly fit the Isabella image. She was one of the few swing shift employees who had stuck around for more than a few weeks, and knew the business of Isabella's inside and out. She reached below Penny's makeshift desk near the fitting rooms, grabbed a can of spray air freshener, and walked up and down the fitting room hallway, spraying like her life depended on it.

"Is it only our store?"

I was shocked that something so malodorous would be seeping through the walls of a store with such a sexy image.

"No," Penny replied. "Just the stores on this side, in this stretch of the mall. We're also by the dumpsters so we get a whole mix of scents and smells."

"Hmm, lucky us."

A couple of nights later, I was starting to get the hang of things at the store, although I had to admit my body ached more than after any large trade show I had ever worked. Well, actually more than anything I had ever done. I didn't know feet, in particular, could hurt so badly. I was forced to go shopping for some well-padded flats and hoped that would end my wardrobe investment for this temporary position.

After the initial dinner rush, things slowed for a bit. I kept an eye on what everyone was doing, trying to learn by observation. When it came to the night shift, Penny and Melody were my two best bets for actually acquiring useful knowledge. Penny usually hung out at her desk in my quadrant while Melody worked the registers most nights.

"Where's Melody?" I asked Penny. I had seen Melody run into the back office about five minutes ago, but she was neither on break nor lunch, so I was concerned.

Without missing a beat, Penny replied, "Oh, she's probably hanging out in the upstairs stockroom."

I couldn't believe what I was hearing.

"We have an upstairs stockroom?"

I was shocked. I had no idea! I wondered where all of the excess inventory was kept.

"Duh. Why do you think there are stairs in the middle of the office?" Penny snarked back at me.

"I dunno. I thought they were for the utility workers. They go almost straight up so I couldn't imagine any other reason to use them."

Penny looked at me, a look that said, "Why is this intelligent woman so clueless?"

"Can I go up and check it out?" I asked.

Penny glanced around the floor. We weren't too busy, so she agreed.

"Sure. Go see what you've been missing. I guarantee those stairs will tell you whether or not you're in shape."

I smiled and nodded at Penny and tore off for the office. I knew we weren't allowed to be off the floor for long, so I tried to sprint up the stairs. Big mistake! I made it about halfway before I had to stop and climb slowly for the second half.

Once I got to the top, a whole new world opened up before me. Box after box, rolling rack after rolling rack, all in various states of disarray covered this vast expanse of the upstairs stockroom. I honestly had no idea it even existed!

I must have startled Melody because she came running toward the stairs as if she were doing something wrong.

"Oh, it's just you," she said as she slowed down, threw the bra from her hand into an open box, and sat down in front of – windows! "What do you want?"

"I've never been up here before," I said as I made my way to the windows to sit beside Melody. "Penny said I could come up here and check it out."

I looked at Melody then stuck my nose up against a window. I could see the entire store from there.

"Wow! That's pretty cool. You can see everything."

"And everyone," Melody said. "Sometimes security hangs out here if they're looking for a shoplifter or making sure the employees are being honest. Sometimes when you can't find a manager, she might be up here. You never know who's watching."

Melody rolled her eyes at me looking out the window in awe, got up and hit me on the shoulder.

"C'mon, I'll give you the lay of the land."

I stood up, excited that someone in this store might actually try to teach me something useful besides bra fitting.

Melody pointed here and there as she described the different zones of the stock room.

"OK, over here on the left we have clothing and fashion lingerie," she said as I looked at a long line of mostly empty rolling racks.

"But I thought we didn't have any fashion back stock," I said. Sure would be nice to know these things.

"Well, generally we don't, but on occasion we do have a piece here or there. Or, we'll get shipments of merch that didn't sell at other stores. But, even if it's really busy and a customer asks you to check the stockroom, you have to do it. If you tell them all the fashion is on the floor they'll complain to the manager. So, it gives you an excuse to come up here and hide for a few minutes before you go back down and tell her what you were going to tell her in the first place."

"I see..."

"This back mess is panty stock. It's marked on the outside of the box what's inside, but we usually have all we need on the floor. The stock team checks it every morning so unless we had a big run on a particular style and size, you shouldn't need to look at those."

I stared at a huge section of the stockroom, stacked with boxes partially opened, panties hanging out, some of them on the floor.

"And, last but not least, over here we have our bras, everything from t-shirt to strapless. This is probably the biggest mess of all."

Melody was right. Some were hanging on rolling racks. Others were in boxes. Still others were in plastic bags on the floor.

"So, if we have a stock team, why is this place such a mess?"

Melody gave me that look, that look that Penny just gave me, the, "How can this woman be so dumb?" look. After a heavy sigh, she replied, in a nearly managerial way.

"Diana, do you have any idea how much merchandise we get in on a daily basis?"

Of course I don't, or else I wouldn't be asking these questions.

"Our stock team barely has time to check in the boxes coming off the truck. They put as much on the floor as they can, then the rest of the merch comes up here."

"But the stairs are so narrow. How do they get those big boxes up here?"

Again, Melody gave me that look. Maybe Melody should be looking into the training program. She has the attitude.

"Next time you're down in the office, look behind the Cupids poster. You'll see a dumbwaiter. The boxes go in there and the stock team can either bring merch down to the floor or send it up to the stock room."

Melody took a quick glance toward one of the windows.

"Uh, oh, we gotta go. Penny is sending us smoke signals."

Melody took off like a shot for the stairs. I tried to keep up with her.

"How do you handle these things? It's worse than going to the gym."

"Trust me. Now that you know about the stockroom, you'll be up and down these stairs about 20 times a day. I lost 10 pounds my first month. Now I'm training to climb Mount Everest."

I knew Melody was being sarcastic, but if I could lose 10 pounds and shape up, I'd have something to be grateful for.

We burst out onto the floor into a sea of customers, timing it just right. The magic show was over and it was time to sell some bras.

Dear Diary,

Men are such slime. Now, I agree, I am still bitter over my divorce, but the quality of men – and I use that term loosely – that shop at this Isabella's is disgusting. On any given night, we'll have at least two or three who come in to purchase multiple sets of lingerie for their girlfriends. They buy the exact same set but in different sizes. At first I thought they did that because if one of the girls found a thong or bra at her man's house that she shouldn't have, she would just assume it was hers that she left by mistake. But, as dumb as some of these women may be, they are still smart enough to know their own bra and panty size.

Someone told me they're not actually purchasing for girlfriends, that these are women who, shall I say, work for them. They must be rather low-end girls to be wearing Isabella's – not that there's anything wrong with that. It's just that, if these were women capable of earning their boss big bucks, they'd be shopping at a high-class store and not here.

I can't believe how much time I spend thinking about these idiot customers! I should be focused on building my business but, here again, those slimy men are still making false promises to me about potential contracts.

"Let's talk next week, Diana. I'm sure I'll have some news by then."

"Oh, sorry, Diana. Looks like I was misinformed. Budgets are still on hold for another two weeks, until the next board meeting. Everyone really likes working with you so I know we'll get a contract processed as soon as possible."

And on and on it goes.

I have learned a new skill during this time – how to properly fit a bra – but unless I can create an app for that, it's still only going to get me one dollar over minimum wage. Oh, and I know how to straighten panty tables. Whoopee.

I think it's time to consign more furniture.

More tomorrow!

All my heart,

Diana

Panty Tables

{ SEVEN }

Panty tables are the bane of my existence.

Isabella's panties are the number one selling product in the company. Although the profit margin on bras is much higher, panties are the entry point to the Isabella's image. Even a high school student could afford some of the cotton numbers and proudly proclaim herself to be an Isabella's devotee.

Every closing shift, I would take a deep breath, look around and try to find the table that needed the most amount of work. The store had several tables piled high with panties, all different styles, colors, sizes. Last inventory, they estimated there were between 15,000 and 20,000 panties total on the tables on a daily basis. Each and every panty had to be in place by style, color and size before we left for the night. I would complain to Helen about how much effort it took, and she would just reply, "I can't even straighten my own panty drawer!"

Usually, four or five girls closed, but it takes an enormous amount of time to straighten that many panties. It amazed me that the company determined this was the most beneficial and efficient use of their employee time. It was more like torture and punishment than a positive entry into the world of fashion. I can only imagine how many dollars were spent on labor, just to straighten those nasty little things.

So many hands touch a pair of panties before you make a purchase that I swear I will never again wear a new pair of panties without washing them at least three times first! And you never knew what you'd find in a table of over 1,000 panties. How could I forget the blood-stained blue and white striped thong, buried deep in a pile?

Straightening the panty tables was as much an art as a process. Big companies are built because they are able to develop repetitive processes that work. For this company, that meant chunking rather than fanning.

Chunking is the art of stacking panties by specific color, style and size, then layering them. So, if I was working on cottons, I might stack the blue low-rise size small, then medium, then large and extra-large. Each stack becomes a chunk, and the layering process is begun. As you can imagine, pulling one panty from the stack can disrupt the entire table. Sometimes, the tables were in such disarray, we'd simply throw everything on the floor and separate them into piles from there, hence, another reason to wash before wearing.

The company should have supplied us with rubber gloves to do the chunking. Although a lot of panties were sold without ever being tried on, many were, and the customers often did not adhere to our dressing room rules.

Isabella's requested that its customers try them on over their own, not placed directly next to the body. If the customer was commando, we could supply them with a paper style like you get for a wax. But most customers just ignored the rules, took off their undies and tried ours on. And, honestly, even if you keep your thong on and try on one from the sales floor, the string is still going up the butt. I'm sad to say, the panty situation was so gross it provided another reason for the health department to come in and cite us with violations or even shut us down. But, the health department has bigger fish to fry and we hoped our customers cleaned with antibacterial soap.

It was always a rush to get the tables done, and when we could, we'd start to straighten them at about eight o'clock. The tables were basically split into two, with one half of the table mirroring what was on the other. When the back half was straightened, we would lift the table skirt up and over the panties and tuck it in so no one would touch it. The customers still had access to the exact same items on the front half of the tables, but covering created some sort of mysterious draw. Invariably, there was a customer who thought we were keeping something from them, and they picked up the table skirt and dug through the straightened panties, rather than the ones in the pile. Then, we'd have to start over again.

One time, it was nearly midnight and I had just completed the cotton thongs. I didn't have a chance to cover the table before I went off to help a customer. When I turned around, a woman in her 50s and her son – well, at least I think they were related – were in the process of destroying it. I just glared at the son as he pulled one or two panties from each chunk. Why was he touching them, anyway? Gross.

"Is there something I can help you find?" I asked the mother when I approached the table, grabbing each of the displaced thongs and putting them back in their piles.

"No, just looking. I really can't decide. I know it's late and everything is so neat and organized, but I'm a visual person so I really need to see everything before I can make a decision."

"Well, there's no need for your son to pull out your selections. I'd be happy to do that for you. We'll be closing in a few minutes and everything needs to be straightened before we leave, as I'm sure you're well aware. If I could help you, it would save us both time."

The mother and son looked at each other and shared a mischievous grin, whereupon the son picked up pile after pile of thongs and said to me, "Too late now!"

"Come along, son," the bitch said. "I can't possibly make a decision in such a messy establishment. We'll have to go somewhere that can keep a tidy store."

The two of them left, laughing, while I began once again to chunk those thongs.

I learned a lot during those panty-straightening nights, not necessarily things that would improve my quality of life. Once the doors closed, the atmosphere completely changed. With loud music playing in the background, the conversations were over the top. Was that how I was just a mere 10 years ago? I can't imagine, because the topics of conversation were so shocking to me. It seems every night I learned more about this younger generation – and sex – than I ever thought possible. Tonight was no different.

We took our stations at the panty tables, turned up the music and began the monotonous task of straightening the unruly undies. While I kept my mouth shut and my ears open, the chatter began. The employee turnover on the night shift was high, so high that I rarely knew anyone's name. They stayed for a few weeks then were replaced by someone who looked surprisingly like them but with a different moniker. It didn't matter. The chitter-chatter went on for hours.

I was halfway through straightening my table when the urge to urinate overtook every cell in my body. I tried really hard to make it home before I had to use the bathroom but tonight I just couldn't wait. On a typical night, we were so busy before the store closed that it was impossible to take a break. And, once the store did close, the girls were vicious about keeping everyone on the floor to straighten, so we could get out of there. Honestly, they had bladders like camels. Must be all that late night partying.

Most days, we didn't leave until at least two in the morning. Oftentimes, later. That meant I would go six or seven hours, even longer, without a break, without eating, without sitting down, often without using the ladies room. Not only was it a shock to my system, I have no idea how Isabella's got away with it legally.

But, tonight, I just had to go!

"I'm running to the bathroom," I yelled, not waiting for permission or negative comments.

"You'd better hurry your ass up!" one of the girls screamed at me.

"Yeah, if you're not back in three minutes, we're going to mess up your table."

The girls laughed. I didn't care. I had to pee!

Even though I came back in record time, my panty table was partially destroyed in retaliation for satisfying a critical bodily function. I thought technology executives could be juvenile, but I was wrong. As I started to fix the new mess, Penny ran by in her five inch stilettos, on her way to the office. I tried to grab her attention.

"Penny, seriously?"

Penny just kept walking.

"No time, Diana. Deal with it."

The girls just laughed. Didn't really matter. We all left together, so if I wasn't done with my table, they would have to come and help me. Who gets the last laugh now? I slowed my straightening to a near crawl. Ten minutes later, the whole crew was circled around my table, silent as ever, finishing with a fever-pitched flourish.

Dear Diary,

Work sucks. The shift sucks. The pay sucks. The whole thing sucks. Retail is nothing like I had expected it to be. I hate it!

When I decided to get a job, I thought retail would be fun and I'd meet a lot of new people. It would get me out of my home office, I'd enjoy the discounts, and I'd make a little play money until the technology industry picked up or I'd find something more in tune with my skills and interests. Well, retail isn't it.

This job is hard work. I originally loved the shift because I'd have all day to work on my own business. Well, I usually get home about 3 a.m., so by the time I relax a bit and get to bed, it's 4:30 a.m.! That, of course, means I don't wake up until noon or later. I've never been an early riser, but this schedule has me totally thrown off balance. I'm constantly tired. Not only that, I have horrible nightmares about straightening the panty tables! They're hard enough to handle when I'm awake. I don't need them to infiltrate my dreams, too.

And, I have a new vice. During a panty table talk, one of the girls mentioned how much she loves Taco Heaven's hash brown sticks. I hate her! I'd never even been to Taco Heaven, let alone had breakfast there. I was informed that the drive-thru was open 24 hours, so I should stop on my way home. One day I did. Now, I'm addicted to their breakfast burritos and hash brown sticks. I stop every day on my way home from work. The guy who works the drive-thru already knows my voice. I just have to order "the usual." Once I get home I grab a beer – yes, a beer – and eat my treats before retiring. Real healthy, huh?

The good part about this work schedule is that I do exercise daily. Long about 3 p.m. I manage to get my butt out to the community club house and walk the treadmill. I know things will get better, but for now, this is my life.

I had another sad situation hit me today. I can no longer afford payments to the country club, so I had to resign my membership. That's OK. I'm certain they didn't appreciate me driving up in my vintage Buick. I'll bet it was an embarrassment to both of us.

Keep the faith…

More tomorrow!

All my heart,

Diana

Drive-Thru Guy

{ EIGHT }

"What'll ya have?"

The voice came booming over the speaker as I finally got to place my order in the long line of cars snaking through the drive-thru. It was 3:30 a.m., and this was my first visit. I'd been disciplined in the past about going straight home, but there was just something about breakfast that sounded good to me right now, and I suspect it sounded good to everyone else in line.

"I'll have two breakfast burritos and an order of hash brown sticks," I said. I'm not sure how big any of this is, but if it's too much, I'll just refrigerate it and finish it in the morning.

"Anything else?" he asked.

"No, that's it.

"Come around."

He didn't seem particularly friendly. In fact, he sounded more like a bartender than a Drive-Thru Guy. But, with so many early morning customers straight from the Vegas nightlife, I suspect that his manner was appropriate.

When I got to the window, he was a bit older than I had expected, looking to be in his late 30s. He seemed friendly, but most workers I ran into at this late hour were exceptionally friendly. The folks at the grocery store, gas station and other stores all had a big smile on their faces whenever I came by. There must be something about working the graveyard shift that kicks up the endorphins.

"That'll be $2.84."

"Wow! That's cheap!" I exclaimed. Pretty darn cheap in this town for breakfast nowadays. Gone are the 99 cent breakfast buffets. Everything is at least 10 dollars.

"You're pretty busy tonight, huh," I said. I thought I'd make conversation. I guess that's just the kind of girl I am.

"No, this is pretty normal for a Friday. At least it makes the night go by fast."

"How late do you have to work?" I asked, later realizing it probably sounded like a pick-up line.

"The shift starts at 11:30 p.m. and goes until 9 a.m. It's a long shift, but as long as people keep coming, it goes by fast. Plus, you get to see the sunrise every morning."

"That sounds like fun," I replied. "You must meet some pretty interesting people."

He handed me my order. "You don't know the half of it," he said.

I smiled a big smile and said, "Thanks," and was on my way. I always try to be courteous to other service workers because I know how much we get shit upon.

When I got home, I grabbed a beer, put some hot sauce on my burritos, and settled down to late night television. One bite and I was hooked! This was the best fast food breakfast I had ever had. Danger! Danger! It'll be hard to stay away.

"What'll ya have?"

"Hey, how's it going?" By now, I'd been here like 50 times in a row, so Drive-Thru Guy knew my voice and my order. Scary, but true.

"The usual?" he asked.

"Yep."

"OK, come around." And just like that, I had my own version of Cheers, where everybody knows your name. Well, maybe not my name, but at least my order.

"How are things tonight?" I asked. I always tried to keep a smile on my face, but limit the conversation. However, no one was in line behind me tonight, and he felt like talking.

"Work's alright but I just got kicked out of the house."

Ouch. Not the line of conversation I wanted to pursue. It's too late. I'm too tired, and I don't even know his name.

"Oh, that's hard. But, you found a place to live?" I inquired sheepishly.

"Yeah. My sister kicked me out. She knows I'm struggling, but she has a new boyfriend, and he and I don't get along. So, she kicked me out. I moved in with one of the guys from here. I only get a sofa, but that's all I really need. The rent is cheap. It'll be OK for a while."

He handed me my order. I was never so happy to see that little paper bag.

"Well, you hang in there, OK?" I said as I started to creep away.

"Yeah, it'll be fine," he said and waved good-bye.

"May I take your order?"

What? Where's Drive-Thru Guy? The voice on the other end of the speaker was a young female. I'd never heard it before. Maybe Drive-Thru Guy got fired. Or maybe I finally discovered a night he's not working. It seems as though he's here every single night, but maybe, just maybe, he's off tonight. Whew! It would be nice not to have to make conversation with him. I'm way too tired.

"I'll have two breakfast burritos and an order of hash brown sticks."

"Is that all?"

"Yes."

"OK. Your order comes to $2.84 at the window. Thank you."

Well, I had to admit, she certainly was much kinder and more professional than Drive-Thru Guy. It was a pleasant change.

I came around to the window, and to my horror, there was Drive-Thru Guy. The woman was behind him, handing over the headset. Shit!

"I didn't think you were working today because she took my order," I said, trying to be nice.

Drive-Thru Guy put on his headset as he answered. "I had to get a box of sauces down, so Dawna helped me out. I'm here every night, I think."

Yes. Yes, you are.

"So, how's life?" I asked. It had been a few weeks since I came by. I was trying to keep myself from eating here every single night. Not only was it adding up financially, I still wasn't sure of the nutritional content of the food. I don't think it's too bad, but you never know.

"Oh, life's been hell. That mother fuckin' son-of-a-bitch that I've been living with. Turns out he's into drugs, big time. I tried to get all my stuff out of his apartment tonight, but I had to leave for work. He's probably there trashing the place right now."

OK, bad time to be nice. I know he obviously needs someone to talk to, but I really can't help him. I'm barely making ends meet as it is. I wonder if he talks to all his customers this way.

"Do you have someplace to go?" I wasn't going to offer. I just wanted to know that he had shelter.

"Yeah, my sister said I could come back for a couple of weeks, but that's it."

"OK. Well, you hang in there."

"Thanks."

"What'll ya have?"

Oh, he's still there. It had been a while since I'd been by. I didn't give up on my late night snacks. I'd just been going to a different drive-thru, about five miles out of my way. But, tonight I was just too tired and this one is so close to my house.

"Two breakfast burritos and an order of hash brown sticks, please."

"Come around."

Oh, he recognizes my voice. What in the world is he going to tell me today? I hope things are going well because I just can't deal with his drama, as well as all the drama at work.

"Hey, how's it going?" I asked cheerfully.

He looked at me kind of odd then said, "Well, you know. Life has its ups and downs, its good news and its bad news."

Shit. Now I have to ask. Why do you do this to yourself, Diana?

"So, is everything OK?"

"I just got out of a weekend in jail," he said, matter-of-factly.

Jail. Yikes! He doesn't seem to be the type. Regardless of what's happening in his life, he always manages to get to work. He's responsible, just not lucky.

"Jail. So, that's the bad news."

"No, that's the good news."

I didn't even want to know what the bad news was. How much worse can it get? Luckily, he didn't press me for more conversation about himself, and changed the subject.

"Hey, have you tried our new quesadilla?"

Dear Diary,

Do you know how long you need to work at my hourly wage to be able to afford a new pair of Manolos? My calculator blew up when I tried to figure it out. It's so hard working retail. I can't believe I'm subjecting myself to it. I'm so much more talented than this.

My whole mindset has changed. I look at everything I buy in terms of how many hours it would take for me to earn it, and it's overwhelming. Shopping is no fun anymore. And, even though I get a discount at Isabella's, I still can't afford anything. It's so sad. How do people live?

Maybe if I was in a commissioned position, it would be better. I've been checking the job postings regularly, but I haven't seen anything worthwhile. I'll just have to update my resume and start pounding the pavement again. At least now I have six months in a retail job, something HR managers might view positively.

The only downfall I know is that I'll have to give up my perfect schedule. Having time during the day to market my business and meet with potential clients is the ultimate. Unfortunately, so far I haven't signed any clients and I need to be realistic about earning more money. Retail is just a transient job anyway, right? I mean, who works retail as a career? So, even if I get a full time position, I'm certain I'll have relative flexibility to adjust my schedule as opportunities arise. It should be fine.

I also need to look into getting another car. It was 117 degrees today, and my lovely Buick doesn't have air conditioning. Well, it came with the option, but it doesn't work and it will cost me $2,000 to fix it. I'd rather put that money into a better vehicle, money I don't currently have. In the meantime, I'm grateful that the heat of the day is over by the time I jump into my car to go to work, and I'm thrilled it gets me to and from work safely. Oh, how my life has changed.

More tomorrow!

All my heart,

Diana

What Happens in Vegas...

{ NINE }

It seems on a daily basis, my mind is preoccupied, constantly trying to figure out how to get out of the mess I'm in. As a result, I'm not always present, in the moment. Even when I'm flying around at Isabella's, I'm deep in thought. This particular job has gotten to the point that my brain could multitask 98 percent of the time. Unfortunately, when I do need to be present, it's almost always jarring to my system.

About 8:30 p.m. one fateful night, I heard screaming and yelling from the left front quadrant of the store. We had a lot of drunk, horny shoppers all the time, so an unruly one wasn't out of the question. Suddenly, I saw Penny shoot out the entrance, accompanied by mall security.

I didn't leave my post, lest I be punished for my misstep, but I used my laser vision to try to figure out what was happening. I noticed mall security carrying a brown shopping bag that looked vaguely familiar.

I remembered when I was straightening the nightgowns last night there was a brown paper shopping bag behind one of the racks. I thought it might belong to the stockroom staff, who left it there so it was easier to carry merch back and forth. I honestly was too tired to ask about it and, knowing the staff on hand, wasn't sure I'd get a straight answer any way. It had no writing, no logos, no company name – just a plain, brown shopping bag with handles. I kept straightening and forgot about it.

But there it was, seemingly involved in all the brouhaha. Melody was making her way back to the office for her break, so I cornered her to get the scoop.

"What's going on, Melody? I heard a lot of hollering."

"Oh, it's one of those theft gangs again."

"Theft gangs?" I had never heard of a theft gang.

"Sure. They hide shopping bags lined with tinfoil in the racks of clothes. One team leaves them and another picks them up so the team members are hard to track. Then, while they're trying to get away, a third team comes in and does a grab-and-run."

I'm a well-read person but I really had no idea what Melody was talking about.

"Why the tinfoil?" I asked, feeling a pain in the pit of my stomach, knowing I had found today's bag of choice.

"The tinfoil keeps the sensors from going off. That part of the gang tries to get the higher-end merchandise. When we find the bags, we toss them so when the second team comes, they can't take anything."

Damn. My laziness had just cost the company hundreds of dollars.

"And what is a grab-and-run?"

"While we're trying to nab one team, a second one runs into the store with another empty bag, goes to a rack or a table and just grabs as much as they can, sensors and all. Then, they run out of the store and into the mall crowd. They usually hit different stores so we can't track them either. They blend into the crowds and they're out of here in just seconds. Sometimes it's an inside job so they leave through the rear door of another store."

"Wow! I had no idea."

I really didn't. I was sure retail theft took place. I just hadn't a clue how organized it was.

"They always nab the quality merchandise then sell it online. It's a huge business."

I truly had a lot more to learn about retail, and not always good things.

Pointing behind me, Melody said, "Looks like you have a customer."

"Oh, thanks, Melody."

I turned around, proudly wearing my lowest-cut top with the most pushy-uppy bra in my closet, ready to meet that bra wardrobe goal for the evening, when I suddenly realized I actually could run into someone I know in this place. There he was, gulping down a margarita by the yard, his significant other wearing a dress so tight neither a bra nor a panty could fit for fear of VPL. He pulled her close, his hand gently rubbing her backside, the two of them sharing an intimate chuckle.

Omigod, omigod, omigod! It can't be! This isn't happening to me.

I thought about spinning around and engaging with another customer – unfortunately there was none – or Melody – but she had already left – or making a mad dash to the stockroom, but just as that thought hit my brainwaves, he looked up and caught my eye. Aside from the credit-card toting Cupid pendant strategically dangling from the center of my bosom, I could have passed for any woman out having a fun time on a Saturday night. Alas, I was not.

Tarek looked up and recognized me immediately. Surprisingly, aside from his gaze which seldom left my chest, I don't think he realized I was part of the help.

"Diana, so good to see you! How strange to run into you here, of all places."

Tarek was one of my best clients who always returned my calls and promised me that the nanosecond the economy picked up and budgets were available, he'd have me back on board.

"Well, this is Vegas. It's one big city of unexpected synchronicity."

"Well, that's not exactly how I'd describe Vegas, but OK! I don't believe you've met my wife, Krissie. Krissie, this is Diana. She's the industry's uber-marketing guru."

"A pleasure, Diana. So nice to finally meet you. I've heard so much about you."

"Nice to meet you as well. What brings you to town?"

I asked, but I really hoped the conversation was short. I couldn't possibly go into Isabella sales mode at this instant. The sooner I passed them off to one of the front quadrants, the happier I'd be.

"We're celebrating our 10th wedding anniversary, and what better place to come than Vegas!"

"Congratulations! That's fantastic!"

I took a deep breath. Since I had Tarek face-to-face, I might as well ask.

"So, any good news on the budget front?"

Tarek took a sip of his margarita. His goal this weekend was fun, not business, but I knew he would answer my question.

"Sure, budgets opened up about a month ago."

A month ago? And Tarek hadn't called me? I mean, that's good news but what's going on?

"Fabulous! Can I update any proposals for you?"

"No, not necessary. We have all we need."

Whew. That sounds like good news. In a week or two I could be back in business.

"I thought you heard, Diana. Maybe living out here you're not in the loop. We signed a two-year contract with Martin Heller."

"What? No, I hadn't heard anything. I thought Martin Heller didn't take on any clients for less than $30,000 a month. I know you don't have MH money."

Tarek snickered.

"Actually, we do. In light of the economy, MH opened a new small business division. They take clients for as little as $5,000 per month. We discussed it with the board and it was a no-brainer. Working with the largest PR agency in the industry is something we aspired to but never thought we could afford. Jonathan and Emanuel did the same. The division is going gangbusters."

Jonathan and Emanuel were two other faithful clients who also conveniently forgot to mention they were no longer looking for me to implement their marketing strategy. What none of them realize is MH only wants to deal with the biggest and the best. The new division will bring in cash flow during these slower times, but it will be staffed with interns and recent college grads that have no clue about the industry or its players.

If they worked with me, they would have top notch talent at their beck-and-call, seven days a week. Just try to reach an MH staffer on a Saturday. Fat chance. Six months into the contract and they'll be licking their wounds but unable to get out of their two-year commitment. MH was known for having cancellation clauses as ironclad as the Chris Christensen prenup.

"Wow, that's unexpected news, but I'm glad to hear that you're happy. Please keep me in mind if circumstances should change, or if you hear of anyone who might need my skills."

"Always, Diana, always. Well, we're heading back to the room. Good to see you again, Diana. You look great. Vegas must agree with you."

"Nice to see you, too, Tarek and a pleasure to meet you, Krissie. Enjoy your celebration!"

After air kisses all around, Tarek and Krissie went back to their snuggle walk, finally making it out the entrance. If he realized I worked in the store, he didn't make it known. Krissie would have figured it out long before Tarek and sometime this weekend she'd be sure to spill the beans about my Isabella's Intimates connection. My reputation in Silicon Valley was ruined.

"Can you believe it? How can they do this to me, Helen?"

I was still shaking, first from frustration over my encounter with Tarek last night, and second from lack of sleep due to my inability to call Helen immediately following my shift. With the time difference and Helen's schedule with work and her two kids, I had to impatiently wait for an appropriate time to ring her.

"Well, at least you know so you can move forward with your life rather than hanging onto hope they'll come through with a contract."

"How can you say that, Helen? They didn't even have the decency to tell me – none of them! I can't believe after all the great work I did for them that they'd just ignore me and sign with an agency that isn't going to give a rat's ass about them in a few months. I gave them everything and they know it. Why would they not even give me a chance?"

"They did give you a chance. You worked with them and did a great job, and you got paid well for it. But, when you're dealing with the board of directors, you don't have an opportunity to battle. Chances are, someone on the board knows Martin or Heller or both and they're sending company money to their friends."

Helen had a point there.

"I know. I've had good and bad experiences with BODs before. Once, I'd submitted a bid but a small agency got the contract because the chairman's friend owned it. One year and $180,000 later, they had done nothing for the company and I got a call to take over the account for far less. Within six weeks, we were doing a complete product launch and full press tour."

"I remember that. It was such a great experience for you. But, what about the time you got kicked off the account in a similar situation?"

"Yep, I'll never forget that one. I'd done a great job for the client but when the chairman's best friend's wife started consulting, they gave the account to her. She was charging $475 an hour and did nothing! She said she was the strategic powerhouse behind the marketing team but she was never a team player. The company got bought out and she made her money right up until the acquisition."

While I appreciated Helen's attempt to help me justify in my mind why I was no longer a power player in high tech marketing, it still hurt. And, I was totally lost.

"So, Helen, what do I do now? I'm divorced, with no business or clients, folding panties in a town where I don't know anyone."

"Diana, you know I've always believed you're exactly where you're meant to be. For some reason, you were supposed to find your way to Las Vegas, even if it meant the end of your marriage and business. Maybe you're not supposed to do marketing anymore."

"But it's the only thing I know! I can't stay at Isabella's. I just don't see myself there long term. I continue to scour the job postings for something interesting, but nothing is calling me. And, it's just not worth it for me to move back to California right now. Not only has Martin Heller muscled into my territory, Gizzi said two of my old colleagues have started consulting. In our industry at our level, there just aren't that many potential clients."

"But, Gizzi said you might be able to get a job at a startup. Have you explored that option?"

"It's enticing, but honestly, I'm just not interested in the grind of a startup. I'd have to really love it to make it work for me."

"Well, then, there you have it. You're obviously looking for something new. Now's your time to find it. It might take a while, but it sounds like you're ready for a career shift. Chris went to Las Vegas to change his life. Maybe that was supposed to be your plan, too, only you weren't aware of it. You have to be open to dropping into your destiny. Or, in this case, your destiny dropping onto you!"

"I have to say, Helen, for a long time I didn't even want to say I was from Las Vegas. I miss California so much! But now that I've been here for some time, in spite of everything I've been through, the city is growing on me. There were always aspects that I loved, but being able to afford a big home and a country club membership is not everything. And, now that you and Gabe are planning to move here, I have even more reason to stay."

"We should be moving in a few months if everything comes together as planned. I'm really excited. No more snow to shovel!"

"No, but when it's 117 degrees outside, you'll wish you had some to cool you off!"

"Oh, I know I won't miss it at all! As for you, I think you'll be fine, Diana. You're smart. You're just a train that's temporarily derailed and you have to get put back on the right track. Regardless, you're going to have to look for a better paying job. Like, now! Everything will be fine eventually. You have to trust what you're going through and learn from it."

Well, if Gizzi was the voice of reason and truth, Helen was the one in the family who always had a positive attitude. No matter how low things may seem, Helen just blew it off and moved on.

"OK, sister, thanks for your wisdom. Can't wait for you guys to get out here. I really miss you."

"Miss you, too, Diana. Now, get some sleep and sell a lot of bras tonight!"

"I'm on it! Later, lady."

"Later, lady."

'Later, lady' was our little thing. As kids, just before we went to sleep, that's what we said to each other instead of 'Good night.' Now that we're older, we don't use it very often, but when we do, those words bring me great comfort. I think back to those days when we shared a bedroom with great affection. It will be good to have Helen and her family in town near me.

Dear Diary,

What's happened to me? I didn't think I changed that much.

I was lucky enough to get a short gig working PR at a tradeshow in San Jose for one of my old clients, a tiny European company. I hadn't seen my friends or past clients in quite some time, so I was thrilled at the opportunity to kiss the ground in the Bay Area once again.

I packed my bags, grateful for the work – read: money – and headed back to Silicon Valley for two days. I'd forgotten what life was like back there.

Everyone tends to dress very conservatively. And, in the land of geekdom, khakis and a polo shirt are proper attire. In fact, many times, it's the only attire. It was everywhere. At a big show like this, business suits are even appropriate.

Well, living in the desert Southwest, particularly Las Vegas, I hadn't really worn a suit for a while. In fact, I hadn't worn pantyhose in forever. Closed-toe shoes are also something I'm not used to wearing, except at my menial job. I guess I hadn't realized how my clothing habits had changed.

I showed up today wearing a designer outfit, a diffused, understated animal print pant with a solid color-coordinated top. I had low-heeled open toe pumps with a bit of sparkle to them. In Vegas, this would have been perfectly fine for a luncheon meeting. In San Jose, I looked like a Madame.

Have I really changed that much? Is life really so different here that I've succumbed to the changes without even
realizing it? The answer was never more apparent than
when I shook hands with my client, and his eyes went
straight to my chest. Oops! I guess I'm confusing my day
job with my night one.

I'll have to be more careful next time I go back to the area
to work – if there is a next time! I'm also going to take a
good look at my wardrobe to make sure that what I'm
wearing is really me, and not just the influence of the
area. I know it gets hot here, sometimes over 110 degrees,
but I still have to be me. After all, that's what life is all
about, isn't it?

More tomorrow!

All my heart,

Diana

The District Manager

{ TEN }

What the...

I walked into the store for tonight's shift, but I was stunned at its condition. I wasn't exactly sure what I was looking at. The whole setup of the front cashier quadrant looked completely different. Usually it was a mix of fashion and standard bras, corsets, bustiers and panty tables. What I found was what looked like my closet when I did a spring cleaning. Stuff was everywhere.

Racks were pushed against walls. Panty tables were on their sides. Assorted items were on the floor. I wondered if we had been robbed by an aggressive faction of the retail theft gangs.

I noticed something else was different, too. The entire staff was working. Usually the cashiers were busy the bulk of their shift. They had to be, as long as customers were waiting in line with their selections. But, today, everyone was working, even the greeters in the other front quadrant. Usually they were texting or talking to their friends. Something big was definitely going on.

I saw Melody running to the front of the store, near the same place I stood dumbstruck, carrying about 50 hangers of merchandise.

"What's going on, Melody?" I asked.

In a panting voice, she replied, "Can't talk. Cruella's here."

Cruella? I didn't see any Dalmatians!

Melody didn't stick around to explain. She dumped the hangers on a rack and ran back to the stockroom. A couple of shoppers were a bit caught off guard by the severity with which Melody plopped them on the rack, but as a whole, the customers simply ignored the mess, climbing over clothing piles and weeding through stacks of bras to find what they came for – the Isabella image.

The atmosphere in the store was palpable. I'd been there several months now, and it never felt like this before. I looked at my watch and realized I'd better clock in and get ready for my shift.

I wended my way through the hot mess, nodded a cheery, "Hello," to a grimacing Penny, and turned into an unexpected confrontation in the office.

"Is she the one?" an unknown female asked Mila, pointing at me. "Is she the reason I didn't get my full bonus?"

Ah, Cruella in the flesh.

"Are you? Because if you are, I'm going to march your sorry ass out the door right now."

Mila, thankfully, got between us and pushed Cruella away.

"No, Alyssa. Diana here is actually one of our top performers. She opens at least one account per shift, in addition to selling a boatload of merchandise."

Alyssa looked me up and down before she responded.

"Good. Then get out there and perform."

I looked at Mila who didn't have to tell me that now was not a good time to be hanging around in the office. I put my handbag in my locker, clocked in and went to the restroom. While I was in there, the screaming began.

"It was you! You're the reason I didn't get my full bonus! You dare to show your lazy, shit-ass divaness in here after what you've done? Pack up your things, you're outta here!"

"But, but…" I could hear one of the nameless nightshift employees stutter.

I opened the door to the restroom, hoping to slip by the tense triad, when I realized I got there just in time for the show. Alyssa, standing tall, raised her batwing arm and pointing to the sky screamed, "Gone!" with such a roar, I expected the heavens to open and lightening to strike.

Nameless girl didn't have a chance. She picked up her belongings and left.

I ran out to catch up with Penny who immediately shoved a pile of bras in my hands.

"Walk with me," she said.

I followed Penny to a rack in the middle of our rear quadrant and we began sorting, hanging and straightening the grab bag of goodies she'd given me.

"We're completely resetting the store," Penny finally spoke.

"Resetting? Why? Mila is always moving merchandise around."

It was true. Mila, Penny and any of the other management team had no choice but to reset the merchandise on a nearly daily basis. We sold so much on any given day, the store never looked the same.

"It all boils down to Alyssa's bonus," Penny whispered. "We may think we're doing a good job, but if Alyssa doesn't receive the entire bonus she has available to her, then she shits on us and this mess is what happens."

Turns out, Alyssa's bonus is based on three characteristics: total sales volume, fashion merchandise selling at full retail and the number of Cupid charge accounts we open. We were the number one store in the country, so total sales volume was a given. However, we ran a bit short in the other two categories.

Because we were Las Vegas, the company shipped some of the most expensive merchandise to our store, thinking the drunk tourists would snap it up at full price. But, while Isabella's has a strong following, many of her customers don't have the discretionary income to purchase most of those items, regardless of the circumstances. And, shoppers whose wallets easily could purchase them, quite frankly, shop elsewhere. That meant that the high-end merchandise either sat around for a very long time, eventually looking a tad scraggly from being tried on so many times by aspirational shoppers, or it had to be marked down to move it. No one wants to buy a red velvet corset trimmed in marabou in July, even in Las Vegas.

Our other downfall was the Cupid accounts. Each employee was expected to open one Cupid account per shift. We weren't tracked on any other sales goal except for that. From the moment the customer entered the store, she was accosted by employees trying to get that elusive Cupid account. Because the store was so big, by the time shoppers made it to the back, they may have been asked five or six times to open an account with the company. Since we received numerous complaints about it, management didn't push it but obviously, it was important to Alyssa.

Many shoppers were from other countries, so they wouldn't qualify to open an account even if they wanted to. And, others preferred to use their own credit cards rather than add another piece of plastic to the purse. Sales volume was simple, but these other two items were near impossibilities.

Penny and I spent long into the wee hours, cleaning, straightening, sorting and displaying more merchandise than I'd ever seen in my life. I stayed quiet pretty much through the whole thing, lost deep in thought. I knew, on some level, Penny's goal was to get me into the management training program with the company from the first day we met. After what I'd heard today, I concluded there must be some sort of financial incentive for her to do so.

And, while I had contemplated joining up, my encounter with Alyssa rubbed me the wrong way. Although the bulk of my interactions with Isabella management had been with Penny, I'm a true believer that the company culture comes from the top down. Alyssa didn't get to be the way she is without someone brow beating her in exactly the same way.

I'd met some bullies in my time in high tech, mostly because the male-dominated industry didn't always shine kindly on intelligent females. But, after today's experience, I realized I couldn't thrive in this environment either. It was cruel and unusual punishment.

I went on the hunt for a new job.

Dear Diary,

I spoke with Mom today. She's really not happy that I'm struggling so, and she begged me to move back to Detroit to live with her and Dad. I can't. I'd feel like such a failure. Besides, the technology business is based on either coast, so living in the Midwest won't help me to build my business back up. It's hard enough when I'm just an hour flight away from California. Can you imagine what it would be like to try to fly from Michigan? People wouldn't take me seriously at all. Besides, my sister and her family are planning to move here soon. I don't need to move to Michigan because family is moving to Vegas.

I went to work a bit earlier so I could wander through some of the designer boutiques at the mall. I'm hoping that I'll meet a sympathetic manager who will hire me. Unfortunately, I'm not sure that they pay any better.

I met the assistant manager of a very fashionable designer boutique, and he said that most of the boutiques in the mall were money losers. They were only there because they feel they need to have a presence against their competition. He said they'll go days without selling anything, and when they do, it will be about $10,000. Other times, he gets requests from customers who want a particular item in a particular size. The request goes to New York, then Italy, taking weeks to get a response. By that time, the buyer has lost interest. After all, weeks in fashion can mean a whole new trend.

I was disappointed, but I know there's something better out there than Isabella's. I just have to keep searching.

More tomorrow!

All my heart,

Diana

Sherborne

A New Job

{ ELEVEN }

Hallelujah! I'm finally out of that rathole they call Isabella's and into a real job. Well, real for retail anyway. I have no idea how people survive at Isabella's. I guess their managers never start out on the sales floor. They're hired in directly as managers, so they don't experience all the shit that the lowly employees do. How they get away with some of that stuff legally I'll never know. No bathroom breaks. No lunches. No nothing. Okay, enough about Isabella's. I'm now an employee of the glorious Sherborne.

When Sherborne called me – finally – I jumped at the chance to work in a more professional environment, and to make more money, of course. Since my only retail experience to date was Isabella's, I was hired into the lingerie department at Sherborne. Not my first pick of departments. I'd rather be in one of the designer boutiques. But, after six months if I'm so inclined, I can switch departments.

However, one of the advantages of lingerie is that it's one of the highest commission departments in the store. I had no idea that each department earned a different percentage. Most clothing departments raked in a paltry 6.5 percent commission. Lingerie earned 9 percent, and shoes and men's suits were the top at 10. Regardless, it was definitely more than the insulting dollar above minimum wage I earned at Isabella's. And, if I'm stuck in retail for a while, who wouldn't enjoy working at Sherborne? It's the epitome of retail. The peak of success. The ultimate shopping experience.

What a relief to be able to park in the garage directly adjacent to the store. Already I felt appreciated. At Isabella's I had to park in the casino employee parking garage, nearly a mile from where I worked. Sherborne obviously knows how to take care of their employees as well as their customers. After that mile-long trek from my car to my job over at Isabella's, this is indeed a blessing.

Today is training day and I can't wait to get started and meet my fellow Sherborners. I shot down the I-15, then took the back streets to the mall like any local would. I turned into the parking garage and parked on the fourth floor, as instructed by my new manager, Holly. Employees park on the fourth and fifth floors of the garage, although I can see already that some people cheat. Must be management. The store isn't even open yet this morning and there are cars on all the other floors.

I locked my car and headed for the elevator. I saw other employees take the stairs while I waited an interminable length of time for the lift. Once I boarded, I realized why they were walking. The elevator was a glass-enclosed cell, a solar oven. An 80-year-old with two bad knees could walk down the stairs faster than this elevator moved. And talk about lack of air flow! In the heat of the day in the middle of summer, you would bake in here. Note to self: take the stairs.

I exited the elevator and crossed the roadway to the employee entrance. Once I punched the code into the keypad, the door unlocked. As it closed behind me, I was left all alone in a small entryway, with nothing but a stairway to my left, and a door with a buzzer to the right. I suspected the door was for visitors, but I wasn't sure where the stairs led. More people came in behind me – fellow employees I presume – and quickly ran up the stairs. One after another they came, and they all went up the stairs. Therefore, so did I.

I started the climb, and just for grins, I counted how many steps there were. As I huffed and puffed along the six, seven, eight flights, I realized how out of shape I was, even after running up that steep, narrow staircase at Isabella's. That was just one flight; here there were eight. I definitely need to improve my cardio training. I'll get right on that.

When I began this journey mere seconds ago, I assumed there were just one or two flights to get up to the secure employee area. When my step count hit 100, I had a hard time thinking clearly as my heart was beating out of my chest. How could a company expect its employees to climb eight flights of stairs every day, then work for eight hours? Still, one by one, they came. Some running, some skipping steps, some dragging, but somehow all making it through this incredible climb. I can't believe my manager didn't happen to mention it, or that I wasn't put through a stress test as part of my screening package.

I pray this is not a foreshadowing of unexpected things to come. I have so much need for Sherborne to be great for me. An image of a bitter job divorce flashed across my mind, but I sent it scurrying away. Sherborne is great. Sherborne is great.

When I arrived at the top, I was swallowed up in the usual hustle and bustle of an employee check-in area. The extremely large security guard, the kind who can't move very fast but you definitely don't want to run into in a dark alley, assigned me a locker where I left my handbag and jacket, then he gave me directions to my orientation class. By now, my heavy breathing had subsided, and I gently wiped the sweat from my cheeks, hoping it didn't leave a trail through my blush.

I walked down the long hallway and into the store, searching for the escalator. I guess once you're inside, you're allowed to behave like a normal person. No more stairs here. I stopped for a minute to survey my surroundings and to absorb all that is Sherborne. The soft music, the beautiful architectural details, the racks and racks of fabulous clothing. Pinch me!

It's always been such a pleasure to shop at a Sherborne store, and now I get a discount. It's like fashion heaven! High tech may have been a great way to earn a living, but nothing beats pure unadulterated fashion when it comes to overall happiness. I can shop, and I get paid for it! Yes, I believe, this is where I belong. At least for now, anyway.

I made my way to the second floor training room. As I surveyed the array of tables, I realized I was one of about 35 new employees. That worried me, in a way, since the store only employs about 220. Is their turnover rate really that high, I wondered? And, they hold these classes twice a month. Hmm…

I sat at an empty seat, next to perky Tammy. A mere 19-years-old, Tammy came from a long line of Sherborne employees. "I don't plan to stay here forever," she said, "but it's certainly good while I build my wardrobe."

My sentiments exactly.

Sally, the hiring queen from HR, was selected to be our instructor today.

"I've been with the company 17 years and hopefully, one day you, too, will be able to say that."

Not hardly, but whatever.

"You are here because you are the best. Sherborne searches high and low to employ only those who truly understand and can deliver 10-star customer service. We are the best because you are the best."

I think it's more a matter of hiring anyone who has applied and doesn't have a criminal record, but I digress. After all, they never even checked my references. What is it with this town?

Anyway…Sally was really laying it on thick, and everyone in the room was sucking it up. We all have egos, you know.

"The folders in front of you contain a unique seven digit code. From now on, that is your employee number. Everything you do with this company requires that number. One day on the register and it will be embedded into your minds."

I'd rather first dibs on the latest fashions to be my focus, but this is the life of a retail clerk.

The longer I'm here, the harder it is to believe that this will be a great experience, and it's only been a couple of hours. The elevator, the stairway climb, the bullshit from HR. It seems so different from a customer perspective, but what can I do? I'm stuck here until something better comes along. Maybe it's just opening day jitters. It must get better.

My heart dropped when Sally got into an explanation of employee earnings. I had friends who made a decent living at the Sherbornes in California, so my expectations were high. Unfortunately, the average Sherborne employee salary in Las Vegas was significantly lower than their expectations for customer service from their employees.

"We're a small store, but we're proud of the high wages we can deliver to our associates. The average salesperson in the store earns approximately $24,000 annually. Our platinum sellers in shoes and men's suits are earning approximately $40,000 annually. Combined with our comprehensive benefits package, Sherborne is proud to offer the best to the best."

I about threw up my breakfast. The best of the best should be earning far more than that, particularly since I'm certain a large percentage of everyone's paycheck goes right back to the store via employee purchase.

Tammy nudged me. "What department are you working in?" she asked.

"Lingerie. You?"

"Men's suits."

Of course. Where else would perky Tammy of the Sherborne dynasty work? I'm screwed already. Or am I?

"Before we begin our videos, I want to introduce you to the general manager of the store, Mr. Gene Thompson."

The door opened and in walked one of the most gorgeous men I'd ever seen. About forty-years-old, dark, thick curly hair, six-foot-two, well defined body, and impeccably dressed. He could be a model.

"He's a hottie," I whispered to Tammy.

"Too bad he's gay," she replied.

What? How could she tell?

"Why do you say that?" I asked.

"Because I know. He and his husband just had a baby with a surrogate. My mom used to work for Sherborne, and now she's their nanny. They have a magnificent house in Lake Las Vegas, right next to Cher. Ironic, huh?"

Ironic, indeed. Why are all the good-looking ones taken or gay? Story of my life.

"Thank you for joining our team here at Sherborne Las Vegas. We've been tops in the region since we opened, and I know that you'll continue to provide the complete customer experience on which we pride ourselves," Gene said.

He rambled on and on about how great we were. He must have attended the same employee motivation class as Sally. Or, taught it.

Once he left and I got over my shock and disappointment that he was gay, Sally fed one DVD after another into the monitor. We learned all about the history of the company, which any good Sherborne shopper would already know: how they started out as a men's suit store in Virginia, how they merged with some other companies and added exclusive fashion merchandise, and now they are the largest specialty goods merchandiser in the country. Blah, blah, blah. Whatever. I'm just here to make money.

I'm quite amazed that a store like Sherborne has such poor employee training. Today we sat and watched videos for hours. Tomorrow we'll learn the registers. That's it! No customer service training. No client book training. No sales or product training. Nothing.

Our employee handbook consisted of one sentence: All we ask is that you use your best judgment always. I live in this town. I'm not sure too many people have good judgment. That might explain the high turnover.

I'm pretty handy with the computer so the registers shouldn't be an issue, but it is a change from Isabella's. Over there, I was strictly sales and straightening. I left the money to others. Here, I don't have that option. Everyone who sells also rings. I haven't been very good with my own money. How am I going to handle the register?

I wanted to stretch my legs after sitting and watching videos all day, so I made my way to the lingerie department on the third floor. The department was definitely much smaller than that behemoth of sex, Isabella's. Far less merchandise, far older sales associates and a more traditional inventory. Not to say that people who shop here don't have sex. They just do it in the dark in their own bedrooms, that's all.

"Oh, good, you're here," said Holly, the department manager. "How did your first day of training go?"

"It was fine. I learned so much more about the company than I could ever have imagined just shopping here."

"Yes, it is a real eye opener," Holly laughed.

I could see two of my co-workers – Duchess and The Witch – eyeing me with disdain. This was a commission-based position and anyone new on staff meant money out of their pockets rather than more sales for the department.

Holly walked me over to the cash wrap and pulled out a clipboard with some papers on it.

"Here, let me go over the schedule with you. Just so you know, the best shifts are given to the top sellers and the staff is listed on the schedule from highest to lowest seller, so you always know where you stand in this department. Since you just started, you're listed on the bottom, but I know, given your experience, you'll be rivaling Duchess and The Witch for that top spot."

I glanced at Duchess out of the corner of my eye. She was snickering a little too slyly.

"I'll post the schedule every Thursday night and each new week begins on Sunday."

"OK, sounds easy enough," I said.

Putting the clipboard down, Holly began to walk me around the department.

"Each sales associate is given a defined area to stock, straighten and clean on a weekly basis. If you slack off on stocking, you'll lose a lot of time running to the stockroom to find sizes that should be on the floor. Always make it your priority to keep your area stocked."

"OK, will do," I said.

Again, snickering from the peanut gallery.

"We have such a vast array of merchandise you'll just have to learn about it on your own. During down times or when you're straightening the department, read the hang tags or manufacturers' content labels. That will give you a lot of information. Before you know it, you'll be a walking lingerie encyclopedia!"

"I'm a fast learner, so that should be no problem, Holly."

"Great! Now, we do have regular department meetings with manufacturers' reps where you'll not only get to see what's coming into the store in the next several months, you'll be able to ask any questions you might have about the merchandise."

Wow! That's pretty cool! I had no idea Sherborne would have such a level of continuing education for its associates in the lingerie department! I could see the designer fashions or shoes or accessories managers insisting on training for their staff, but here we are in lingerie. I'm impressed.

"OK, I know you've had a long day, so one more thing before you go. The lowest person on the schedule is responsible for filling all the cash wrap supplies – bags, tissue, ribbon, register tape – and for clearing out the hangers. Since you're here, Duchess can show you where to find everything and you can get started right now."

"Oh, OK, thanks Holly," I said, not expecting that I would have to do anything else after that mind-numbing day of training. "I'll get right on it."

Duchess, a tall, imposing, prison guard kind of gal, nodded her head at me, and I followed her to the main stockroom where there was a massive section of register supplies.

Duchess looked down at me and said, in a very intimidating voice, "If we run out of supplies at the cash wrap, you will hurt."

She then walked out of the stockroom and left me to grab some supplies on my own.

Hmm…maybe Sherborne isn't the dream job I wanted after all…

Dear Diary,

I just can't catch a break.

I'm shocked that a manager can treat an employee so poorly, someone they hardly even know. Maybe it's just a department hazing for the newbie on staff. Whatever it is, I hate it!

Right from the start, Holly mentioned that I would be responsible for filling the cash wrap with supplies. OK, I get it. I can handle that. It's the schedule that is really killing me.

The top salesperson gets the best shifts and the worst salesperson in the department gets the shifts when hardly a shopper walks in the store. Now, tell me, how is that person supposed to reach number one? Or, make a decent living? I think, to be fair, everyone should get a good mix of best and worst shifts, but my private little world of fairness doesn't seem to have any impact in the commissioned retail world.

I'm also amazed at just how many store and department meetings Sherborne has. And, it never fails, they are always on my day off or, given that nearly every shift I work is closing, I have to come in for an early morning meeting, go home for an hour, then come back and close. What a pain! And, so much wasted gas! Once a month, I could handle it but it's often twice a week. So unfair!

I'm not even sure Holly looks at the schedule week to week because she often schedules me more than seven days in a row. I feel like I live in the place! If I could, I'd save on rent, for sure. I've noticed I'm the only one in the department that gets this special treatment. I have to start increasing my sales so I can move up and leave the worst to the next newbie. I mean, Holly just hired Jordan into the department and she's getting better shifts than me! Something is wrong here.

At least there is one positive thing about working at Sherborne. The highlight of my Sunday is consistent. After I clock out and pick up my handbag and jacket from my locker, I make my way gleefully down the eight flights of stairs, knowing that I don't have to climb them again until tomorrow. I walk out the employee entrance, make my way to the parking garage, and climb the ten short flights of stairs to my car. As I stop to catch my breath, I look to the west to the most magnificent sunset you can imagine.

I climb in my car, make my way home through the hordes of tourist traffic, turn on the television and pour myself a nice glass of wine. Here's to Sherborne. Here's to my life.

More tomorrow!

All my heart,

Diana

The Client Book

{ TWELVE }

"That's it for today's meeting," Gene screamed into the mic, over the shouts and claps of the throng. "Our goal is a 30 percent increase over last year's numbers."

The crowd is now on their feet, screaming, like we're at some sort of religious revival meeting. Or, a political convention. Cue music, loud and strong.

"Let's give it a YIP, YIP, YIP!"

Gene is dancing on the stage, pounding his fist into the air. Everyone is clapping and YIPing, the company's signature cheer. The lights are flashing, the music throbbing – boom, boom, boom – and Gene yells again into the mic, "YIP! YIP! YIP! You can do it! You are the best! You're Sherborne Best! Go and be the best that you can be!" A cross somewhere between Liberace and Yoda, Gene is eating up the moment.

All the YIPing and yelling comes after we've been stuffed with freshly squeezed juices, fresh bagels, muffins and donuts, coffee, tea, milk, mineral water and fresh fruit. I'm surprised that the company doesn't supply a chef to do waffles and omelets. The entire store has to attend, so the company goes all out to draw us in and keep us awake.

We have to sit through at least three speakers before Gene. Usually it's one of the regional vice presidents, one of the buyers, and one guest speaker to get us motivated if the others can't. As the meeting goes on, each speaker gets louder and more animated. They certainly must attend acting classes, they do it so well.

I'm amazed at how much the company spends on these monthly shows – uh, I mean meetings. They are shows, really. The flow is so finely orchestrated. The budget alone is probably enough to feed a small African nation for a year. Custom music, original videos of Sundance quality, guest speakers, custom lighting packages, at least three technicians to run the show and a screenwriter from L.A. to put quality words into Gene's mouth.

While the meetings are interesting, they don't make up for the fact that we have to be here at 7 a.m. for this little motivational number, and even if we're not working immediately after the meeting, we have to show up in professional dress. At least at Isabella's, if I closed the night before and worked until 3 a.m., I could show up for a meeting at 8 a.m. in my sweats without makeup. Not here.

After another series of YIPs, most employees got up to go to their individual department meetings, Lingerie no exception. Our small but estrogen-laden group made their way to the department, skipping to the beat. After all, it was only 8:30 a.m. on a Saturday morning. We still had a long way to go.

"Gather 'round, ladies," Holly said as she took her place in front of the empty chairs in our department.

Maintenance had shifted several rounders to the back of the department and set up folding chairs facing the cash wrap so we'd have a place to sit while we heard more motivational drivel – and occasionally something important – regarding our department.

"We still have lots to cover and we only have about an hour."

Holly was definitely a Sherborne lifer. She'd only been with the company for a couple of years, but she was already a department manager. Just a year or two younger than me, I knew that 10 years from now I could walk into a Sherborne somewhere – or the corporate offices – and still find Holly hard at work. She was almost like a senior citizen and her doctor. Once she bought into the philosophy, she didn't question anything. She just did as she was told.

We all grabbed additional drinks and snacks and found our way to a chair. I hadn't slept very much last night so I was anxious to get this meeting over with so I could rush home for a quick nap before I had to return for my shift. Whatever Holly had to say, I'm sure would be in a memo somewhere that I could read in far less time.

With a huge smile on her face, Holly began.

"Well, as you heard Gene say, our goal for the year is a 30 percent increase in sales compared to last year. That will put us into a bigger category of store, which is a good thing and a not so good thing. You know that the stores break down into three levels by sales volume – Superb, Mid and Growing. Since we opened just a short time ago, we've been number one in Growing."

As if on cue, the entire department raised their hands and gave it a big, "YIP! YIP! YIP!" I was mid-gulp in my coffee so I didn't participate. I felt like I somehow bought football tickets in the opposing team's student section.

Holly noticed I wasn't YIPing, but said nothing. I know she kept it in the back of her mind when she made out the schedules but, I'm sorry, I'm just not that kind of gal. Not for retail, anyway.

Holly picked up her notes and continued.

"So, I'm sure you're wondering just how we're getting to Mid. A 20 percent increase in sales will get us to Mid, but it's such a huge group of stores, Gene really wants us to break high into the category. A 30 percent or greater increase will do that."

And, again, YIP, YIP, YIP…

I wasn't told during orientation but I eventually found out YIP stands for Yes I Perform. Honestly, it's like a secret society around here.

"And, the company has outlined a plan to get us there."

Well, I should hope so.

Everyone put down their drinks and snacks, grabbed their notebooks and started writing. I'd forgotten to bring my notebook this morning. It was in my locker but I was running late so I didn't stop for it. Holly tore off a sheet from her legal pad and handed it to me. Jordan got up from her seat, ran to the cash wrap and grabbed a pen I could use. I really hope this is important.

"OK, so, the first step is to work our client books. Now, I know we all keep the binders with critical client information, but I have a surprise. Sherborne has invested millions of dollars upgrading our register software to have an electronic client book!"

More YIPs from the crowd. I've worked in high tech. This is not for our benefit. This is so the company can track our productivity and adherence to corporate policy.

"Now, when you make a sale, if the client is already in your book, the sale will record automatically. Of course, you can always print out a second receipt if you prefer to keep an additional paper record. If the client is not in your book, you can ask if they would like to be. One simple question and we now have the opportunity to offer exemplary service to another customer. Yes, Tina?"

"We'll still have to get additional data from them, like address, phone number and that sort of stuff, right?"

"Good, question, Tina! And the answer is, it depends. If the customer has shopped at one of our stores anywhere in the country using that credit card and they are in another associate's book in a different department, that information will automatically pull up. You can always verify the information with the customer. Also, during down time you'll be expected to hand enter your current client books so all that information is contained in one database. If they're not in anyone's book or their information hasn't been entered yet, you will need to fill in their record as much as possible. Any other questions? No? Good.

"OK, so the reason the company is doing this is to make it easier to contact those customers in your books, not only for calling circles for special events but just to follow-up and create a constant stream of repeat business. I know we have tourists here from other parts of the country who may have stores in their areas, but there are many who cannot travel to a local Sherborne and it's our pleasure to reach out to them and service them. Remember, Sherborne ships any purchase at no cost to the customer."

"Holly, what are our percentage goals for our client book?" asked The Witch. Of course she would. No one else would even think of that.

"Wow, another good question! You ladies are sure on fire this morning. What's in that coffee?"

"YIP! YIP! YIP!"

"OK, calm down. Let's save some of that energy for when the store opens. Gene has outlined specific goals for the electronic client books, and the great thing is, you can check it anytime to see how close you are to goal. We're aiming to have 65 percent of shoppers added as new customers to client books, and 50 percent of your sales should be to existing client book customers each quarter. That should help us to hit our store goal easily while providing each and every one who walks through our doors with the ultimate shopping experience!"

"YIP! YIP! YIP!"

While everyone else was sucking up to the finely crafted corporate message, I was analyzing what it meant to me as an employee. Client books were such a sham. The purpose of being in someone's book was so you could always work with the same associate on your shopping trips as well as count on that person to do special favors like notify you when new merchandise comes in that you might like, or hold sale merchandise for you for days on end when another associate might only hold it for the corporate guideline of 24 hours. It was created to help build a rapport between client and associate.

In actuality, most Sherborne shoppers could care less. They purchase something when they need it or when they are in the mood to shop, particularly when it comes to lingerie. If they want more specialized service, they shop strictly through the personal stylists provided by the store.

If you ask a customer if you can add them to your book, they either agree or decline. Chances are, if they agree, they are probably in everyone's book in your department as well as several other departments in the store. So, when it comes time for calling circles, the customer will receive as many as a dozen calls, then request that we add them to our Do Not Call list which means that reduces the chances of repeat orders to our existing client book. And, since this is a store that welcomes shoppers from around the country, they will not only receive calls from us but from their local store as well.

Considering the lofty goals the company will now be tracking, the competition on the sales floor will be intense. After all, who does a customer really belong to when they are in four associates' books? And, entering data or viewing a customer record will also get tricky. Although the department has four registers, very seldom are they all open and available to use. If money is not in the register for that day, the register won't function. So, between helping the customers on the floor and trying to sneak in time when a register has availability will be a finely choreographed dance.

"OK, ladies, gather 'round the cash wrap. I'll show you what this baby looks like!"

One by one, we all left our seats and headed the few feet to the registers to see this marvel of modern technology. I glanced around quickly to see nearby departments were all doing the same thing. This rollout was superbly organized, I had to admit.

Jordan followed behind me and just couldn't squelch her enthusiasm.

"This is so great, isn't it Diana? I can't wait to get my hands on it. Thank goodness I took that typing class in middle school."

"Sure, it's great. Whatever," I replied.

Holly heard that, and once our lesson was over and I went back to my chair to gather my things, Holly pulled me aside.

"Diana, I'll not have the company disrespected," Holly said as she glared at me.

"What did I do?" I asked.

"Using the term 'whatever' the way you did is a sign of disrespect. Whoever you were before or whatever you accomplished in the past has no bearing on who you are now. You are an associate of Sherborne, a fine establishment that provides the ultimate shopping experience to its customers. If that doesn't work for you, let me know."

"Uh, no, I'm fine, Holly. Sorry if I seemed disrespectful."

"OK, as long as we have an understanding," Holly said as she turned to go into the stockroom.

Sure, Holly, we have an understanding.

Whatever.

Dear Diary,

Commissions are such a complicated mess at Sherborne. I can't believe I'm saying this, but I much prefer the sucky hourly rate I was making at Isabella's. At least I knew how much I earned each day and there were no surprises in the morning.

At Sherborne, you just never know. First of all, the classic Sherborne shopper buys a lot but also returns a lot, given their extremely liberal return policy. They'll take anything back at any time, doesn't matter how many years old it is, whether new or worn. And, since your employee number is emblazoned on every item, the company knows just exactly who gets the credit – and who gets docked.

Take for instance what happened this week. Friday, Tina had an amazing day. She sold over $4,000 and decided to treat herself to a fabulous dinner. However, when she came in on Saturday morning and looked at the company-wide sales reports, she was in the hole by $300. Seems many of her past customers returned merchandise at other stores. The report is only updated overnight so she had no idea she was truly having such a bad day. Rumor has it one customer returned $1,700 worth of merchandise that was over 10 years old – and still had the tags.

I may be a slow learner when it comes to sales because I've seen my fellow associates sell things that didn't look or fit quite right, just to get their numbers up. After all, there is a faction out there who won't return a single item once they make a purchase and your mission is to hope that each and every shopper you help belongs to that group.

I'm just too honest a person when it comes to selling. I don't have it in me to lie to a customer, and I worked in marketing! I'd hate it if an associate lied to me so why would I do it to someone else? My numbers are OK but if I sucked up some of that YIP juice the company feeds to its employees, they might be even higher.

Then, there are other unwritten rules about commissions. It's so frustrating when you've spent a long time helping a customer, only to have them mention just before they go into the fitting room that so-and-so has items on hold for them. That's the kiss of death. Whatever they purchase, whether items on hold or something you selected for them, is credited to the original sales associate. The entire sale. All of it. The company's position is that you wouldn't have had that customer if it wasn't for the other associate, so they deserve all the credit.

I try to keep a smile on my face during those situations, but I know my entire demeanor changes. I've had customers specify that I should get the commission but I have to follow the company rules. I don't feel there's a fairness in this situation either. I'm surprised more people don't quit over that policy, oh, which just happens NOT to be in the employee handbook, thank you very much! What a farce!

I keep trying to wrap my head around this magic formula of how to make a living in commission sales, but I'm still confused. I can tell you the state of the consumer electronics industry, how to get through customs at Heathrow, where to find the best breakfast at DFW and how to set up a trade show booth in Taipei, but this

Sherborne commission formula is an elusive beast as far as I'm concerned. Oy, I need a beer!

More tomorrow!

All my heart,

Diana

Gratis

{ THIRTEEN }

"Well, that's it for the next six months," said Trevor Guest, Sherborne's sales representative for Whisper Brand bras. "Are there any questions?"

Trevor looked at the small group of female lingerie sales associates sitting in front of him, most half asleep since the meeting began at 7 a.m. In between yawns, sips of coffee and nibbles on bagels with cream cheese, Trevor commanded the presentation of the Whisper fashion bras, not only for its house brand, but for its two designer brands as well.

Trevor was tall, probably six feet three or four, mid-thirties, lots of darling dark wavy hair, a little bit of stubble, just enough to make you want to crawl into bed and scratch it. Well built, he had the perfect pyramid shape with broad shoulders and narrow waist, long strong legs. One would think this is enough to prop your eyes open in the early morning, but today, it just wasn't working.

Trevor has the ultimate heterosexual male job: he travels year-round with a beautiful lingerie model, presenting the upcoming product releases to the lingerie departments of all the Sherborne stores in private fashion shows. Two or three mornings a week, he starts his day with Melissa romping around, modeling the company's latest designs. Melissa and Trevor appear to be good friends, and nothing more, but I do hear that he's getting a divorce. Hmm…

In addition to his good looks. Trevor has a kind heart, a witty sense of humor, and a great fashion sense – at least where lingerie is concerned. He's the utmost professional, as one in his position should be, yet there's something that's just not right. I guess if I was his wife, I'd be a bit concerned about his constant travels with Melissa. Hence, the rumored divorce?

"Okay, well, if we don't have any more questions, then we'll just wrap this up by giving out your gratis sheets, and I'll be back again in six months."

Trevor had some papers in his hands, and everyone – except me – gathered quickly around him to get a sheet with her name on it. I had no idea what he was talking about, so I decided to help fold up the chairs from the meeting and reset the sales floor since the store was opening in just a few minutes. Once the crowd thinned, I'd sneak in and ask Trevor what the gratis sheets are. Or, if he's still busy, I'll check with Holly.

After the chairs were stacked and the clothing racks were back in their respective places, I looked around to see if Trevor was free. Instead, what caught my eye were my co-workers running around the department like kids trying to clean the house after they hosted a party while their parents were away.

Faster than hummingbirds in a hurricane, the gals flitted from rack to rack, picking up bras and panties, then heading back to the counter to discuss their selections and calculate their choices.

"Do you think Angie would like this?"

Tina held up a demi bra and thong set, asking The Witch for her opinion.

"It's a bit similar to one I got her from spring, and the same colors as two years ago, but I really like the way the cup fits her."

Tina was referring to her twenty-eight-year-old daughter, Angela.

"Oh, Tina, I think it's perfect for her. She's got such a cute shape, the demi cup fits her really well," The Witch concurred with her co-worker.

Now, holding up her own selection, she questioned Tina.

"I think Michaela would like this. What do you think, Tina?"

Tina took a good look at the set.

"I think it's perfect for a twenty-two-year-old. It's certainly her colors."

Tina was now referring to The Witch's daughter.

"But for a twenty-two-year-old mother?" The Witch asked.

"Yes, of course. She's still a young woman, and I'm certain her husband would appreciate her being feminine underneath her sweats."

The Witch stopped and looked at her paper.

"How much did you get?" she asked Tina.

"$228. You?" Tina asked The Witch.

"$275."

"Wow! You had a great quarter. Good for you!"

The words sounded congratulatory but the meaning was, "Bitch!" Tina walked away a bit upset that she'd been outsold another quarter by The Witch.

Duchess came over when she heard The Witch's totals.

"You got $275! You must have really been pushing the Whispers."

Duchess sneered as she went back to gathering her goodies.

"I only sell what the customers want," The Witch called to her back.

I wasn't so sure of that. I've rarely seen The Witch sell any other brands to her customers, even when I know that another brand would fit the customer better. I just didn't realize there was incentive to do so.

Jordan, Duchess, Tina and The Witch continued their hunting and gathering, comparing notes and making choices for the next five minutes. But, before I could corner Trevor to ask him about the gratis sheets, Rowan from the women's sports department next door caught my attention and called me over.

"What's up Rowan?" I asked.

Rowan didn't look too good. Her face was white as a ghost, and her petite body was bent over, holding her stomach.

"Oh, Diana, I have a terrible stomach ache. I feel like I'm gonna be sick."

She obviously was in pain, but she's a conscientious employee who never missed a day of work. Rowan was one of the few responsible twenty-one-year-olds in the store, attending college, working full-time and helping out around the house rather than partying until the wee hours of the morning, so easy to do in this town. But, if she was sick, she shouldn't be here.

"Rowan, why did you even come in? You should go home."

"I called in but Tess my manager said she didn't have anyone else to open. No one else is scheduled until 5 p.m. and Tess has meetings all day."

Rowan let out a small squeal and clutched her stomach even harder. I knew all about Tess. She was cut from the same cloth as my manager, Holly. Life is all about the company, not about you. Tess had been with Sherborne for over 15 years, opening new stores around the country. She played a hard line with her employees, and she had one of the highest employee turnover rates in the store. Still, they kept her as a manager.

I faced a similar situation to Rowan's when I had a really bad sinus infection a few weeks back. I had the closing shift, and I called Holly to let her know I was sick. She said she was sorry to hear that, but it was my responsibility to find someone to take my shift, or else I had to work it. The company obviously didn't want me to come to work if I was sick but she needed to have floor coverage, so if I couldn't find someone she'd expect me at my scheduled time. I worked.

I wasn't as sick as Rowan is, but she can't exactly wait on people if she's throwing up.

"Rowan, it doesn't matter if Tess doesn't have any help. You're sick and you need to be home."

"I think if I have some tea and crackers and sit down for a few minutes, I'll feel better." She saw the concern in my eyes. "Don't worry, Diana, I'll be OK. Just look out for me to make sure I don't pass out behind the counter or something like that."

Rowan went to the café to get some tea and crackers, but before she could make it back to the stockroom, she grabbed a waste basket from behind a counter and threw up.

I felt sorry for Rowan and I'd offer to work her shift, but I was working a crazy schedule as it was. I closed last night, was here for the 7 a.m. meeting, I close tonight, then I open again tomorrow morning. If I work the rest of Rowan's shift until 5 p.m., I won't have a break all day.

Plus, I hadn't been here long enough to know just how far I could push the rules as far as working straight through. Wait a minute. Rules? What rules? This company has no stinkin' rules! That's what they tell us in orientation. All we ask is that you use your best judgment always. Yeah, right.

Every day I encounter new rules, only they're not written down. Management just makes them up along the way. How convenient for a company, in the event of a lawsuit. Nothing in writing. That's what helps to create the Stepford environment here at Sherborne. By not having any written rules, it's easier to keep the employees in line. Everyone is constantly on edge, not knowing what will be thrown at them next.

It was now 10 a.m., the store was open, but the gratis party was still going on. I had customers to attend to, so I took a break away from the madness, both in my department and next door, to make some sales. Because of the meeting, I was working a split shift today – four hours in the morning, then returning to close at 5 p.m. I would be closing with Duchess tonight.

I put a customer in the fitting room, and saw Rowan scurry off to the restroom. A few moments later, I noticed there were customers at the women's sports counter. I ran into the stockroom to let Tess know so she could help them.

"Where's Rowan?" Tess snapped at me.

"She's in the ladies room. She's not feeling very well."

I tried to support Rowan in her hour of need.

"Well, what the hell is that bitch doing there? She's supposed to be on the sales floor. I don't have time for this today. I need to prepare for my meetings. I'll write her up as soon as she gets back for leaving her department without permission."

With that, Tess left the stockroom and went out on the floor to help the customers.

Rowan came back, three shades paler than she was just a half hour ago. I could see that she and Tess were having a very heated conversation, but I was busy closing a sale with my customer so I couldn't pay too much attention. Tess eventually went into the stockroom and Rowan stayed at the counter to ring sales.

Midway through a transaction, Rowan bent over and hurled into the waste basket. The customer simply grabbed her handbag and left. Rowan dragged herself over to human resources and requested that she go home. By the time Rowan got back to her department to gather her wallet and keys, Tess came out onto the floor, screaming at her.

"How dare you go to human resources and report me! You know we're short-staffed here. I need you to work, and that's all there is to it."

Tess threw Rowan's wallet and keys at her.

"When you come in tomorrow for your shift, we'll be sitting down to discuss the written warning you'll be receiving. This type of behavior is totally out of line for my employees."

Rowan left and never, ever came back.

While all the drama was taking place next door, things finally calmed down in lingerie after the store-opening rush. The gals were still finalizing their gratis choices, so I snuck up to the counter to find out what the big deal was about gratis.

"Oh, we live for gratis here," The Witch said. "It's one of the few perks the company gives that we really like."

Perks? I didn't know the company gave any perks.

"So, how does it work?" I asked.

Tina filled me in.

"Diana, it's so simple. Whisper Brand bras is our largest vendor. They include the two designer lines we carry. The company tracks how much you sell each quarter. You receive twelve dollars' worth of gratis for every thousand dollars you sell, with minimum sales of fifteen thousand dollars. So, if you sell less than fifteen thousand that quarter, you won't receive any gratis."

So far, it sounds easy enough. I hadn't been here that long, so I guess I didn't make the minimum selling requirements. But... how did Jordan make it? How did she even know about gratis when I hadn't a clue? Maybe they had a similar arrangement at her last place of employment.

Tina continued, "At the end of the quarter, you'll receive a report with your gratis dollars, just like we did today. Then you can select any item the company makes for free, as long as we have it in stock. That includes sale merchandise, too."

"But you can't go over the amount, so be sure to select wisely," Holly added.

She had joined us at the counter to see how gratis selection was going.

"When you're done, you just fill in the UPCs of all the items, and their cost, and hand it to me. I take it to security so they can verify your selections, record the amount and you can pay taxes on it."

"You mean sales tax?" I asked.

"No, the amount gets added to your earnings so you actually pay income tax."

So, how is that a perk?

"Oh. Okay, anything else I need to know about gratis?"

Holly answered, "Sure, this isn't the only type you get. Sometimes vendors will have contests for money or for free merchandise. The process works basically the same way. Just remember that gratis is not a purchase, and it's against company policy to return it for any reason."

There we go again with those phantom rules.

"Just wait, Diana, you'll see. Before long, you'll have drawers full of free lingerie. Soon you'll be like us, having to use the gratis for other family members. Even my daughter's drawers are full. It's a beautiful thing."

Tina obviously liked getting gratis, and I'm certain that, as time goes on, I'll be thrilled, too. Of course, it would be better if I had someone to wear them for.

But, right now, it's time to go home to have a little break before I have to come back to Stepfordland for my closing shift.

After a refreshing nap and nutritious lunch of canned turkey chili and a small salad, I made my way back to Sherborne to close with one of my favorite people, Duchess.

Working with Duchess was like working by myself. She claims each and every customer as her own, and when she isn't busy selling, she simply broods in one corner or another of the department. Her imposing stature makes you fearful, regardless of the circumstances. So, on nights like tonight, I pretty much keep to myself.

It was an extremely slow night. There were so few customers we could have bowled down the marble aisles and we wouldn't have hit a soul. I decided to busy myself with writing thank-you notes to those in my client book in order to kill time. I staked out my corner of the cash wrap and, one by one, knocked off my to-do list of thank yous. Duchess seemed to be content in the pajama section, straightening, folding, re-hanging.

About 8:30 p.m. a young blonde came into the department, and she and Duchess recognized each other right away. I'd never seen Duchess so animated, so lively. The two talked and joked and laughed for a few minutes, then made their way to the cash wrap behind me. The blond had a bag of lingerie she threw on the counter, and one by one, Duchess rang the return.

"So you just didn't need these anymore?" Duchess asked, a smile on her face.

"No. It's all gratis from when I worked here the last two years. I just have so much of it in my drawers, I decided it wasn't worth hanging onto, so I'll just return it. It will practically make my Sherborne charge payment this month!"

The two women laughed. My ears perked up.

"OK, so you're going to get $326.58 credit on your charge. How's that sound?"

"Fantastic! Nothing like gratis to make a woman happy!"

"Are you sure you don't want cash back?" Duchess asked.

"No, I'm always in here shopping, so this will open up some room on my account. At least I'll get something I want instead of whatever the company wants to give me."

"I know what you're saying, girlfriend. I know what you're saying."

Duchess swiped the blonde's credit card through the system, the blonde signed, and away she went. Duchess hung up all the merchandise like any normal return. I was still a bit confused about the whole thing, but I didn't say anything to her. Not that she'd do more than snort back at me.

The next morning I cornered Holly at her desk in back and relayed the events of the previous night.

"Are you absolutely certain that she said it was gratis?" she asked.

"Absolutely. She said she got it when she worked here for the last two years.

Holly glared at me.

"Don't say anything about this to anyone. Not a word. It's as if it never happened. Understood?"

"Sure, whatever. Did she do something wrong? Was I correct in reporting it?"

"Not a word."

And with that, Holly left the back room.

A few days later I was working a mid-shift. When I came back from lunch, I saw Holly and Duchess walking toward the employee service area. I thought nothing of it. Holly often walks with employees when paperwork needs to be corrected, which in this company is more often than you think.

About an hour later I saw someone from security go into the stock room and come out with Duchess's wallet. As security walked away, Tina looked at me and started shaking her head.

"That's not good," Tina said.

"What's not good?" I asked.

"Whenever security comes here to take your personal belongings, that means you're not coming back. I guess we can kiss Duchess good-bye. I wonder what happened. She's not the friendliest gal but she is top seller in the department."

"I don't know," I replied. "Security is always watching us. It must have been something major to get her fired like that."

Rumors spread quickly about Duchess, none of which were what I knew to be the truth. At the end of the week I scanned the Fired Employee Report at the employee entrance to gather insight into her departure. The report showed the store number of each location in the region, and a bulleted list of reasons someone was let go. Under our store number there was only one reason listed and it stated: Stole $100 from register.

Hmm…

Dear Diary,

What day is it? What the hell day is it? I'm so exhausted, I just can't think anymore.

My schedule is so inconsistent I truly don't know what day it is. When my alarm clock rings, I panic. Is it my day off and I have something fun planned? Or, do I have the day off but a meeting to go to? Or, is it really– shudder – a work day?

When I was at Isabella's I didn't start until evening, so it was much easier to keep track of things. Plus, I felt about ten years younger then. (Was it really only a year ago?)

Now, at Sherborne, I work a completely different shift every day, and it changes from week to week. I can't plan anything, and I freak when I get up in the morning because I have no idea if I've overslept. I have to walk outside and pick up the newspaper to find out what day it is. Well, at least I used to be able to locate the day on the front page of the newspaper. Nowadays, they plant a sticker advertisement right in that prestigious spot. And, God forbid it's a holiday, because the paper only tells you the name of the holiday, it doesn't tell you the day of the week!

I haven't had a weekend off since I started, except when I took a vacation but I couldn't afford to go anywhere anyway. Most weeks I don't have two days off together, like a weekend. Every day is a different shift. Some days I open, but my start time can vary from 8 a.m. till 9:20 a.m. Or I can work a mid-shift, but that can also vary from 10-6, 11-7, or 12-8. Closing is the only thing that's consistent, from 1-9:30. And, if you work a mid and it's slow, you might get to leave early. So often when I have a day off they schedule either a department or store meeting at 7 a.m. and I have to go into work. Now, perhaps other managers scheduled differently, but in our department, the only one who gets regular days off is The Witch, although Tina does always have Sundays off so she can spend time with her husband.

After I pick up the paper and put the coffee on, I pull out my cell phone to check my schedule. The one good thing about my phone is that when I touch the calendar, it always goes to the right day. As long as I remember to charge the damn thing. I used to live by the appointments typed into my calendar, and now I look at it twice each day. First thing in the morning to check my schedule, and the last thing at night to type in my sales for the day. I can't believe my $800 cell phone has been reduced to this.

I have no time for a social life. It's too hard to plan anything, and on those few days that I get off early, I generally open the next day. So, I have to get up at 5 a.m. That's not conducive to any late night activities, especially in this town.

Not that I have anyone to plan things with. There really isn't anyone at work who interests me. There are a couple of people who are nice and we might keep in touch when I finally get out of this place, but friends – well, I wouldn't exactly call it that. And dates? I can't even think about them. I thought it was hard to find a guy to put up with my schedule when I was flying all around the world. Now, I'm in the same city all the time but my schedule is so convoluted I don't even try. And, working in lingerie, where exactly would I meet a nice, available guy? Any man who walks into this department is taken.

Retail sucks.

More tomorrow!

All my heart,

Diana

The Witch

{ FOURTEEN }

"Eeewww! What is that! It's sooo gross! Get it out of here! Get it out of here!!!"

The Witch was looking at something on the counter, upon which Jordan had just dumped a load of bras and panties from the fitting rooms. Jordan hates to be bored, so she frequently makes a clean sweep of rejected merchandise and dumps it on the counter for a communal hanging.

The Witch yelled and screamed and carried on, jumping up and down, holding her nose, then her mouth as if she were going to vomit. She spun around on her three-inch dance heels, then ran into the stockroom. Jordan just continued to grab from the pile, hanging the stack of bras and panties. It was so unusual that The Witch was even helping to hang dump. She was typically too busy selling to be saddled with such mundane tasks.

We weren't sure at first what caused The Witch to be so offended, but the antics of this adult child could hardly be considered professional. Unless there was a dead body in the pile of dump, she had no reason to be screaming and carrying on so.

Being that we do live in the desert, she could have seen anything: a cockroach, a cricket, a gecko, a scorpion or even a rat. But no, what The Witch saw was something even more despicable than that - a nine-year-old bra.

The bra belonged to my customer. She had gained a reasonable amount of weight over those nine precious years, and because she felt self-conscious about her body, she delayed venturing into a proper bra fitting for a very long time. Not only did she postpone the fitting, she didn't buy any new bras either.

I had just spent almost two hours with her in the fitting room. She tried on 57 bras – I counted – before we finally found one that not only fit, but also met her requirements for comfort. It was a tough job, but she was completely satisfied and intelligently decided to wear one of her new bras home.

As customers often do, when she took off her old bra, she flung it onto the fitting room chair, so as not to get it mixed up with all the new bras. Unfortunately, we went through so many options, she eventually had to throw those on the chair as well. Ultimately, her old bra got mixed in with the new ones. It's not the first time it happened, but I felt embarrassed for my customer because her husband had to listen to The Witch's untimely screams.

You see, my customer's husband was sitting in a chair opposite the cash wrap when The Witch began her ranting and raving. At first, he stared at her, unsure of the cause of her distress, just like the rest of us. When I realized what the culprit was, I simply took a tissue, wrapped the dirty bra in it, and tossed it in the trash. Very professionally, very quietly. However, when I lifted the bra, the husband recognized it as his wife's, and he started squirming in his chair. He obviously had never been subjected to such demeaning behavior at an upscale store like ours.

His wife came out from the fitting room, prouder than she was two hours ago, her twins lifted six inches higher. She waved a thank-you to me, then turned toward her husband. He shot up from the chair, grabbed her hand, and ran them out of the department. I never saw that customer again, and frankly, I don't blame them. But, I do blame The Witch.

The Witch has been a thorn in my side since the day I started working at Sherborne. A lifelong cocktail waitress at the casinos, when she bends and turns to speak with the customers you can almost see the tray of drinks in her hand. Of course, her career in cocktails was excellent training for retail sales. She's easily able to handle multiple customers while providing good service. However, I can't imagine her reacting to a situation so rudely at a casino. Surely, management would have written her up or walked her out the door.

The Witch is 42-years-old, strikingly beautiful in a Demi Moore sort of way, with long dark hair, about five feet seven inches tall, thin as a rail, with the requisite silicone enhancements most cocktail waitresses in this town employ. She works out constantly, watches everything she eats, and works hard to please the customers. She always dresses exquisitely, almost too exquisitely for a lowly commission-only lingerie sales clerk.

Her two signatures are her professional ballroom dance shoes and the lovely rose quartz crystal that hangs around her neck, a gift from her mother. She's punctual to a fault, blissfully organized, and takes only half the allotted time for lunch so she can busy herself with sales. She's intelligent, loves old movies and even older starlets, and is environmentally and politically conscious. She's the number one salesperson in the department. And, you ask why I hate her.

No, it has nothing to do with how perfect she is. It's what's behind the façade that throws me off-kilter.

First, let's look at the punctuality issue. Now, I'm a firm believer in being punctual, especially when it comes to work, family and friends. However, The Witch takes punctuality to the extreme. One morning I was working an opening shift. I wandered into the employee lounge to see what was on the news, and I noticed her sitting in the corner reading a book. I knew from the schedule that she didn't start for another hour and fifteen minutes!

"Hey, what are you doing here so early?" I inquired. "Your shift doesn't start for over an hour."

The Witch peered up from a biography of some silent screen siren and responded curtly, "I don't like to be late."

Then, she went back to reading her book.

I was a bit puzzled by this. I mean, most people get to work at the last minute, or within a reasonable timeframe. But, over an hour early! To me, that's just ridiculous.

"Wouldn't you rather be home sleeping or cleaning or, perhaps, reading your book in the comfort of your living room?"

She now glared at me over the pages of her book, and once again replied, "I said, I don't like to be late."

And that was the end of that discussion.

The Witch prides herself on her nearly fat-free body, and lives for comments from customers. When people ask her why she would give up a lucrative career as a cocktail waitress to work in retail, she simply replies that she felt that it was time to leave the smoke-filled arenas of debauchery, and follow a path of respectability.

"After all, I'm not just a wife and mother, I'm a grandmother as well," she'll say. Over and over and over again.

"A grandmother!" a shocked customer will reply. "My, you certainly have a fantastic figure for a grandmother. How lucky you are."

A smile of satisfaction will grace The Witch's lips as she coos, "Yes, I certainly am lucky." Over and over and over again.

But the price of beauty is sometimes obsession, and I soon learned that The Witch was diagnosed with OCD twenty years ago. It became more and more evident the longer we worked together.

Turns out, she was bulimic as a teenager, and anorexic for a period of time as an adult after her daughter was born. With the help of a therapist she threw away her scales, and now measures her health by how her clothes fit. "I refuse to be a slave to numbers," she says.

Even at this mature age of 42, she still worries about gaining an ounce of weight. She works out for two hours every morning upon rising, and generally an hour after work. She carefully measures everything she eats, so in some sense, she is a slave to numbers. Not on the bathroom scale, but on the kitchen scale. And, to the number of hours she works out in the gym.

Her OCD is noticeable in other facets of her life as well. As a consequence of her OCD, she became one of the world's biggest germaphobes. When she works, the cash wrap counter is spotless. Sneeze or cough in any way, and there she is, spraying down the registers, phones and counters with disinfectant. It gets so bad, that when you talk on the phone, you can't help but cough from the remnants of the disinfectant, which only makes The Witch spray it again. It's a never-ending cycle.

She feels uncomfortable wasting time, finding it quite hard to relax. So, when she's at work, she works. When she takes more than 20 minutes for lunch, we're shocked. But, that doesn't mean she does all her chores. She might be the top salesperson, but she rarely, if ever, cleans her customers' fitting rooms and puts back the dump. She seldom even straightens or stocks her assigned area. To her, work is simply sell, sell, sell. She's not hired to do anything else.

But why do I call her The Witch? Because she is one. The white magic sort of witch, you know. The good type. Although, with her judgmental behavior, I'm not totally convinced she's not hiding a voodoo doll of me somewhere, or a secret potion to make my day miserable.

She and her mom are Wiccan. Hence, the lovely rose quartz crystal that graces her neck. I'm not offended by it, supportive or judgmental. As long as people are respectful of one another, that's fine with me. That's a critical element for us all to get along in this big world. And, I'm certain it has nothing to do with her behavior. I simply bring it up because it intrigues me. I've never met a full-out witch before.

I found out quite accidentally. The Witch was chatting with a few friends, and while I was straightening and stocking my area, a task totally foreign to my co-worker, I did a bit of eavesdropping.

It appears that her friends were from Southern California. They worked at Castleland amusement park, in the wardrobe department. I guess The Witch had worked there for a brief period of time when she needed a break from cocktailing, and before she discovered retail. I'd seen her friends before, but until now, I didn't know much about them. I was a bit jealous of them, working at the funnest place on Earth, compared to the Stepford environment we had here. Most of their conversation was horribly mundane, but my ears perked up when they started talking about witches.

"Are you getting any flack being Wiccan here in Vegas?" one of the gentlemen asked.

"No, most people don't know about that part of me," The Witch replied. "It's not like I share it with anyone. If someone notices my crystal, and I feel comfortable with them, I might share. Otherwise, I wait to be guided to people I feel I can trust."

"Yeah, I know what you mean," a different gentlemen commented. "Can you imagine the nightmare we'd have if people found out that the Castleland Princess costumed characters at the park are all witches? I mean, Mr. Castle knew and he was fine with it, even encouraged it. But I don't think the rest of the world would agree."

Omigod. Omigod! Are you serious? The Castleland Princesses are Wiccan? Not that there's anything wrong with that. Who knew? That was a shock to my system. I'll have to check it out next time I'm at Castleland.

But, being Wiccan isn't the only reason why I call her The Witch. It really has to do with how she judges people, especially me. We had a major falling out, and I can no longer stand to be near her. When we work together, we're on opposite sides of the department. And that suits me just fine.

You see, a few months back, I seriously contemplated moving to Southern California. I thought, maybe I could transfer with the company, then look for some consulting work. L.A. is a much shorter drive than San Jose, so I wouldn't be that far from my family here in Las Vegas, once Helen and the clan move out.

I spoke with Holly about it, and she suggested I explore the possibilities. What I didn't know is that she would basically write me off as a transfer the minute I selected a few dates to go and talk to the other stores. When I got back from my weekend in LA, I discovered I was off the schedule, and Holly had hired Jordan!

I told Holly that after my trip, I didn't want to move. It would be too complicated right now, and I wanted to be near my family. Holly, surprisingly, understood and agreed to keep me on staff. Well, that didn't sit well with The Witch. She cornered me in the stockroom one Saturday afternoon. She had been treating me rather rudely since my return, and I didn't know why. But I do now.

"You really have a lot of nerve screwing over Holly like you did," she screamed at me. "Do you know how it hurt her? First you're leaving, then you're staying. You need to just make up your mind. You should go back to California where you belong. Then we won't have so many people on staff and maybe we can make a little bit more money rather than sharing it with you!"

Well, I must say, she didn't take long to get to the point. First of all, she had no idea how I felt about Holly basically kicking me out of the department, and she wouldn't let me explain. Her mind was made up. I was judged.

But the kicker, I see, is that she was now losing money. One more person on staff means everyone takes home just a little bit less in their paychecks. She doesn't like that. Well, too darn bad. I never submitted my resignation so Holly had no right to hire my replacement. She technically didn't have an open req. She found someone who had lingerie experience, and she grabbed her. Not my fault. Go pick on Jordan and Holly. Leave me alone, bitch.

Now, I'm certain that there are Wiccans all around us. And, I believe they are a kind and peaceful people. The fact that The Witch is a Wiccan has absolutely nothing to do with the reason I can't stand to work with her. It's simply that episodes such as these from this second-generation Wiccan are enough to make me want to burn her at the stake.

Dear Diary,

Who am I and how did I get here?

It's as if I've fallen down this deep well and can't climb out. I'm sure other people have been through a similar ordeal, but I honestly don't know how they get past these bad times and create a fabulous future for themselves. Everyone knows I'm capable of doing far more than I currently am, but for now, I feel stuck. I'm lost without a map. I'm not sure where that light is at the end of the tunnel. Maybe I need new batteries in my flashlight.

Gizzi keeps asking me to come back to Cali. Can't do it. I looked north and south, and there just isn't enough money in it to justify the move. Besides, I've been out of high tech for so long, I'm not sure I could still be viewed as the marketing guru I once was. Technology changes so quickly, I wouldn't garner the respect I had in the past simply because I don't honestly know what's going on in our industry any longer and couldn't stand behind any opinion I might offer.

But, ask me about bras! I can spew out the type of bra that works for every woman on every occasion. I seem to have developed a niche of talent, one that doesn't bode well for my future financial picture. Sure, I could go into management here but I really have no desire.

Gene tells us that we should act as if we're running our own businesses, but that's such a hoax. I can't market, advertise, travel, select merchandise or set my own hours. I can only operate under the unwritten rules of this company.

Is Holly right? Have I become bitter and now, disrespectful? I was always so happy, joyful and had such a positive attitude. Now, I go to work bitter and come home
angry. I absolutely hate what I'm doing while at the same
time I'm appreciative I have an income. Oh, and my feet
hurt.

With my crazy schedule, it's nearly impossible to look
for other work or to even schedule a meeting. I'm sure
the company does that on purpose. Besides, the economy
is worse than ever, so not a lot of people are hiring. I'm
grateful we still have customers. As Tina said, the two
things women buy during a recession are lipstick and
lingerie. I guess she's right. Otherwise, we would all be
out on the street.

I don't even contemplate a social life. I'm so exhausted,
my head hurts just thinking about it. Then there's that
whole schedule thing. How people in this town are able
to find romance is beyond my current comprehension.

I know this is just a phase, but it's a long one I'm not
thrilled about. I wonder how Chris is doing.

More tomorrow!

All my heart,

Diana

Employees Aren't Customers

{ FIFTEEN }

I shot up the stairs, clocked in, and practically ran to my department. I was running late and I had a lot of stuff I had to get done before the store opened in thirty minutes. I closed last night, and I was opening today with Holly. You just never know what additional projects Holly is going to hand you when you step foot on that padded carpet that defines our department.

I rushed past the robes and pajamas, and was about to cut through the sale panties, when something caught my eye. I turned, and stared in shock. Holly was standing at the cash wrap, her head down, and she was sobbing! Now, people had told me that Holly has a heart, but I'd never really seen any sensitive emotions emanate from this shill of a manager. Yet, here I had it. Proof! Whatever was troubling her had reached deep down inside and made her cry. Hopefully, it wasn't anything traumatic, but it had to be bad enough to trigger such a display.

I gingerly walked across the carpet and stopped short of touching her shoulder for fear that she might tap unknown martial arts skills and I'd be on the floor in two seconds.

"What's wrong, Holly? Why are you crying?"

Holly slowly lifted her head from the counter, her eyes red and swollen, snots dripping from her nose. Very unattractive. She'd been crying for some time.

"We have to put the blankets out."

Then she put her head back down on the counter and sobbed heavily.

We have to put the blankets out. What is she talking about? Let me think here for a minute. Blankets. Blankets. Oh, I think I get it.

"Do you mean the ones we've been holding for the employee sale?" I asked.

She turned and glared at me scornfully.

"What other blankets do you think I mean?"

OK, Holly really wasn't a pretty picture right now, and the store opened in just a few minutes. I've got to get her talking to see if I can offer any suggestions, although I'm sure she'll just ignore them. Her comments were puzzling as I thought the blankets were reserved for employees and everything had been approved through the management chain.

See, every year around Thanksgiving, Sherborne does a special Thank You day for its employees. The date will vary from store to store, but on that selected date, employees can purchase anything in the store for 40 percent off, instead of our typical 20 percent discount. It's like their Christmas present to the employees, since we don't get anything else.

This year, the hot gift is these fabulously soft blankets. From the time we first got them in July, they've been selling like hotcakes. Even in the desert, people have been snatching them up the second they hit the selling floor. Some folks buy two, three or even four at a time, some even more than that. Some are for gifts, some are for multiple rooms in multiple homes. They feel like a baby blanket, and as soon as you touch them, you want to curl up in front of the fire with a good book, then take a nap. It's amazing what an effect these blankets can have on people.

Holly knew that employees would want to purchase them for Christmas gifts, so she asked the buyer, and Gene, the general manager, if she could survey the store employees and place a special order. Both granted them her approval way back in September. The order came in, and they were all set aside on the top shelves of the stockroom. They'd been there for weeks. Our Thank You day was next Sunday, so they would all be gone in a matter of days.

However, the company that manufactures the blankets ran into a snag. They just couldn't keep up with demand nationwide. Our inventory showed we had a huge quantity in stock, so stores from throughout the country were calling, asking us to sell them to their customers. Whenever we got such a request, we simply stated that our inventory numbers were off, and we didn't have any to sell. Everything was fine with that little white lie (they were, after all, on hold for legitimate customers) until yesterday when Jordan was chatting with a manager from another store, and she slipped and told her about the stock we had on blankets.

That was it. All hell broke loose. The manager contacted the buyer, and the buyer called our ball-less wonder, Gene, to tell him we had to sell the blankets. Holly fought back, Gene said he'd tell the buyer we weren't going to do that, but obviously, things had changed.

By now, Holly stood erect, wiped her smeared mascara and eye liner from her puffy eyes, and put on her manager face.

"Well, I'd better get moving and put the blankets on the sales floor before the boss comes around."

Oops, too late. Just as we both turned to head toward the stockroom, Gene was in front of our faces.

"You got my message?" he asked, knowing by the way Holly looked she certainly got it, loud and clear. "Good. Do you need any help putting them out?"

I was in shock by this exchange. The ball-less one actually giving an order, and the emotion-less one taking it. Let me write this day down in my diary.

"What's the deal with this, Gene? These blankets were promised to the employees."

I figured, what could it hurt, I'll throw in my two cents.

Gene bristled back and pushed out his chest, just like a rooster does when trying to be studly and protect his territory.

"This came down from the buying office, Diana. I don't have any say in this situation."

Like hell he doesn't. He's the store manager. He can determine what is right and wrong for his own domain, if he even knows the difference.

"What exactly is the problem, Gene? Why can't we keep these blankets for the employee sale?"

Holly was now huddled in the corner of the cash wrap, fearful of what might happen if Gene should strike. I knew he didn't have it in him, but I wasn't sure if it was worth wasting my breath. Something, somehow, just kept me going. It was the principle of the thing.

"Thank you for being so interested in this situation, Diana, but it really is none of your business. However, since you asked, there's a huge customer demand for these blankets, and we can't get more inventory for the customers until we sell the ones we have in stock. So, they have to come out onto the sales floor."

Think, Diana, think. There must be another solution.

I piped up, "Well then, why can't the employees buy them today? Just give them the discount. Or, let them buy it at full price and refund the discount on Sunday."

Holly awoke from her daze to counter my suggestion.

"Good idea, Diana, but we don't get paid until Thursday, so most of the employees won't have the money to purchase them until payday anyway."

Gene was being adamant. He can be a little twerp at times. Well, OK, most of the time.

"Doesn't matter, Diana. I can only do the Thank You discount for items purchased on Sunday. We have 80 blankets in the back, and they have to be on the floor by the time the store opens." He looked down at his watch, and smirked. "Oh, yeah, and that would be now."

As he walked away to unlock the doors, I rolled my eyes and muttered, "Whatever."

He stopped for a second, looked at me, then turned and headed for the doors. In a few seconds, we would be surrounded by throngs of holiday shoppers, and Holly would be a broken spirit for a while.

Holly threw her paperwork across the counter, slammed her pen into it so hard it broke and shattered into pieces, and glared after Gene. Then, she took a deep breath, looked at me, and said, "Come on. We have blankets to put out."

My first customers of the day were three 40-year-old women who were away from their husbands and children for the first time in several years. They were bound and determined to find new bras that would make them look perky again. Well, at least their breasts, anyway. We spent a long time roaming the racks of merchandise, discussing what each one was looking for, and her specific bra issues. It wasn't always easy, but it was definitely a lot of fun. They hadn't been to sleep yet, and although they had breakfast and coffee, you could still smell the strawberry margaritas and cranberry martinis they'd drunk the night before. Every little thing made them laugh, and I'd nearly forgotten about the morning strife.

We gathered quite a selection of bras and made our way to the largest fitting room we had to house all three women. They kept laughing and telling stories. It was almost as if I wasn't there, while at the same time, as if I'd always been part of the group.

While I listened to their chatter, I picked up a very distinct accent. I knew it was true, even before I opened my mouth to clarify, but it was just something I do. I guess I like to prove to myself how intelligent I am by having people acknowledge that, yes, I did correctly identify their country of origin. There's not much to make me feel intelligent lately, so this is just a little ego-boost for me. And, I think it helps to make the customers more comfortable, that I would be able to determine where they are from. Most times, they're impressed. Ah, that illustrious ego.

One of the ladies had just taken off her top and bra, and I handed her one of the stash to try on. Everyone was laughing and having a good time. I just had to say it.

"You're from Canada, aren't you?"

The naked woman was in shock, covered her breasts with her arms, and turned 50 shades of red.

"How can you tell? Do my breasts look different? Do I have… Canadian breasts?"

We all burst out laughing so hard, I was sure I'd be calling maintenance any moment to wipe up puddles from the floor.

"No, it's just the way you talk, the 'eh' thing."

I could barely get those words out, I was still chortling over her comment.

One of the other women contained herself quickly.

"Okay, Miss Smarty Pants. If you know so much about Canada, what is our capital?"

"Oh, that's easy. It's Ottawa."

I grew up in Detroit, so it was just one of those things I knew, being so close by.

They all stared at me in amazement.

"Wow! You're the first American we've asked who knew the answer. You're smart. We'll buy bras from you."

Why this question would be important for them to ask during their visit to Sin City was beyond me, but who am I to judge.

Ms. Canadian Breasts put on one bra after the other, and true to their words, the three of them spent a ton of money – and time – with me.

Jordan finally came in, so as I wished the Canadian women a happy day and much thanks, I realized it was now time for me to go to lunch. We had to take an early lunch here and generally I'm not hungry when it's time for me to go, but for some reason, today I was. I hadn't brought anything to eat, so I went to the stockroom, grabbed some money from my wallet, and headed down the escalator to the coffee bar on the first floor to grab a salad and a cookie. They have the best chocolate chip cookies I've ever tasted, and while I try to limit myself to just one a week, today definitely begged for one.

I thought about sitting in the mall courtyard to eat my lunch, but sometimes it just feels too open. I never know who's going to spot me here. Then I'll have to explain to them that I have to get back to work, and before you know it, I'm a loser in their eyes. So, up the escalators I went to the employee lunch room.

I got off the escalator, turned and BAM! Who do I run into but Gene. Just when my day was getting better. It was as if he watched me on the security cameras and knew I was going to be there just at that precise moment.

"Oh, uh, sorry. I didn't see you there," I apologized to him.

He was, after all, our store manager. I thought the apology would be enough but he obviously had other things on his mind.

"Diana, so glad I found you."

Yeah, right.

"I got the distinct impression that you don't support the decision I made regarding the blankets this morning."

Oh, no, here it comes. I won't be able to control myself. He opened the flood gates, and now every little thing I have against this company will come out. Sorry, buddy. You started it.

"Yes, you're right, Gene. I don't support your decision. You made a promise to the employees months ago that they would be able to purchase those blankets on employee sale day. Now, you're going back on your word. What does that say about the company?"

"It says that we're very concerned about our customers," he snorted back.

"Well, employees are customers, too," I said.

Gene took a deep breath, rolled his head, then focused his eyes on mine, kind of like a Dad does when he's about to tell you that you can't have the convertible for the weekend.

"Diana, employees aren't really customers. If anything, they're discount shoppers, and the company cannot survive on discount shoppers."

I about threw my salad in his face. The cookie was mine, but he'd look lovely, standing here in the middle of the third floor with carrot strips hanging from his mustache.

"Is that what you think of us? Puhleeze. How many of your employees spend all of their paychecks – and more – shopping here at Sherborne? How long do they stay here as employees? Most of them were regular customers before, and will be again when they leave their jobs."

"Diana, it's a bottom line thing. We have customers who are willing to pay full price for those blankets. I can't justify holding them for another week just to get a discount price."

"And, what about promises? You'll do more harm to the morale of your staff by refusing to honor your promise than you will in the amount of money you'll lose on the extra discount. I calculated it. We're talking about $3,200 difference between the employee purchase price and the customer price. However, you'll lose far more than that in respect and trust with your staff by not living up to your promises."

I was on a roll now. Look out!

"This place really sucks. It's all a lie, from the first day of orientation until the day you walk out the door."

Something piqued Gene's interest, although I'm not sure I cared.

"What do you mean it's all a lie? We have one of the best employee programs in all of retail."

"Yeah, right," I responded. "That employee handbook is such a sham. It says we as employees should use our best judgment and the store will support us in our decisions, but I've yet to see it."

"You're wrong, Diana. I support my managers and employees in their decisions all the time."

"That's bull, Gene, and you know it."

By now my blood pressure was through the roof, and all I could think of was how he was wasting my precious lunch time arguing about something that would never change.

"It's never about our best judgment. It's all about having made the right decision at the right time as your boss who forgot his coffee and his boss who might not have gotten laid last night and decides to take it out on her staff. It's always about doing what the boss says, not being empowered to run the department like your own business. And, how convenient, that the employee handbook consists of only one line, that nothing more is in writing. It's harder for employees to sue you if nothing is in writing. It's all just whim."

I started to walk toward the lunch room when Gene grabbed my arm.

"You're wrong, Diana, that's not how it is. If I have a manager that makes a decision, even if I don't agree with it, I support them on it."

I looked down at my arm, which was still in his grasp. He finally let go.

"All I'm saying is, I don't see it. I haven't seen you support a manager or an employee since the day I walked in the door."

"But this morning is a great example. I supported Holly in her decision to put the blankets out for the customers."

He couldn't actually believe that was true, could he? Is his mind so twisted he thinks it was Holly's decision to sell the blankets?

"No, Gene, this time you're wrong. I don't see it. Holly made a commitment to her fellow employees, that she would order and hold their Christmas purchases until employee sale day, per your approval. And, this morning you came along and told her she couldn't do that. That's what I call a lie, a sham, and I don't care who you are, you don't live up to the corporate ideals."

With that, I ran to the lunch room to eat my salad in the few minutes I had left before I had to be back on the sales floor.

When I finished my lunch, I went out the rear door of the lunch room, so I could use the restroom before I clocked back in. To my surprise, Holly was sitting there on a chair. She looked up at me with her doe-like eyes, still smudged from her tears.

"I saw you and Gene talking by the escalators," she said.

"Well, I wouldn't exactly call it talking. There were comments going back and forth, but I wouldn't consider it a conversation."

Shit, am I in trouble? Am I going to get fired?

"What did you say to him?" she asked.

No emotion here, hard to read her thoughts.

"Nothing in particular. I just told him how I felt."

That's it. Now I know I'm in trouble. I wonder how hard it is to find a job this close to Christmas.

"Well, you must have said something to him, because when you finished, he came over to me and told me we could hold the blankets until the employee sale, and that he would contact the buyer and tell her he supported my decision."

What! Something I said actually had an impact in this place?

Holly got up from her chair, and touched my arm, much kinder than the way that Gene had grabbed it just a short time ago.

"Thanks, Diana," Holly said. "No one has ever stood up for me before."

With that, she walked away and headed back to the department.

I was stunned by the turn of events, but the only thing that popped into my mind was, "Just remember that, Holly, the next time you schedule me 12 days in a row."

"Diana, sweetie, I can't believe you're still at Sherborne," Gizzi said with her usual concern. Between my work schedule and her travel schedule, it seemed we hardly talked any more. It was good to hear her voice. "I recognize that you have a life to live, but darling, you're not living! I'm not quite sure you're even existing!"

Gizzi always hits the nail on the head. And, she realizes things that I hope others don't. Unfortunately, I don't live in a vacuum or on some deserted island. I'm in Las Vegas, for chrissake.

"Trust me, I know, Giz. I can't believe I used to manage multi-million dollar marketing budgets. Now I'm thrilled if I can afford a visit to Whole Foods once a month when I used to practically live there. I'm off-stride and I don't know how to get it back."

Gizzi chuckled.

"Off-stride? Honey, you're not even on the same highway any more. I haven't a clue how to advise you. Until you make the decision to move your life forward, you'll be selling bras. That's just reality."

Gizzi took a long drag from her ever-present cigarette. I knew there was a martini close at hand. I just couldn't hear it.

"Well, enough about me, girlfriend. What's new with you? We hardly talk now that I'm working these crazy schedules at Sherborne."

Gizzi cleared her throat before she spoke. Whatever she was going to say was important to her, but for some reason I could tell she was reluctant to share it with me.

"Um, yes, well, I was promoted to vice president of sales last week," she kindly blurted out. "It was totally unexpected. I felt we had such a good team in sales that it would be some time before the VP position opened, but, heh, here I am!"

"Gizzi, that's wonderful! Congratulations!" I said.

Sure, I was thrilled for my friend, but her promotion was a slap in the face to my current situation. It would take me a number of years to recoup what I lost since the economy tanked. I'd probably have to go back to B-school to even compete at an entry level any more.

"Yes, thanks, Diana. It really was a shock. Turns out, Dave, the prior VP, had been working on the side with an engineer friend of his to launch a startup. They finally got funded and off he went. Budgets are tight but we really couldn't go very long without someone in that position. It's just too critical in our business. I thought they would give the title to Maurice, but instead, it was entrusted to me. Big raise, big office, business class seats. I couldn't have asked for anything more."

"I gotta hand it to you, Gizzi. You really have stayed focused and all your hard work has paid off. Before you know it, you'll be president and CEO!"

"Well, not yet, Diana. Give me a couple of years!"

We both laughed although it truly was just a matter of time before Gizzi hit the top spot.

"And, what about you, Diana? Where will you be in a couple of years?"

"I wish I had an answer for you, Giz. I really don't know. It seems everything I learned in Silicon Valley is pretty useless to me here, even regarding plans and proposals. The whole style of business is completely different in Vegas. I've even tried to snag some clients who come to town from Europe for the many conferences and trade shows that take place here, but that hasn't worked either. I don't have any recent experience or current clients I can use as a reference. I'm lost in a sea of opportunity without a rudder. No motor. Not even paddles. I'm happy for you, Giz, I really am, but I don't even know how to begin defining my future."

After another long drag off her cigarette, Gizzi responded.

"You'll find it, Diana. I know you will. It's right around the corner, I'm sure of that. Keep your eyes and your mind open. Something wonderful will come your way."

Wow! Gizzi never got so inspirational. Must be all that yoga she's doing.

"Thanks, Giz. I know you're right. My future is right around the corner."

Dear Diary,

Oooohhh, I can't believe how condescending those customers can be. They think that just because I'm a sales associate, that I'm a piece of trash. I work at Sherborne, for chrissake! They hire intelligent people from all walks of life, or so their reputation goes. Do they think that just because they have money they can treat me like PWT?

I had a customer today that was so rude and pompous, I wanted to spit on her. She was shopping for her trip to Hong Kong next week. When I told her I had been there several times, she looked me up and down with all the attitude she could muster and said, "Why in the world would Sherborne send you to Hong Kong? You're just a sales clerk."

Just a sales clerk! Just a SALES CLERK! I'm an intelligent, well-educated, well-traveled, successful business person who just happens to be in a slump right now, rebuilding my business. How dare she be so rude!

And she's not the only one. I get so many customers who look at me and just can't understand how I could possibly have traveled outside the country, let alone outside the state of Nevada. How could I afford it? After all, I'm just a sales clerk. (They do have a point there. My vacation dollars have diminished significantly in recent years.)

I've been to 27 countries, and throughout most of the U.S. I've visited more places than a lot of my customers. And they have the nerve to talk down to me?

Retail is typically a transient profession, something people do as they're passing through from one career to another. Certainly, there are a few who make a career of it, but that's definitely not me. EVER! I'm just passing through on my way to a life.

I'm so much better than this. Why am I here?

More tomorrow!

All my heart,

Diana

The Social Club

{ SIXTEEN }

It's Sunday, 12:15 p.m.

It doesn't matter the date because every Sunday is exactly the same.

I hear the phone ringing on the counter, and instinctively check my watch. No, it can't be 12:15 p.m. already! It seems like I just got here. We've been super busy since the doors opened at 10:45 a.m., 15 minutes before the posted time. It's a Sherborne tradition. Rather than leave the customers anticipating the store opening by lining up outside, Sherborne opens its doors early. And, most days, we're busy right from that fateful moment.

But, this is now another fateful moment. It's time for the weekly Social Club members to pay their visit. Unfortunately, these aren't women that we want to socialize with. These are women who make the hair on the back of our necks stand on end, and we are fiercely competitive about avoiding them. If you can hide, you don't have to abide.

We instituted a telephone alarm system in the store to give us at least a few minutes of warning. When the first member of the Social Club enters, the handbag department immediately calls the lingerie department. That gives us enough notice to get busy with customers or hide. We all know that when the phone rings at 12:15 p.m., there's no need to answer, but we do anyway, just in case, by luck, it rings for some other reason.

I look up from my watch, and shoot a quick glance to my fellow employees. Jordan and The Witch are working with me today, and both are quite familiar with the Social Club. The two of them are busy with customers so I run behind the counter to answer the telephone. I check the caller ID with a wishful heart, but I'm disappointed to see it read HANDBAGS. When my co-workers see the look on my face, they scatter faster than I can blink my eyes.

"Get the perfect fit at Sherborne Lingerie. This is Diana. How may I help you?" I answered the call with our required script.

"Oh, give it up, Diana. You know why I'm calling," sneered Morgan from Handbags into the phone. "Petunia is on her way. Have a good day!"

I could hear the sneer through the receiver. Morgan had obviously escaped the wrath of Petunia. I, however, could see that I was now the only sales associate on the floor. My commission-hogging co-workers had fled for cover.

I felt my stomach churn the minute I noticed those signature black leggings. Petunia strode across the floor like a dancer who never quite made the cut, but continued her exercises to this day, hoping just one more audition will land her in the chorus line. Every Sunday she arrived precisely at 12:15 p.m., attired in black leggings, black ballet flats and a colorful top. Her hair was staged in a bob, gray streaks giving way to her 63 years. Her left hand held a diamond the size of martini glass; how her fragile bone structure supported it is still a mystery to us all. A bigger mystery is the man who manages to put up with Miss Petunia Puss, the personality that killed many a sales associate.

I took a deep breath and prepared for the worst. Today was my day, and I had to survive. The Witch had had it out with Petunia in the past, and was unofficially banned from helping her. Jordan had one experience and that's all it took to keep her distance. I, on the other hand, have such a loving heart that I somehow get suckered into waiting on her nearly every Sunday. Sometimes I'm so busy that I get blindsided and don't realize that she's here. However, most of the time I'm just the unlucky one whose name she recalls.

"Diana, darling, you know I don't like to wait."

I recoiled at the mention of my name from the lips of that wicked, wicked woman.

"I need to purchase something for my daughter."

"Why, yes, Petunia. How can I help?"

If only it were a simple request, but I knew better.

"See this lavender robe?"

Petunia held up a super soft, microfiber robe in a lovely violet shade.

"I need one in a size small, but I want it to be the exact hue of this size large."

Like I can control dye lot variations.

"I have a nightgown that I purchased for her birthday, and I'm certain it will match that color. I need it by Wednesday and I won't pay for shipping."

Of course not, you bitch. If you weren't such a wealthy pain in the ass, the company wouldn't kiss yours. Besides, I know how this scene will play out. I'll spend the next hour on the phone trying to track down the robe in a small, regardless of color. We'll ship it overnight on Monday, to arrive at your house on Tuesday. You'll return it next Sunday because the nightgown is actually lime green, not lavender, because the drugs you're on affect your sense of color. So, the colors won't match, I'll be out the commission on this sale, and the ones I lost during the hour I spent on the phone trying to find the item for you. May you rot in hell.

"I'd be happy to find that for you, Petunia. We'll ship it to your house as usual, correct?"

"Of course. Where else would you send it?" she snorted at me. "But call me on my cell the second you locate one so I can be assured of it arriving in time for her birthday."

"Absolutely, Petunia. I'll get right on it."

She strode out of the department as quickly as she slid in. I leaned back on the counter, relieved that I had survived another visit from Petunia. I took a deep breath, and as I congratulated myself for my efficient handling of the situation, I was brought back to reality in the harshest way.

WHACK!

I didn't need to turn around to know that Lucy had arrived, because the sound of her cane slamming against the counter was all the notice I needed. Dammit! The second member of the Social Club was here and I was stuck waiting on her, too. There was not another customer on the floor, and Jordan and The Witch were huddled at the entrance to the fitting rooms, giggling hysterically like prepubescent teenagers.

Quite the opposite of Petunia, Lucy hasn't seen a treadmill or a barre, or her toes for that matter, in years. Reaching just barely over five feet tall, Lucy would need to grow another foot to have the correct BMI for her size. And, while Petunia has a style all her own, Lucy spends a lot of money at Sherborne but always looks like she shops at the local thrift store.

Lucy flung a Sherborne bag on the counter, and whacked her cane on top of it.

"These didn't fit," she screamed. "I want a refund."

"Why, of course, Lucy. Let me see what you have here."

"It doesn't matter what I have. I want a refund. Sherborne will refund anything I bring in here."

Well, technically that's true, but I can still hassle you a bit if I want to. On second thought, it's probably better if I don't.

I gingerly moved Lucy's cane off the bag and looked inside. I could have vomited right then, but I chose to keep my composure

– and my breakfast. The bag held a bra and panties that had been worn since Lucy was a teenager. She was now 52-years-old. She also obviously used moth balls in her house as well, their toxicity one perfect explanation for her obnoxious behavior. If only there was some way for me to understand why the company catered to her.

"These are our basic stock items," I lied, "so I can give you an immediate refund."

I rang the return on the register while she snarled at me impatiently.

"That will be $85.32. How would you like that refunded?"

"I want it on my credit card."

She dug through her handbag, at one point feigning that she would pass out. Eventually, she located her Sherborne card and threw it across the counter at me.

"Here. And I want it credited immediately. None of this 30 day stuff."

"Why, of course, Sherborne will credit it immediately to your card, no problem," I happily replied.

I ran her card through the machine, she grudgingly signed, and I braced myself for what was yet to come.

"Give me two of those shopping bags," she barked at me, "and I want a few yards of that ribbon you use for your bows."

Yes, of course, Lucy needed empty shopping bags so the next time she cleaned out her closet, she could find more disgusting merchandise that wasn't ours to return for credit on her account. Her need for ribbon threw me for a long time, until I finally found out her fascination with it.

I originally thought she used our ribbon to wrap gifts, although knowing her cheerful disposition, I couldn't imagine that she knew anyone that would accept a gift from her. Or, even for that matter, anyone else she knew but us and her husband. Still, I wanted to believe that she had family and friends and used our fabulous ribbon to decorate packages for them.

Sherborne had quite exquisite boxes and ribbon for gift wrapping. The copper and gold boxes were an easily distinguished trademark. Just a glimpse at a Sherborne box and you knew you were getting something special.

The ribbon was a fabulous silver tulle, fit for a princess. It had precisely the right combination of softness and stiffness, so bows had a fluidity to them impossible to achieve with grosgrain ribbon. However, without a signature box, the tulle had little value, or so I thought. Still, I always try to think the best of people, and hoped that Lucy was using Sherborne tulle to make people happy.

I held this imaginary thought until Rowan proved me wrong. Sometime before her untimely departure, Rowan had the unfortunate experience of hand-delivering a rather large purchase to Lucy's house. Since she bought so much, she requested an entire roll of ribbon, gratis. Rowan complied and had hoped to simply drop everything off at Lucy's front door.

However, that was not to be. When Lucy answered the door, Rowan was swept into a scene from Cinderella. Lucy demanded that Rowan reorganize her enormous closet so that all her new purchases fit in properly. Three hours later, Rowan caught a glimpse of Lucy at her bathroom mirror, scrubbing her face. She was using Sherborne tulle! Impossible, Rowan thought. Impossible.

When Rowan questioned Lucy on her inordinate use of the ribbon, Lucy confessed.

"I love the texture of the ribbon. It has just the right exfoliating properties for my skin," she admitted. "I've never found another cleansing cloth that makes my face feel as smooth as Sherborne ribbon. I must have it! I can't be without it!"

While I gathered the ribbon for Lucy, out of the corner of my eye I caught Jordan pulling a fast one on The Witch. Jordan must have seen Marjorie – Social Club member number three – coming up the aisle with her handlers, so she quickly ducked into the stock room. Before The Witch could even think about hiding, Marjorie was at The Witch's side.

Every Sunday afternoon, Marjorie comes in to buy a new bra for some special event she plans to attend during the week. No big deal, right? Wrong! It takes her anywhere from two to three hours to decide. So, during that time, you're stuck with her in the fitting room. She not only expects you to find the bras for her to try, she refuses to help in any way. She will barely lift her arms so you can slide the bra on, then hook it and make sure her breasts are sitting properly in the cups. Marjorie is in her late 70s and it's not a pretty sight. It's not that she's not capable, she just views the sales staff here as her personal slaves. She does keep everything she buys, but she really doesn't buy enough to make up for the hassle.

Marjorie is definitely the wealthiest of the bunch. Old Money Vegas, her family helped to found the town in the early 1900s. An exquisite dresser, she rarely buys anything at full price. She prefers to give her money to charity. And, while she does look stylish, she's not ashamed if she's wearing last season's clothing as long as she can give an extra thousand dollars to her favorite cause. Marjorie never goes anywhere without her handlers, two bodyguards cum servants who are well paid and quite enjoy the opportunity to partake of the millionaire lifestyle, if only from the outside looking in.

Once Lucy left, I decided to take my lunch. An hour later when I returned, The Witch, as expected, was still in the fitting room with Marjorie. I'd take Petunia and Lucy every Sunday versus spending time with Marjorie. However, she couldn't have found a better salesperson than The Witch.

I don't think the members of the Social Club actually know each other, but they should. Maybe they'd stay away from us. All three women are married to extremely wealthy men, but they have no life – not even a family life, or so it appears. They're creatures of routine, visiting Sherborne every Sunday afternoon and we, unfortunately, are their social life, their family – the only consistency in their lives. How sad that they have so much money but their lives are so empty.

It had finally slowed down, so Jordan and I stood at the counter chatting. The Witch came out of the fitting rooms smiling, Marjorie in tow. Shockingly, The Witch had a pile of bras, panties and nightgowns in her hands. Jordan and I looked at each other, a bit inquisitively, a bit in shock. She can't actually be buying all of that, could she? Marjorie never buys more than one bra a week!

The Witch made her way behind the counter to the cash register.

"Marjorie is going on a month-long cruise to the Italian Riviera," she said to no one in particular.

As we stared in silence, The Witch kept ringing, item after item.

"That will be $745.51, Marjorie. I'm so glad we were able to find the right assortment for your fabulous trip," The Witch spewed, laughing eyes catching us off-guard.

"You really must consider taking a trip like that yourself, after all the hard work you do in this place," Marjorie answered back.

"I'd love to, but I'd hate to leave my grandchildren for so long," The Witch replied.

"You have grandchildren! My Lord, you're much too young to have grandchildren. How lucky you are to keep that fabulous figure."

There she goes. Marjorie said the magic words. The Witch, as always, will eat up every compliment she gets on her shape.

"Why, yes, yes I am lucky. Thank you so much, Marjorie, and I'll be sure to put you in my personal client book. I'd be happy to help you any time you're shopping with us. And, remember, I can assist you in any department in the store."

The Witch was definitely on a hunt for money, as always.

"Why, thank you. I have several presents to purchase when I return from my trip, so we'll make an appointment and spend a few hours together. I enjoyed your company immensely."

"And I, yours," The Witch replied.

She handed Marjorie's handlers her bags, and the two air-kissed before Marjorie headed down the aisle to the elevator. Jordan and I stood there in shock, recognizing that The Witch was just a bitch in witch's clothing.

Dear Diary,

I try to be observant about my life, and lately I've been struggling to determine what makes a top salesperson in retail. At least in my little world of retail. I've been listening to a bunch of motivational and self-help books on selling, but there really aren't any that pertain to selling in retail that I've found. If I were selling widgets, the words would mean something. But retail is a whole different world.

I've watched several women become Queen in our business, and what I see I don't like. To them, my issues are trivial. They are hired to sell, and sell is all they do. But, to the rest of the team, the issues are valid.

It seems that once a woman decides she wants to be the top, she changes. She doesn't do anything that doesn't result in actual sales. She doesn't clean her fitting rooms or other mess. She doesn't stock the register supplies. She doesn't stock her assigned area, nor does she straighten it. She doesn't share her customers, so she takes on as many as she can at once.

Unfortunately, that also means that she doesn't service the customer properly. The other gals on the team wind up answering questions and getting items for the customers because the Queen of Sales is just too busy looking at dollars, not service. In fact, the Queen is sometimes able to recruit the manager into helping her out, while the rest of the team stands idly by without a single customer.

We also ring the sale for her customer because the Queen is never around. She's always helping someone else, and it's poor customer relations to keep the customer waiting when all she wants to do is checkout.

Of course, management never sees any of this. When a manager is on the floor, the Queen is as sweet and compliant as can be. But when the manager goes back to her office, the Queen turns into a major bitch. When the team complains to management, the managers just think that we hate the Queen because she's number one in sales. Management thinks it's a conspiracy, that we're all ganging up on the Queen. So, the Queen actually gets management's sympathy!

What the Queen doesn't realize is that she wouldn't have the top sales if the rest of the team didn't clean and stock for her customers! It's a sad reality, but I've now seen it too many times to even think that there's a solution.

I just don't have it in me to be the Queen. I would have to be rude and heartless and only think in terms of dollars. Even as a high tech consultant, to me the pay was simply gratitude for taking good care of my client. I'd treat them with the utmost respect while defining and implementing the proper marketing strategy for them.

Here, I just sell bras. I somehow can't get fired up over it. I keep renewing my business license because I know my consultancy will be successful once again, but as fiercely independent as I once was, I still cannot be ruthless just to grow my bank account.

Where, oh where, do I go from here?

More tomorrow!

All my heart,

Diana

The Shop at Positano

Wolves in Sheeps' Clothing

{ SEVENTEEN }

"Great! I think that's it. I'll send your file down to HR for processing. Then, they'll contact you for a drug test and we'll get you on the schedule."

And just like that, I was now an employee of Positano, the premier hotel-casino-resort on the Las Vegas Strip. Built for almost six billion dollars, it epitomizes lavish extravagance to the fullest. The attention to detail and meticulous maintenance helped Positano stay at the top of the heap, regardless of the ever-increasing competition.

I've always loved to visit Positano. You feel wealthy just walking through its doors. The non-stop mosaic flooring, gilded trim, fresh flowers and waterfalls were like wrapping yourself in a cashmere robe and nestling in front of the fire with a magnum of Dom Perignon. You feel special, appreciated, and yet, in spite of the crowds, you feel calm, serene, peaceful. It's amazing what a few billion dollars can do.

Destiny Drop

I'd met with Lily, the store manager for The Shop at Positano after applying on the company's website. I'd reached the end of my rope at Sherborne, and I had to get out. If I looked at one more set of 80-year-old breasts, I'd kill someone. I couldn't hack another day of lingerie.

One night when I couldn't sleep, I decided to check out several employment websites. When I saw the position at Positano, I didn't hesitate. I applied immediately, and received a call the next day. I was thrilled!

Lily seemed like the world's greatest manager. She appeared to be about my age, maybe a bit older, tall, thin, beautiful. She grew up in California, but like so many Angelinos, made her way to the desert.

Lily had been with Positano since it opened several years ago, and had a pretty stable staff. Nearly everyone had been with her since the store opened, and some with the company even longer. That indicated to me that she was a great manager and great to work for. Otherwise, people usually don't stick around.

I would be selling fabulous designer clothing for a whopping 10 percent commission. Lily needed someone to work swing shift, and it sounded like heaven to me. I could sleep in again! Oh, and hopefully make more money.

I was really looking forward to learning a lot from Lily. With my marketing and retail background, maybe I could move into management one day. Lily would be a great mentor. It was as if the universe had dropped this opportunity into my lap, just when I needed it most. It had to be destiny.

I liked Lily. I liked Positano. In fact, I was so excited about joining the company, I thought I was going to jump out of my skin! Gizzi was right. My future was right around the corner – and a mile or so down the street. However, I'd been wrong about Sherborne and Isabella's before, so I'm hoping I'm not wrong again.

Lester, one of Lily's assistant managers, met me at uniform control after I completed orientation. This is the area in the bowels of the hotel where unstylish polyester is handed out by the truckload to the hapless saps who keep the place going. The good news is I can keep more of my paycheck now because I won't have to sink it into new clothes. The company dry cleans our uniforms, too, if we like. Shoes will be my only expense. And, since the company feeds us one meal a day, I can save my lunch money for a new car.

I felt it would be good to work with a man on-staff again. Technology is quite the testosterone-laden industry, and fashion is oh-so-estrogen. After working in lingerie for so many years, I'd about had my fill. It was time to find a little x-factor. Here was Lester, six feet 3 inches tall, in one of the best-fitting suits I'd ever seen on a man, perfectly tan, highlights of perfection, and just the right amount of jewelry.

"You must be Diana," Lester said as he held out his limp hand.

Damn. No testosterone here.

"Yes I am. So nice to meet you, Lester."

"Let's get you into the procurement area so they can fit you for your Valentino original."

Lester smiled sweetly but I knew it was a joke.

Lester led me down a long, dank hallway with folks in uniform far as the eye could see. We finally got to the fitting area. I told the clerk behind the counter my size, and it was just like the racks in Cher's closet in Clueless. Round and round and round they went until suddenly, there it was. The perfect color and perfect size. My uniform. A lovely three-piece wine polyester suit – jacket, shell and pants. Basic 1980s blazer, shoulder pads and all, scoop neck shell and high-waisted pants with pleats. Just like Grandma wore. I guess we're not supposed to look better than the customers, but given the quality of the merchandise we're selling, I would expect to be wearing something more fashionable.

I tried on a uniform two sizes larger than I normally wear. These people must use the same size chart bridal shops use.

Surprisingly, it fit perfectly. No hemming, no alterations needed here. I should have been a model. I removed the uniform, and the clerk sewed my ID number into all three pieces, then gave them back. I was ready to work!

"They have your requirements in the system now," Lester said. "You can pick up two more suits tomorrow. You're provided with three suits, and it's up to you to maintain their condition. If anything rips or buttons need to be replaced, you need to bring the uniform down here for repairs. Other than that, you're on your own. Now, let's get you some money."

Once again, Lester took the lead. His long legs had quite the stride, and I struggled to keep up the pace. A few minutes later, after several rights and lefts, we were at the satellite cage.

Man, I hope I don't have to find this place on my own! I should have dropped breadcrumbs. Maybe they have 'you are here' signs posted along the way.

Since so many people at casinos handle large amounts of cash, each employee is provided with a bank, a designated amount of money that you check out at the beginning of your shift, then return when you leave with the additional amount of your sales. You'd better balance, or you're outta here!

I completed my check-out form and headed to the counter. My, aren't these a happy lot. If I didn't know better, I'd think they were all constipated. Maybe it's the food in the employee café. Not a smile among the bunch.

I walked up to the first available cashier, showed her my ID badge, handed her my form, and watched her count out my $500 bank. When she was finished, I recounted all the money to confirm the amount, put it in the designated bag, and turned to search for Lester. He was in the back of the cage flirting with a dealer.

"I'm ready, Lester," I said.

"Oh, OK, fine. I'll see you later, man," he said to his conquest, and once again, utilized his big, long strides to lead the way.

We went down still another long corridor, this one with offices on either side that were identified as Casino Marketing, Slot Marketing, Scheduling, Poker Room, Retail and so on. They all had windows so I could see inside. And, it was just as I expected. A lot of men in suits, looking like they were all part of the Mob. There's just something about a casino that does that to a man.

We made our way to an elevator that took us to the casino level. "Now, I hope you remember how we got here because that's the route you'll take to the store every day," Lester said.

Great. Now he tells me. I really should have paid more attention.

The doors opened and there we were, in still another dank hallway. Only, this one stunk like fresh fish. I'm guessing we share the hallway with the sushi restaurant.

Again, down another long corridor and past another series of doors, these without names, numbers or windows, just keypads on the handles. If you don't know the secret code, you can't get in. We finally stopped.

Geez, it seems like we've walked two miles plus the walk from the parking garage, and I still have to be on my feet for another eight hours. I don't like this already.

Lester stopped at a non-descript door, punched in a code, and suddenly, there was life. Maybe more than I anticipated. I thought I was hired to work in a high-end designer boutique, not a restaurant kitchen or a mechanic's garage. Am I in the right place?

"You bitch! You stole my sale," Claire screamed at Sophia.

I could tell who they were because we adorned our lovely polyester suits with exquisite plastic name badges. Claire looked to be in her late 50s, obviously a loser to menopausal spread. These uniforms really didn't do a thing for her. Sophia was much younger, probably in her late 20s, and I'm guessing a size 0. They were both Hispanic, though, from the sound of it, Sophia had a much better grasp of the English language.

"I did not steal your sale, you fucking cunt. I put the guest in the fitting room. You were off in the bathing suits sucking up to some celebrity. Don't tell me I stole your sale."

Sophia, I suspect, is not one to back down.

"I'll get you, you stupid bitch, and I'll get you good," Claire shot back. "You just wait."

With that, Claire stormed out of the stockroom and back onto the sales floor. Sophia let off a bit of steam, then followed her.

Behind me, I felt a big puff of wind. The door opened and in blew Jazzy.

"Oh, the traffic. And, it's so hot, my hair just won't keep a curl."

Yippee. Another drama queen. This one with the worst fake British accent I've ever heard. Great. Three high-maintenance women so far and I haven't even met the customers yet.

"I've had such a rough day that I'll have to nap at lunch. I'm lacking in beauty sleep."

Oh, honey, you're lacking so much more than that.

Lily finally got up from her chair.

"Jazzy, I want you to meet Diana. She's our new swing. Let her follow you tonight so she knows what to do."

Please, Lily, please don't stick me with her!

"Oh, Lily, lovey, must I? Can't one of the others help her? I just don't have time for that."

"No, you're up Jazzy. It's your turn. Pamela broke in the last one."

Lily turned to me and laughed.

"Welcome home," she said. "Are you still excited to be here?"

I was beginning to rethink my decision-making skills. I'm way out of practice.

Dear Diary,

Omigod! Omigod! Omigod! I can't believe it! I finally
have some good news! Helen and Gabe are officially
moving to Las Vegas!!!

Helen called this morning before work. Her job offer
from the school district finally came through. She'll begin
teaching second grade in the fall at a school not too far
from where I live. And, Gabe was able to land a job as an
electrician with one of the major casinos in town. Grace
and Justin will finally be able to spend some quality time
with their Aunti Di!

The way my life has been lately, it will be so awesome to
actually have family out here. I miss celebrating holidays
and birthdays with them. With kids around, holidays
always take on a different and funner perspective.

They've already started packing, getting ready to make
the trek from Michigan, but once they're here we'll have
a great little family unit going on. And, when I finally
find a husband of my own and we, perchance, have kids,
they'll all be part of each other's lives. OK, so that's a
down-the-road pipe dream, but a girl can dream, can't
she?

More tomorrow!

All my heart,

Diana

Initiation

{ EIGHTEEN }

Once I made it through the stockroom door and past the fitting rooms, I was in all the grandeur that is Positano. Even in a retail boutique such as this, opulence abounds. From the beautiful tapestry-inspired carpets and mosaic walkways, to the velvet drapes and non-stop gold leaf, I wasn't sure if I was in an exclusive Nevada bordello or Buckingham Palace.

In the 6,000 square foot store there are two cash wraps, one in the center back and one closer to the front. Between the two is a sort of lounge area, with two Victorian sofas and a glass coffee table. I suspect the men sit there and wait while the women shop. The back center wall is covered with designer sunglasses on acrylic shelves that climb the wall. The back left is filled with Italian and French lingerie, from bras and thongs to silk nighties. Next to lingerie, toward the front of the store is Genesis, an all-organic make-up and skin care line owned by Positano.

The back right contains shoes and handbags in the floor area, with dresses, gowns and business attire displayed on the walls behind. More casual clothing, including jeans and swimsuits are in the front section of the store, on beautiful soft gold racks. Throughout the store, small gold and glass display cases house the various jewelry lines the store carries.

Architectural elements such as columns, molding and drapery break up the sales floor so you feel more as if you're in a mansion than a hotel boutique. Exquisite artwork lines the walls. Three large canopies of wine-colored velvet hang from the ceiling along the main walkway. The store has two entrances, one on either side of the front counter, and it connects to the gift shop next door through a gate near lingerie. A light mix of contemporary hits and classical music is played through the sound system. I can't believe I'm working in such a fabulous place!

"Clean up your fitting room, bitch."

I looked around to see who was talking to whom. Much to my surprise, one of the other sales ladies was talking to me!

"Excuse me?" I said. "Are you talking to me?"

Julie, a tall, beautiful African-American woman in her 50s turned around and stared me down.

"Of course I'm talking to you. Now go in there and clean up your fitting room."

Julie stood tall and strong, and it didn't appear that she would take no for an answer. However, I wasn't going to clean up other people's shit. I'm here to make money.

"Sorry. Not on my list today," I responded coolly.

Julie came nose to nose with me.

"Clean up those rooms, bitch, or you'll regret it."

Lily walked out from the stock room and caught the encounter.

"Oh, Julie, leave Diana alone. It's her first day. She doesn't even know where the fitting rooms are."

Lily was laughing.

I'll bet she's seen this sort of behavior before...

Turning to me, Lily continued, "Don't pay attention to any of the girls. They try their best to make each other's lives miserable. Just stay out of their way and they'll stay out of yours."

And, with that, Lily turned and went back into the stockroom.

Great! She couldn't have told me about the shit and the drama here before I quit Sherborne? Had I known, I might have looked elsewhere for employment. I don't mind a little fun until I get used to this place, but from what I can tell, I'm in for more of a fraternity hazing and I thought those were outlawed.

I slowly made my way out onto the sales floor to find a register where I could bank in for the night. I approached the first one I came to, and the lovely Claire snapped at me.

"You have to go to Sophia's register. These are taken."

"OK, thanks," I said and made my way to the front to share the register with Sophia.

Once I got that settled, I looked around and noticed it was quite busy. What I didn't know is that during this hour of overlap, between the day and swing shifts, was the busiest hour of the day. It's also the time when nearly the entire sales staff was on the floor, so each sales associate might have one or two customers max, but that's about it.

Sometimes it's also busy in the morning right when the store opens, and sometimes just before closing after the shows let out. But, often it's not. It's during this one hour that you make most of your money for the day so everyone is extremely aggressive.

Lily magically appeared from the stockroom again, headed to my register, with someone new in tow. She was a thin, older lady, probably in her late 70s, someone who should have been retired long ago. This must be our Madame.

"Diana, this is Polly, your night manager. Polly, this is Diana," Lily said as once again, she left the sales floor.

"Well, nice to meet you, Diana," Polly said in a soft Texas twang. "I hope the girls aren't being too rough on you."

I desperately tried to stop myself from rolling my eyes or hurling over the counter.

"Oh, everything is just fine. No worries!"

"Good, because I have to leave early tonight. I have a meeting very early tomorrow morning. You normally close with Lynn, but she's out of town for a few days. So, tonight you'll be closing with Jazzy and Pamela. I'm sure they'll show you what needs to be done."

Polly turned quickly to eye my two co-workers at the back counter. I looked up to see Jazzy and Pamela at their registers. They knew what Polly was telling me, and Jazzy let out a hysterical squeal. I knew she would be trouble from the minute I saw her. This is just going to be a never-ending mess at Positano.

"It's really quite simple: straighten, turn off the sensors, the music, the lights, lock all the doors and cabinets, and take out the trash. And don't forget to turn in the store keys and money to the cage. That's all."

"Don't worry, Polly. I'll be fine."

"Yeah, sure you will!" Lily laughed and shot past us, headed out the front of the store.

"Can you help me?"

A casually dressed woman in her late 30s approached me from behind. I could tell from the diamonds draped around every appendage that I was now working with a different class of people than Sherborne customers. These people have money. Real money.

"What can I do for you?" I asked.

I hope it's something easy like where are the nearest restrooms.

"I'm trying to find a gift for my mother-in-law. She's back home in Toronto taking care of the kids. I'd like to bring her something special as a thank-you gift."

Sure. Just jump right in, feet first. I don't even know how to swim!

"What size is she and what sorts of things does she like?"

I had no clue what to show her. I hadn't even walked the floor to determine what merchandise we had, so it was impossible for me to make suggestions. Luckily, the customer was quite skilled at shopping and quickly selected a gold twin set. It was a nice little gift, a total of $516.

We made our way to the register. I rang the sale, and just when I was about to breathe a sigh of relief, came those awful words: "Can you please wrap that for me?"

"Why, yes, of course. I'll be just a few minutes, so if you would like to come back in a bit, I'll have it ready."

"No, that's OK. I'll wait."

Of course she will. I don't have enough pressure on me.

I rushed back to the stockroom and caught Polly's attention. Luckily, she hadn't left yet.

"Polly! I have to wrap a gift!" I screamed.

Out of the mouth of this petite woman came a trademark shriek, the likes of which I'd never heard before but would hear on a daily basis for all my days at Positano.

"Gift wrap! No one gift wraps here! I don't even know where all the supplies are. Did you offer to do that for her?"

I could tell Polly was easily shaken, and thus, not in a good mood.

"No, she asked me to do it. We gift wrapped all the time at Sherborne, so I just assumed we did the same here."

"Well, you assumed wrong. You Sherborne people."

Polly was up on a ladder talking to herself, digging through containers of gift boxes to find a matched set. She handed them down to me, climbed down the ladder, then started to collect supplies: scissors, tape, ribbon. I followed her to a back table where we promptly wrapped the gift.

"There, now, take that to the customer and don't ever tell anyone we wrap gifts again!"

And, off I went.

After I handed the gift to the customer, I was accosted again by one of my valued team-mates.

"Quit stealing our sales, bitch!"

This time it was Jazzy. I didn't even have to turn around. I could tell it was her by her fake British accent. But, glutton for punishment, turn around I did.

"What did I do now?" I asked, quite stupidly.

"If it wasn't for you, one of us would have had that sale. Now, keep to your own corner and quit stealing our sales, lovey."

The evening continued in much the same vein. I'd wait on customers, close the sale, then Jazzy would come up and say something nasty to me.

I love my job. I love my job. I love my job.

"All right, we're ready to go. See you tomorrow, Diana."

Jazzy and Pamela had their banks in hand, and were getting ready to leave.

"Wait! This is my first day. How do I close?"

Pamela looked like she would relent, but Jazzy clearly had her in control.

"You'll do just fine, lovey. You seemed to handle the sales by yourself, now you can close by yourself."

She grabbed Pamela's arm.

"Come on, Pamela, time to go."

Then she turned back to me.

"Ta ta, lovey."

Oh that pompous little bitch. I've worked with some arrogant assholes before in high tech, but at least they were intelligent assholes worth millions. This pretentious snob can't even get her fake accent correct. She's one of the top sales people in the store, but to me, she's trailer trash. Obviously, we're dealing with self-esteem issues here, but I'm not getting paid to analyze the bitch. Right now, I have to focus on closing.

OK, what was it that Polly said? Oh, yeah, straighten, turn off the sensors, the music, the lights, lock all the doors and cabinets, take out the trash, turn in the store keys and money to the cage.

I walked the floor to make sure it looked presentable, double-checked to see that the doors were locked, took half an hour to find the sensor keys and lock them, took another fifteen minutes to determine which were the correct light and music switches, put the trash out in the hallway and closed the back door.

I made my way through the snaking hallways and down the elevator to the satellite cage, turned in my money and the keys, and headed up the long, dank tunnel that leads to the employee entrance. I practically ran the mile to the parking garage, found my car, collapsed in my seat and cried. The store closed at midnight. It was now 2 a.m.

With all the strength I could muster, I made my way back to Positano for my second day on the job. Polly was there when I got to the stockroom. She looked at me with concern. Had I done something wrong? Yesterday was only my first day, for chrissake. Cut me some slack. But, from what I saw of Polly yesterday, spotting a moth in the stockroom would be enough to ruin her day. Fluster would be an understatement.

"Diana, you know that lady y'all wrapped the gift for yesterday?" she asked.

How could I forget?

"Well, turns out she was a shopper. We normally don't get shopped this time of year, but for some reason, it was a surprise shop."

What was she talking about? Aren't all our customers shoppers?

"What's a shopper? What does that mean?"

"The company pays a service to shop our stores, eat in our restaurants and grade us so that we can maintain our five-star rating. They usually make you jump through hoops for them, like this one wanted it gift wrapped. Sometimes they even record the conversations you have. Then they turn in the reports, along with the merchandise to security, and the purchase is credited back."

"So, not only did I waste time with her, I lost the commission on the sale?"

"Yes, that's right. I have the sweater set right here."

Yippee. That means I only sold $1,050 yesterday. All that shit I had to put up with for a lousy hundred dollar commission.

"The good news is, the shopper liked you and gave you good grades."

"Do I get something for that?"

"Yes," Polly smiled. "You get to keep your job."

"So, where are we today, my friend?"

Through the phone, I could hear Gizzi take a long drag off her cigarette. For all I knew, she was sitting on a balcony, perched above Paris, soaking up the atmosphere and making me tremendously jealous. I was curled up on my sofa, exhausted but thrilled to be chatting with my BFF.

"Actually, sweetie, I'm in Dallas. Just got back from two weeks in Asia. After the conference here, I finally head back home for a bit."

"Ah, listen to us, a couple of world travelers."

Gizzi snort laughed.

"Sorry, sweetie. I haven't heard of you getting on a plane to California, let alone some exotic locale."

Now it was my turn to laugh.

"Ah, that's where you're wrong, my friend. I live in an exotic locale. Within two miles, I can visit replicas of nearly every major tourist destination around the world. The airfare's cheap and the jetlag nonexistent."

"Fine. If that's what you want to believe, Diana."

Gizzi was joking, or so it seemed, but I knew deep down she was disappointed in me and there's nothing like disappointment to deflate your balloon.

"So, how's the semiconductor industry lately?"

I hadn't kept up on much ever since Tarek single-handedly reduced my chance for a Silicon Valley comeback to nil.

Gizzi took another long drag.

"Oh, Diana, it is a bit rough. I mean, I've been very lucky, although there are rumors circulating that changes are afoot at my company."

"Really? How will that affect you, Giz?"

"Not sure, sweetie. Right now, I'm just grateful to have a job, and I have been able to bring in an inordinate amount of business considering the state of the economy. Still, we're a small company and any change affects us all. I'm wondering if we're going to be bought out. Our CEO has spoken recently of wanting to retire soon. I can't remember the last time he got on a plane. He's just not into it any more. Rather than shake things up too much, they might just sell us off."

Whoa, I hadn't expected Gizzi to sound so Debbie Downer. That just wasn't her. Give her a situation and she'll find her way out, always on top.

"How soon do you think this will happen, Giz?"

"Don't know, sweetie. I'm not home that much. Seems I live on a plane and in hotel rooms. Maybe now that I'll be back for a couple of weeks I'll get a handle on the rumors and determine their viability."

Gizzi Boudrot, woman of steel.

"So, what's life like in Sin City these days?"

Great. Now it was my turn.

"Well, you know, I'm still sort of in survival mode."

"Diana –"

"No, Gizzi, no pep talks. No admonishment. I have to do things my way. My sister is moving out and I want to stay near family. I'll figure things out."

"Well, sweetie, you know I only want what's best for you but I find it hard to believe that someone with your skillset isn't in high demand. Anywhere."

I laughed.

"You mean my ability to fit bras?"

I thought Gizzi would choke on her martini, which I'm sure was the beverage at hand.

"I agree. I thought a whole world of different things when I first moved here, but it's almost as if I died and I'm reinventing myself. This new me certainly doesn't earn as much, but eventually, I'll figure things out."

Gizzi was never one to sit on her laurels. With her, life was all about planning and implementation. Mine was, too, at one point in the past, but I now faced life outside the nerd capital of the world.

"I know you will, sweetie, but if I don't speak my mind, I wouldn't feel I did my job as your friend. We're in this together. I'm there for you wherever life takes you. I just hope you find the path soon and it's on a high speed train."

It was good to hear Gizzi still had my back. Good friends are hard to find and I cherished Gizzi.

"Agreed. Now, pull up your martini and your cigarettes and let me tell you all about the drama at work."

"You got it, girlfriend!"

Gizzi spent the next hour listening to me regale her with stories from the front lines of retail. Never in her life did she imagine such a world existed so close to her American Express card. Truthfully, neither did I.

Dear Diary,

When I first started working at The Shop at Positano a couple of months ago, I was grateful to be wearing a uniform. I went through so many clothes at Sherborne, wearing a uniform meant that I wouldn't have to buy new work clothes every three months. I wear a three-piece polyester suit every day, adorned with a watch, no more than two rings, earrings smaller than a half dollar and a simple necklace. The uniform is not exactly flattering on me but hey, it's free. And money is important nowadays.

But, now, I'm so bored with it. Maybe it's because I'm selling such beautiful designer clothing. I love each and every piece. I want to buy them all! I just can't afford them, at least not right now. When things go on sale, even at 75 percent off, I'm still in no position to purchase any of them. Seventy-five percent off $1,000 is still $250 – two and a half days' work if I'm lucky.

And, it's not just the beautiful clothes I see at Positano. When I read the fashion magazines, or see something on TV, or even check things out online, I quickly dismiss anything I'm drawn to because I really have nowhere to wear it. I've become a social pariah – I have absolutely no social life at all.

When I worked at Sherborne, it sometimes felt like a chore to decide what to wear each day. Still, I had such a vast wardrobe that I had options. And, I got a discount there, if only 20 percent, whereas I don't get a discount at all at Positano.

But, I did go through a lot of clothes at Sherborne. I had no idea how much running around I would do, and how quickly my clothes would wear out – getting snagged, pulled, nipped, ripped. No wonder they give you a discount!

Still, I'm desperate for some new clothes, something that makes me feel good and looks great on me. But I need to get a life first. Five days a week I'm working, one day I wear jeans to run errands, and my other day off I stay home to clean and get caught up with my sleep. I haven't been on a date in forever, and I don't see a potential suitor on the horizon. Oh, how I hate my life!

More tomorrow!

All my heart,

Diana

The Bitch

{ NINETEEN }

"Aaarrrggghhh! I can't stand that woman!"

I was screaming to no one in particular as I ran into the stockroom. I just had to let off some steam. I'm working with The Bitch tonight, and it always sends me over the edge. I can't stand to be within a hundred feet of her, let alone spend hours on the floor and closing with her. I thought Jazzy was bad but The Bitch takes the cake.

Polly was at her desk in the office. She heard my screams and lifted her head to find out what was wrong.

"Now, what woman are you talking about, Diana?"

"You know. The Bitch!" I responded.

I was pacing in very tight circles in the stockroom, and I was afraid I might set off a round of vertigo if I kept it up. I finally sat down and rested for a bit.

"I loathe working with her."

"So what has she done now?" Polly asked.

"Oh, what hasn't she done? The list would take all night. The biggest thing is that she spends the entire night on the telephone. I have no idea who she's talking to, but she leans on the counter and talks all night. Then, when a customer comes in, she has some sort of radar, like she knows they're going to spend a lot of money, so she puts her call on hold, helps the customer, then goes back to her call. I don't know how she does it, but that's not the point. I thought we weren't supposed to make calls longer than a couple of minutes."

I knew I was wasting my breath. Polly and The Bitch were good friends, and whenever I raised an issue with her, she said she'll deal with it, but her way of dealing with it is not to discipline The Bitch. Instead, she simply tells her to cool it a while so I won't complain to Lily. Not like she'd do anything either.

"Well, I'll have a word with her, Diana. She knows she's not supposed to be doing that."

Polly seemed unaffected as I suspected she would, and went back to her reports while I continued to let off steam.

Now, most people think I should be happy that The Bitch is spending so much time on the phone, because then I don't have to talk to her all night. But, it's not just that she manages to still snatch all the good customers, it's her whole attitude. She really doesn't do much of anything else.

Sure, she straightens her side of the store, but she does it in about 15 minutes, while I take over an hour to straighten mine. Her side looks like crap, but she never gets in trouble for it. And she doesn't do any of the other tasks on our list, like fill supplies, empty sensors, do markdowns, etc. All she does is talk on the phone. I have such rage inside for her, I'm afraid I'm going to punch her in the face one day. I hate working with her.

However, personal finances got the better of me. I knew I couldn't sell anything if I stayed in the stockroom, so I made my way to the sales floor. To my horror, The Bitch was ringing up a $700 handbag for a customer. How does she do it?

"I was looking for you," she said when the customer left. "I already sold $40,000 this pay period, so I thought you might like a sale."

Forty thousand dollars! That's four times what I sold! Now I hate her even more, plus, the fact that she was even attempting to be kind. If she truly meant it, she could have just rung the sale for me.

"That's OK, I'll get the next one," I said, although it was a slow night and there might not be a next one this evening, certainly not another $700 handbag.

The Bitch let out a deep sigh, and leaned on her elbows on the counter.

"I'm lonely. I miss my Mom."

Oh, now she wants me to be sympathetic.

"Why don't you go see her?" I asked.

"Because she doesn't live in this country. She lives in my country."

There she goes again. My country. That's all she talks about. In my country, they only grow organic food. In my country everything tastes wonderful. In my country, my asthma doesn't bother me. In my country, I don't have to work. She goes on and on about how wonderful her country is. And, from the way she speaks, one would think that she comes from a very wealthy family. But, one of the girls in the gift shop knows the town where The Bitch's family lives, and she says it's a very poor little town.

I'd heard this train of thought so many times from her before, I just couldn't deal with it any more.

"Are you an American citizen?" I asked.

"Yes. I just completed my schooling and was sworn in two weeks ago."

She didn't say this with pride, she said it like she had just completed traffic school.

"Well, then this is your country. From now on, when you say my country, you'd better be referring to America, or I'll correct you every time until you get it right."

"But I hate it here!"

"Then why are you here and why did you become a citizen?"

"My husband likes it here. And, now that I'm a citizen, my Mom can come over to live."

"When does your Mom plan to do that?"

"Oh, probably never. She hates it here, too. No one in my country likes Americans."

"Why is that?"

"Why not? You Americans think you're better than everyone else, and you have all the money. Why shouldn't we hate you?"

"Then why don't you just go back home to be with your family?"

"I like to have money. I'm making a lot of money here. I make more in one month than my brother does in a year. And I get to buy all the designer clothes I want at a discount."

Ironic, for this reluctant American citizen…

She was looking at a pair of Gordon & Brease shoes as she spoke. They matched the coat she just purchased at 75 percent off. She hid the coat in the stockroom from the time it arrived until it got marked down so that she could buy it at a discount. Now she wanted the shoes, which just went on sale.

"See the beautiful point these have? I'd never wear round toe shoes. Those look like paupers. I only wear the pointed toes."

She was trying them on and admiring herself in the mirror. They were beautiful, but they looked a little tight to me.

"Aren't those a bit too small?"

"A little, but that's OK. You only wear them for a couple of hours, then take them off. It's OK if they hurt a little. Sometimes fashion has to hurt. As long as they have the pointed toe they will be good."

I was seriously beginning to question The Bitch's sanity when her cell phone rang and she ran off to one of the fitting rooms to talk. That was her other way of getting out of work without getting caught. She talked on her cell phone so the company couldn't log how many hours she spent talking during her shift.

Not that we're supposed to have cell phones with us on the sales floor either.

I was now helping two women in the far back of the store. They were a mother and daughter who were living in the hotel. The family had sold their home in another state, and until they decided where they wanted to live, they holed up at Positano. I helped them for over an hour, finding them clothing to try on, cleaning up their messes. They didn't buy anything, but thanked me and walked away. While I was cleaning up the last bit of mess at the clothing rack, I noticed The Bitch at the counter, ringing a handbag for the mother! They left, and I went up to her.

"You bitch!" I screamed. "I just waited on them for an hour, and you rang the handbag for yourself!"

I was absolutely livid.

The Bitch just snarled at me.

"Did you help them with the handbag?" she asked.

"No, but I helped them for a long time with clothing, and they didn't buy anything. So you just waltz up to the register and sell them a handbag?"

"Hey, I'm innocent in all this. I came out of the fitting rooms, and the older woman was looking around for some help, with the handbag in her hand. When she saw me, she said she wanted to buy the bag. I had no idea you were helping them. And besides, if you weren't helping them with the handbag, it's not your sale."

"But, it's my customer, and if you had been on the floor, you would have noticed that and let me know they were ready to buy something else."

The Bitch was getting really upset now.

"Fine. What's your number? I'll transfer the sale. I'm not a bad person, but I don't need this crap."

She recorded the exchange on the register, and gave me my copy of the receipt for my records.

"I try to be nice to you and this is the thanks I get."

With that, The Bitch went into the stockroom and spent an hour chatting with Polly.

At about 11:30 p.m., The Bitch emerged from the stockroom. She proceeded to spend the next 15 minutes straightening her side of the store, as usual. Then she went into the office, got the sensor keys from Polly, turned off the music, and reemerged from the stockroom. In the interim, a number of customers came wandering through the store.

"Tell them to leave," The Bitch said.

"Why would I do that?" I asked. "The store doesn't close for 15 more minutes."

The Bitch was getting really irritated now. It seemed we went through a similar scenario every time we closed together.

"Tell them the store is closing."

The Bitch wasn't giving up.

"If you want them to leave, then you tell them!"

I'm not getting into trouble for this just because The Bitch is tired and lonely and wants to go home.

The Bitch then went around locking all the sensor removers. I was getting really pissed now.

"What are you doing? If I have a customer, I need to remove the sensors from their purchases. We're not even closed yet!"

"Yes we are," The Bitch said. "And, if you want to sell something you can unlock your own sensor."

With that, she threw the keys at me, and mumbled something under her breath in her native language.

"Right back at you, sister," I said.

The Bitch just glared at me.

She proceeded to her register, organized her paperwork, counted out her bank, and left.

Peace reigned once again at The Shop at Positano.

"How is everything going, dear?"

I'd been so busy, I was a bit lax in calling my parents. I loved talking to Mom and Dad, particularly when we were able to video chat, but as happy as I was to see them, I knew it would take every ounce of strength I could muster to not completely fall apart the minute their faces popped up on screen. My stress level of late has been through the roof and all I wanted to do was cry, something that would throw my parents over the edge.

"It's all good, Mom."

"So, that new place has good benefits, Diana? I hear the casinos pay well and if you can tap in to their retirement program early, by the time you're 60 you should have a good nest egg built up."

Oh, Daddy, always thinking about retirement. I prefer to think about today. How can I make my life better today?

"Well, I am diverting some of my paycheck to a 401k. I'll keep tabs on the percentages as my income increases."

"That's the spirit, Diana! I know I harp on you about this, but since so few companies actually offer a pension nowadays, I feel it's important for you to keep your future in mind, even though you feel it's a long way off. Retirement will be here before you know it."

"Thanks, Daddy. So, it's pretty cool about Helen and Gabe living here, isn't it?"

I could see the look of dread on Mom's face knowing that both of her daughters, and now her grandchildren, are living across the country and not as easily available for a dinner or a hug.

"I am happy for your sister, you know that, dear, but I hate that you're both so far away. No impromptu dinners in our near future, I guess."

Dad rubbed Mom's back lovingly. Obviously, Mom was trying to work through this whole situation and Dad was well aware of her difficulty in letting go.

"I guess now that we're grown up, it's hard to keep us close to home," I offered, knowing it wouldn't be much help. "But, at least we're both in the same city, so when you vacation, you don't have to decide which child gets your time."

Dad chuckled.

"Diana, you know that we vacation in Florida, just like our friends. We'll have to wait until the two of you come back to Michigan in order to see you."

I smiled, but my heart was breaking. I loved my parents, but the thought that they wouldn't come here to visit their children was so like their generation.

"Fine. Then, let's take it one step further. How about following in our footsteps and retiring here?"

"In Las Vegas? Sin City? Oh, my dear. Let me try to wrap my head around that."

Mom did seem a bit flustered by the suggestion. Dad was a bit more pragmatic.

"Honestly, we're not looking to move now or when we retire, Diana, but if we do decide, if you and Helen are still there, I guess we'll have to consider it. Of course, we'd always welcome you here with open arms."

"That's right, dear. Your room is still just the same as when you left. I don't want to touch anything. I'll leave that up to you, whenever you have a chance."

It had been forever since I was in Detroit for a visit and while I enjoyed our video calls, today was one of those days where it completely drained me. We only talked a few minutes, but I did long to cuddle up on the sofa with the two of them, watching old movies, hot cocoa in hand, back to the days when my life was so much simpler than it was now, back to the time capsule that was my old bedroom.

I couldn't go back, I knew that much. I had to keep moving forward. I'd experienced so much in my life I just couldn't consider trying to make a fresh start back home, particularly with the way the economy seems to have just stalled. I was thankful to have a job, even if it was in hell.

"Sorry for the short call, but I have to go. Love you both!"

"Yes, dear. We love you, too. Be well and we'll talk again soon, okay?"

"Yep. I'll try again in a couple of days."

I ended the call, and immediately collapsed in a heap of sobs. I'm strong. I'm Diana, for chrissake. I'll make it through all of this and come out a winner. I must. I'd expect nothing less of myself. But, at the moment, I'm only human.

Thankfully, if I needed a hug, Helen was just a short drive away. She was still settling in but at least we could get together and visit, whether for a family dinner or a sisterly talk. Helen and Gabe moving to Las Vegas was the best thing that had happened to me in the last few years and I cherished every minute of it. There's nothing like family to make you feel loved.

Dear Diary,

People come to Las Vegas to be entertained, but I wouldn't put retail high on my list in that regard. We don't break into song at designated intervals. We don't open and close the store with a chorus line. We don't recite Shakespeare and we don't do a pole dance on the few occasions when we get a tip.

However, if anyone has captured the essence of entertainment in retail, that would be Jazzy. While what she does irks the rest of the staff, the clientele love it! They think she's the bee's knees while we just think she's an annoying, lying, back-stabbing, melodramatic bitch.

Jazzy has a few signature moves that customers enjoy on a regular basis. The first is the Sensor Dance. On our more expensive items, the company will often attach two or more sensors. Sometimes we catch them all when the customer makes a purchase, sometimes we don't. We can't tell until the customer walks out the door. If the alarm goes off, then we missed detaching a sensor and pissed off a customer

Jazzy doesn't wait until the customer walks out the door. Instead, she grabs the item, proceeds to the doorway, spins in a circle, and swings the item round and round in front of the alarm, to see if it triggers. If it does, she goes back and removes the hidden sensor. If not, the customer thanks her profusely, and is content that Jazzy has gone above and beyond the call of duty to please her. Of course, there are days when the alarm isn't working...

Another signature move is the Bag Whack. Jazzy proudly wants to inform the rest of us that she's had a sale, while still maintaining her humble, fake-British demeanor. When she's ready to place the customer's purchase into a bag, Jazzy will loudly shake the bag open with a big whack! That's her own private code for telling the rest of us that we're losers, that she just made a sale and we should all be jealous.

Two other favorites are the money flip and the shoe circle. When Jazzy counts change back to a customer, she flips the bills as if performing a magic trick. Customers shriek over her talents! One would think they were in the presence of Jazzy Copperfield.

The shoe circle is like a theater in the round. Jazzy places her customer in the center of the shoe area, brings out at least five pair of shoes, opens each box and places them in a semi-circle around the customer. She waves her hands over each pair, gingerly lifting and holding the shoes, hoping to entice the customer to purchase simply for the art of it all.

Jazzy is one of the top sales associates in the store, so I guess there's something to her entertaining ways that are worth emulating. However, I just can't be that fake!

More tomorrow!

All my heart,

Diana

What Did I Do?

{ TWENTY }

"Are you still happy you left Sherborne?"

Helen handed me a nice, big lemonade, then sat down in the swivel chair opposite the swing I was on. I loved to sit on Helen's patio at night, and have these heart-to-hearts. It was so wonderful to have her and Gabe living just a couple miles away instead of all the way across the country. These patio talks reminded me of when we were kids, sharing our deepest, darkest secrets before we fell asleep. Now, circumstances were a bit different. Helen had two kids so I tried not to bother her too much on my days off, although I thoroughly enjoyed my visits. Hopefully, Helen did, too.

It was now 9 p.m. Both Grace and Justin were down for the night, Gabe had an early start so he was in bed and in less than an hour, Helen would be fast asleep as well. I had to talk quickly and hope for the best. I could always count on Helen as a sounding board, but I wasn't sure just what I wanted to accomplish tonight.

I took a sip of my lemonade and held the cool glass in my hand. It was a pleasant change from the 100+ degree temperature surrounding me. Welcome to the desert.

"Honestly, I'm not sure how to answer that. I really felt I needed to leave Sherborne. I just couldn't take it anymore. It was a very stifling environment, and the pay was horrible."

"So, are you making a lot more at Positano?"

"Well, not necessarily. This store has a bit of a different rhythm than Sherborne, so I'm not sure how it will pan out at the end of the year. At least I'm up to ten percent commission, and they provide uniforms and food, so I'm saving there. But, the people…"

"You mean the customers?"

"Well, the customers are one thing, but it's the employees who are, well, insane."

"Oh, come now, Diana, don't exaggerate. Every business will have its own culture. This one is just different than the other companies you worked for."

"No, I'm serious. These people are certifiably insane. I had no idea what working straight commission does to you, the stress that you're under. Every day you get up and pray that you have a good sales day. You never know how much you're going to bring home in your check, so you can't budget. You have to become competitive rather than be kind to one another, and there's no team building. Everyone is pitted against one another. And, the company doesn't care about you because they don't have to pay you a dime when you're working on commission. If you don't make your goal, they'll find someone else."

"Is it that way just at Positano?"

"Oh, no. There was definitely some of that at Sherborne, and from what I've heard – and seen – this is the environment for every full-commission retail store. It's just that the women at Positano are much worse than any place else. I have no idea how they can go to work, day after day, with the type of environment that's there. And, most of them have been working together for years. It's like a totally dysfunctional family. They argue constantly."

"Doesn't your manager do anything to correct it?"

"Oh, please. Lily loves the drama and does everything she can to cause even more. When there's a problem, she just lets the employees have a go at it while she sits and works on her reports."

"I thought you were looking forward to working with Lily," Helen reminded me.

"I was, until I did. Now I know better."

I took another sip of lemonade and continued.

"But that's not the worst of it. Everyone is just so weird there."

"What do you mean by weird?"

"Well, let's take Jazzy, for instance. She's a nightmare. There's nothing about her that's real. She lies constantly. She has a terrible fake accent. She says that she lives in a gated community with a swimming pool and a tennis court. She makes it sound like she lives in this big mansion. Helen, she and her husband are renting a one bedroom apartment. Yes, it has a pool and tennis court, but they're not hers! And it's definitely not gated. It's not even a great neighborhood."

"Talk about someone with self-esteem issues."

"And she said she used to live in Palm Beach. What a lie! She used to work there, but she lived in a seedy part of town outside of Palm Beach. You can't believe a word she says because she lies constantly. And, she doesn't see anything wrong with that. She even lies to her best friend, Pamela, and Pamela still hangs out with her. I don't understand that at all."

"Jazzy lies to her best friend and she still sticks around? That's sad."

"And she steals, too."

"Pamela?"

"No, Jazzy. Pamela is a saint. Whenever customers leave behind something, like sunglasses or jewelry, instead of turning it in to Lost and Found, Jazzy hides it in the stockroom, 'just in case the customer returns,' and lo and behold, it's gone the next day. She blames it on Julie, but I know Jazzy's taking it. That would explain all the really expensive jewelry she wears."

"And Lily doesn't do anything about it?"

"Lily could care less. But Jazzy's not the only one. Everyone there has some sort of problem, so far as I can tell. Lynn, the other new hire, seems to be the only somewhat normal person, but she likes Jazzy, too, so I have to wonder about her as well."

"It sounds horrible!"

"I know, I know. And, it seems like nearly everyone is on some sort of meds. Julie and Claire have bottles in their purses, and I can tell the difference when Jazzy takes certain meds and when she doesn't. And, they complain about everything: schedules, music, merchandise, sales, everything. I used to be a really positive person, but lately, I'm getting Clairitis."

"Clairitis? What's that?"

"It's a disease we get from Claire at work. She's so pessimistic, everything that comes out of her mouth is negative. So, we dubbed it Clairitis."

"So, how do you deal with it?"

"I drink. A lot. Have anything for this lemonade?"

I could see Helen nodding off. These late night talks are fun, but with two children, Helen's idea of a late night is 10 o'clock. Oh, well. Time to head home...

Dear Diary,

Jazzy and Pamela really got into a big fight today, and I'm not sure whose side I'd take.

You see, Pamela has this really wealthy customer that comes in from Texas about once a month. Generally, she spends a lot of money, like $10,000 or $15,000 every visit. Whenever we get a new shipment of clothing, Pamela checks it out. If she finds something that she thinks her customer would like, she pulls it off the floor in her size and puts it on hold. Sometimes, this can be for as long as a month! Lily has given Pamela special permission to hold the merchandise an extended period, since the customer spends so much money on a regular basis.

Pamela's customer wears a size 4, so that means almost all the size 4's are unavailable to the rest of us trying to sell items to our customers. If we knew it was a definite sale for Pamela, I don't think we'd have much of a problem with it. However, Pamela's customer doesn't buy everything, maybe only one half or one third of what Pamela is holding for her.

So, when the rest of us lose a sale on a size 4, we all think to that pile of clothes on hold for Pamela's customer. I guess Jazzy had reached her limit with it, and started swapping out sizes for her own sales. If she needed a size 4, she'd grab maybe a size 2 or 6 and swap it out with Pamela's holds. Jazzy got the sale and Pamela was none the wiser.

That is, until today when her wealthy customer finally arrived. Pamela set up the clothing in the fitting room, and her customer loved a few items, but they didn't fit. They were either too big or too small. When Pamela looked at the sizes, she realized she'd been duped, that someone had switched them on her.

Pamela knew who had done it. Jazzy has a habit of swapping sizes no matter who is holding the item. When she needs something for a customer, nothing stops her from getting the sale.

Pamela's customer was upset but understanding, although she didn't buy as much as she usually does. Mainly, because the items she really liked we no longer had in her size.

When the customer left, Pamela cornered Jazzy in the stockroom and read her the riot act. I've never heard such language come from Pamela's mouth, especially since the two of them are such good friends.

Jazzy just laughed it off. She never feels any remorse for what she does, and her best friend yelling at her wasn't going to make a bit of difference. There's a lot of jealousy there, too, from what I've heard. I guess Pamela's customer used to be Jazzy's customer once upon a time, until she met Pamela, then she no longer wanted Jazzy to help her.

Unfortunately, this is just another day in the life of commission sales. I'm soooo over this place! I must move on.

More tomorrow!

All my heart,

Diana

Indentured Servitude

{ TWENTY-ONE }

"I don't want any points! I don't want any points!"

I was in the stockroom chatting with Polly when I heard the sobs and screams coming toward us. Pamela was holding Martha, one of the cashiers from the gift shop next door. Martha was doubled over, barely able to walk. I wasn't sure if she was sick or something had happened. Martha's nearly 70 years old, so it really could be anything.

"Please don't give me any points. I need to leave, but don't give me any points. I can't handle it!"

Martha continued to scream about points, but we had no idea what was wrong.

Points are the torture system Positano uses to control you. It's just one part of the indentured servitude you experience as a valued Positano employee. It's totally opposite the gold star treatment you received in grade school. There are few systems to reward you in this company, but a multitude to punish you. And, everyone fears the points.

Depending on your position, you'll be charged points for any number of missteps. Attendance is probably the biggest issue. If you call in sick, you get a whole point. However, if you call in for four straight days, you still only get the one point. So, if you call in, you might as well take advantage of it. On the down side, no one gets any sick pay, so while you might enjoy the time off, you're not getting paid for it.

If you arrive late, you get a half point. If you go home after working half your shift, you get a half point. If you leave before you've worked half your shift, you get a whole point. None of it matters, whether or not you have a legitimate excuse. It's all charged the same. If you need to miss more than four days, you're automatically put on leave of absence (LOA). After six months, if you don't come back, they fire you.

If you handle money, like cashiers, you have a whole different set of point charges, as do all the various positions within the company. Once you hit five points in a calendar year, you get a formal verbal warning. Six points, a written warning. Seven points, a one day suspension. Eight points, a three-day suspension. Nine points, termination.

At the beginning of the year, everyone's slate is wiped clean if you have five points or less in any given area. Also, if you go six months without another point in the same area, you're back down to zero.

Of course, the company can choose to terminate you at any time for any reason. The only people who have some protection are the folks who are in the Culinary Union. Anyone else works strictly at the pleasure of the company.

No gold stars for us folks, but there is one little bright spot. If you have perfect attendance for six months, you are awarded a free paid holiday. Now, you have to track it, you have to remind your boss about it, and you have only two weeks to take it from the time you hit your six month anniversary, so the onus is on you. If you miss it, oh well. And, you only get paid minimum wage, just like you do for vacation days, but sometimes that's more than you make during an entire shift.

In order to get a week's vacation, you have to work an entire year. To get two weeks' vacation, you have to work another entire year. After that, you can take your vacation time anytime you like, as long as your boss approves. The pay might not be that great, but most bosses will add your weekend before or after, so you actually get nine days for one week's vacation.

Holiday pay is only minimum wage as well. No overtime. No double time. No time and a half. Just straight minimum wage. You work the holiday, or you don't, it just depends how your schedule falls. And, you don't get an extra day off during the week of the holiday, just your normal two days. The company operates 24/7/365, and they expect you to, too.

Points aren't the only disciplinary action. The other feared method is the Add-A-Note. These are notes that are added to your personnel file that aren't bad enough to charge you a point, but that mark your file in a negative way. Oftentimes, it's just a matter of doing the same thing you always do, but the boss is in a bad mood. So, that's the day you suffer and you receive an Add-A-Note in your file.

Martha had been with the company for a long time, so she knew the threat of points. Although she was nearing her 70th birthday, she worked two jobs to support herself and her ailing older sister. In general, her attendance record was better than most of the young girls whose focus was on partying all night. Martha had a great sense of responsibility, but the power of the points was a heavy burden for her.

"What's wrong with y'all?" Polly asked in her soft, Texas accent. "Are y'all feeling all right?"

Pamela sat Martha down, who answered Polly once she got her sobs under control.

"They found him dead. He's dead. Please don't give me any points!"

"Now, y'all don't worry about those points. Who died?"

To me, it didn't matter who died. It's just very sad to think that someone you know passes away and your first thought is not of your love for that person, but whether or not you'll get penalized for grieving.

I left Martha in the caring hands of Pamela and Polly, and returned to the sales floor. Lynn pulled me aside as soon as I got through the door.

"I'm not telling anyone else, but I'm calling in tomorrow. My sister is in town."

When Lynn says she's not telling anyone else, that means she's telling Jazzy and me. She still hasn't learned what a two-faced bitch Jazzy is.

"Why didn't you just ask for the day off?" I asked. "Lily's pretty good about giving people the time off they request."

Lynn was obviously upset about the whole thing. She kept her voice low but smiled at the customers as they passed. She didn't want to draw any attention.

"Maybe she'll give you time off, but I submitted my request over a month ago. I said to give me any time off this month, and I'd be happy. Well, it's the last week of the month, and instead of giving me time off she schedules me ten days straight! My sister really wanted to come out, and she had to use up her vacation by this week or she'd lose it. So, what am I supposed to do? Lily always says to deal with it, so let her deal with it this time."

I thought I saw smoke coming out of Lynn's ears. I knew where she was coming from. I had experienced the same issue when my sister came to town to look at houses for their big move. So many people had requested vacation time, I couldn't get off either.

"You know there are two other people on vacation right now, don't you? That's probably why she couldn't do it."

I tried to reason with her, but I knew it wasn't working.

"Well, too damn bad. I'm not going to give up my personal life just because some forty-something boss takes off all the time in the world but won't make a sacrifice so I can spend time with my family. I'll take the hit on the points and come back in three days. At least I'll have some time with my sister."

Lynn started to walk away, but backtracked. She looked me square in the eye and added, "What are you so upset about? You'll get to work alone those nights so you should make some good money. At least you'll be able to pay your rent this month."

That was true. With two people on vacation and Lynn calling out, there was no one else they could call in to take her shift. If it's busy, I'll have some good sales. And they'll be all mine! Of course, that means I'll also have to straighten the whole store by myself. And, that means I won't get out of here until at least one o'clock. I admire the balls these new college grads have, but there's also a responsibility factor. And, it seems, I end up cleaning up after them while they go off and enjoy their lives. Something is definitely wrong with this picture.

The next day, I ran into Martha in the employee dining room. She seemed perfectly normal. I was shocked!

"Martha! How are you? Is everything OK?" I asked.

"Well, no, but there's not much I can do about it. My nephew died unexpectedly. He was only 42-years-old."

I knew she depended on her nephew to help her and her sister. Martha was widowed, as was her sister, so her nephew was the man in the family. But, if he just died yesterday, what was she doing at work today?

"Martha, why aren't you home? You get bereavement pay, don't you?"

Martha smiled slightly, and wiped a tear from her eye.

"Thank you for being so concerned. Yes, I do get bereavement, but I only get three days. Since he died so young and so unexpectedly, the coroner is conducting an autopsy. It will be a few days before that's complete, so there's really nothing I can do. There are just the two of us left in the family, which means the service will be really small. Rather than sitting around at home, I decided the best thing I could do was come to work."

Well, that's definitely a noble thing to do, but a very old-fashioned concept. Nothing you can do? Doesn't your ailing sister need help dealing with the death of her son? Who's consoling her while you're able to escape to work? I didn't understand her line of thinking, but I know she's strapped for cash, and if she takes off more time than the three days, she won't get paid, and she'll wind up on an LOA. As it is, she hasn't slept much in the last few years, and with this latest burden on her shoulders, the best thing she can probably do is work.

"Well, you take care, Martha. You're in my prayers."

"Thank you dear. I appreciate that."

Martha walked back toward the elevators that would take her to the gift shop. I don't know if I'd have the strength to do what she's doing. But, rather than get points and lose wages, I guess it's the lesser of the two evils.

While I was eating lunch, I saw a very perturbed Lynn storming by. I got up and tried to stop her, but nearly got run over in the process.

"What are you doing here?" I asked. "I thought you were calling in today."

"I did," Lynn snorted. "I called and spoke with Polly. But it wasn't long after that when I got a call from Lily. Seems someone let the cat out of the bag. Lily said there's a rumor going around that my sister's in town, so if I ever wanted to work in this town again, I'd better get my ass into work." Lynn looked up and stared me down. "It wasn't you, was it?"

Oh, puhleeze. I'm the only decent, sane person in the place. And she's accusing me of turning her in! Besides, I know exactly who did it.

"I think it's I-told-you-so time," I snapped back. "Your BFF did you wrong. I saw her talking to Lily. I just didn't know what she was saying. Now it's all clear."

I thought Lynn was going to hit the ceiling.

"You've been waiting for this, haven't you? You never liked Jazzy. You've been waiting for me to get burned."

"I've told you time and again to stay away from that lying, manipulative little bitch, but you love her for some reason. Maybe now you'll see that she's not worth your trust."

"That's it. I'm out of here. As soon as I find a new job."

Lynn spun on her heels and headed to get her bank. I knew she was mad. I also knew she wasn't mad at me. She was upset at Jazzy, for sure. But she was also upset with herself. She really feels she's more mature than her 23 years, but this just proves that we all make mistakes. The sad part is, she doesn't get to spend precious time with her sister.

Indentured servitude trumps logic.

Dear Diary,

The new month, hence the new schedule, starts tomorrow. Problem is, I have no idea what I'm supposed to work for the next four weeks. Lily has generated seven schedules in five days. Most of the staff is confused about which one to follow, but I think we'll just show up when we think we're supposed to be there and hope for the best.

Lily is terrible about schedules. From what I've experienced, she generally gives them out just a day or two before they start. For the most part, we all have the same days off each week, but when someone goes on vacation or requests a personal day, that throws everyone else off schedule. And, I suspect, it throws Lily off, too.

Scheduling the fifteen or so people plus management has to be tough, but she's been doing it for years. She should have it down pat by now. There are no excuses.

However, I do have my own theories for her mistakes in each of the schedules this month. The first time she was drunk, the second time she was hung over, the third time she was mad at her boyfriend, the fourth time she was in a hurry and thought she corrected everything, the fifth time she was tired, the sixth time her computer crashed and she thought she had saved all the changes, and the seventh time she just didn't care anymore.

As Lily says, we'll just have to deal with it. What a caring, concerned boss.

More tomorrow!

All my heart,

Diana

The Diva

{ TWENTY-TWO }

"You know, I don't think the night crew did a very good job of straightening last night," snarled Claire, as she took her reading glasses off and slipped them into her neckline. She accosted me just as I arrived for my shift, totally catching me off guard.

While Claire did her usual hands-in-pocket sway that she does when she's trying to burn off steam, I blew past her ignorant comment and headed for the front to check into a register.

She's got to be kidding. The day crew does practically no work at all while the night crew is like hamsters on a wheel, working, working, working.

As I was putting the money in the register, I noticed a quite heated powwow taking place in the center of the store. Lily, Polly, Lester, Jazzy and some woman I didn't recognize were arguing about something. I could tell because they were under one of the store's canopies which, rather than acting like a Cone of Silence, actually magnified everything that was being said. I could pick up bits and pieces of conversation, but because I didn't know the context, it was hard for me to understand the gist of it all.

In the meantime, Claire sidled up to her counter, totally ignoring the mayhem just 10 feet away. I wandered back to ask her about the situation.

"What's going on?" I asked.

"Oh, it's one of the casino executives, The Diva. She's nothing but a troublemaker. She bitches about something every time she's in the store. She's such a bitch, unless you want to kiss some ass, I'd stay away from her. I think she's sleeping with half the executive team. When she complains, heads roll."

OK, well at least Claire had a handle on the circumstances. However, she wasn't planning to drop her first line of attack.

"I almost lost a sale today because you guys at night aren't straightening properly. The customer needed another size and I found it stuffed into a different rack. You people really have to do a better job."

"Oh, come on, Claire. You should see the mess we have to clean up. If you people put everything back where it belongs, we'd have a much easier job."

I was oh-so-tired of hearing it from Claire. She, of all people, had a lot of nerve. As part of the day crew, she basically did nothing. If she has to move more than three feet from the register except to eat or use the restroom, it just doesn't happen.

Claire was not going to give in on this one.

"I put everything back where it belongs, hung properly. I don't know what your problem is."

I leaned over the counter to make my point.

"Maybe *you* do, but your colleagues don't. We find a lot of stuff hung on the sides of the racks. That means we get to clean up their mess as well as ours."

Claire hid back behind the counter and started busying herself with cleaning the register.

"We get busy during the day. We're not slow like you are at night."

I was really getting upset now.

"You day people are the laziest sons of bitches I've ever met. We're not your slaves. We're busy, too, only we have a lot more to do. You have no clue what it's like to work at night."

Claire just rolled her eyes and kept wiping down the counter while I stormed off to the stockroom.

I grabbed a bottled water and leaned against the shoe racks while I gave myself a little pep talk. Calm down, Diana, calm down. Claire is Claire and you know that. She's been here forever and she thinks she can boss everyone around.

Moments later, Lynn walked in. She and I were closing together tonight.

"What up?" she asked when she saw I was upset. She had calmed down from the scheduling fiasco when her sister was in town, and things were back to normal between us.

"Oh, Claire's bitching that the night crew isn't straightening properly. She almost lost a sale because something wasn't in the right place. Why does she always think it's our fault?"

Lynn grabbed a chair from the desk and sat down. She was always the type of girl I wanted to be: beautiful, fit, at ease in every situation, totally in love with life. She was fresh out of school and took shit from no one. She had a college degree in hand and she was about to change the world. For now, she would graciously console.

"Diana, dear sweet Diana, you're coming at the problem totally wrong. Your first line of thinking should be, 'Fuck you, Claire.' Then, you should go on the floor and sell your little heart out."

I know that Lynn is right, but I guess I've lost a little of my edge since I left high tech. I'm not as strong and opinionated as I used to be. Retail doesn't allow me to speak my mind, and no one wants to hear my opinion anyway. It's all about the sell, sell, sell.

"I know, I know," I replied. "She's a sourpuss. But, come on. We do all the work around here. They don't do a damn thing."

"Oh, now, now, Diana, they are responsible for putting the expired holds back out."

We laughed.

"What is that, like 20 pieces a day? Must take all of five minutes."

"Hey, it's very important to spend those five minutes working every day, cos Lord knows, they don't do anything else."

Lynn and I were always on the same wavelength when it came to a day crew versus night crew disagreement. Lynn, smartly enough, sided with the night crew, of which she herself is a member.

"I did work a day shift once for Pamela, and it just blew my mind. Aside from putting out the holds, the only other important thing they have to do is open the doors. And they don't even want to do that! When it's ten o'clock, everyone scatters. Two girls were back here touching up their makeup and another suddenly got thirsty and had to run down to the café to get a coffee! How lame is that!"

By now, we were roaring. We could barely control ourselves.

In addition to straightening the entire store, the night crew fills the bags and other register supplies, empties sensors, dusts, restocks merchandise, resets the floor, handles all markdowns and empties the trash. Now, there are usually four or five people on days, and generally only two people on at night.

"I'd like to see Claire do what we have to do on a nightly basis. She'd never make it!"

"Do you remember that one time you were emptying Sophia's sensors from her drawer, and she said how nice it was of you to do it, because it was so full there just wasn't room for any more? She was too lazy to empty them herself. They're just lazy ass shits."

"Yeah, and when was the last time you saw anyone besides the night crew stock the floor? If we didn't do it, there wouldn't be anything to sell, and then they'd complain that their sales were down!"

After we had our little motivational meeting, we realized it was time for us to hit the sales floor. Just as we opened the door, we heard The Diva, the casino executive, say, "You're nothing but a bunch of commission whores!"

Yes, yes we are. We all prostitute ourselves for the almighty dollar. But, from what I hear, you do it in more ways than one.

The Diva walked out of the store as fast as her little stiletto heels would take her, and the rest of the powwow broke up. Lily, Lester and Jazzy waved good-bye, and Polly said she was going to lunch. I guess we'll have to wait until later to get the groovy details.

"Can I get some help?"

I heard the plea coming from an impatient female on the floor, but I was busy with several customers in the fitting rooms. Lynn had her own group of ladies in the other rooms at the back of the store. We were really busy tonight and for that we were grateful.

I really couldn't help another customer right now, yet the plea sounded rather pitiful but demanding, so I rushed onto the floor to see if I could help.

Yikes! It's The Diva! What the hell does she want?

"May I help you?" I asked.

"Can you hold these for me? I'll come back tomorrow to try them on."

"Sure, just leave them on the counter. I'll take care of it."

From what I'd seen this afternoon, I didn't want to spend a lot of time with her.

"What is it with you people? I can shop at any store on The Strip, and people treat me with respect. I come here, at my own company, and I get treated like dirt. I'll be talking to your manager."

Oh great, just what I need, an Add-A-Note.

"I'm happy to help you, but I'm really tied up right now with several customers. Here, let me take those from you and I'll put them on hold."

The Diva relinquished the items from her hands, and stared me down.

"I'll be back to talk to your boss, Diana."

And away she went.

"What are y'all doing waiting on her?"

Polly let out one of her trademark shrieks when she returned from lunch to hear my Diva story.

"Lily doesn't even want her in the store! Y'all need to stay away from her. She's just trouble."

"Polly, no one told me I'm not supposed to help her. What was I supposed to do? You were at lunch and the other managers were gone."

"Well, yeah, OK, but just know, in the future, stay away. If she does happen to come in, let Jazzy wait on her. And, if Jazzy isn't here, then let me know and I'll help her. She always looks for the new ones to attack and let you know that she's boss. So, y'all got to be her victim tonight."

What a relief. I was just one in a long line of victims.

"Who is she anyway? And what was that big meeting about?"

"The Diva is our European liaison for high rollers. She's from Italy, and is used to being catered to when she shops. And, she's very demanding. But, she doesn't always follow all the rules."

Hmm, OK, so what's that supposed to mean.

"So what was the deal with the meeting this afternoon?"

"Oh, she was up to her antics again. As an executive, she's not allowed to accept cash tips from a guest, but she can accept gifts. So, she had the guest come down here to buy her a $500 dress, and 15 minutes later, she came by to return it for the cash. Now, she's technically not allowed to do that."

"So, that would explain the 'commission whores' comment."

"Yes. Jazzy waited on the guest for over an hour to help him find the perfect dress for The Diva. She's very particular, and Jazzy usually waits on her, so she knows her style. When The

Diva returned it, she lost the commission, as well as the time she spent with the guest, so Jazzy was really upset. She's pulled this stunt before and she'd been told not to do it again, but she did."

"So how was it resolved?"

"Well, Lily took the dress back and gave her a merchandise credit. That way, Jazzy won't lose the sale."

OK, this didn't make any sense to me.

"Well, if she has a merchandise credit, she has to be allowed back into the store to use it, right?"

"Yes, that's true, but Lily only wants Jazzy to wait on her and only until she uses her $500 credit. But I'm sure Lily didn't think she'd be back so quickly. I mean, that was just a couple of hours ago."

"Does The Diva's boss know she's not allowed in the store?"

"Well, no, that's another issue I have with Lily. She doesn't want us to help her, but she won't go and talk to The Diva's boss, probably because The Diva is sleeping with him. So, if we don't wait on her, then she'll complain and Lily will deny everything and we're the ones who will get in trouble."

What a mess. I'm not supposed to wait on The Diva because the store manager says not to. However, The Diva never comes in when Lily is here, so Polly and the night crew are the ones who really have to deal with her. And, if we don't, she'll complain to her manager who is much higher up on the executive scale than ours and she just happens to be sleeping with him. Hmm...I think I'll just treat her like any other customer to save my job.

"Do you still have those items I put on hold?"

Oh, goodie. Graced with The Diva's presence once again. Why does she always come by when I'm the only one on the floor? Does she have some sort of radar or something? And, the least she could do is say hello.

"Why, yes, I do. Would you like me to put them in a fitting room so you can try them on?"

The Diva looked at me like I was a child locked in my terrible twos.

"Did I ask you to put them in a room? I don't think so. I simply asked if you still had them on hold."

"Yes, yes I do. What would you like me to do with them?"

"Keep up this line of questioning and I'll get you suspended. I'll do the talking. You only need to respond yes or no."

"Yes, ma'am."

Whew! What a nightmare! She's more high maintenance than Jazzy and The Bitch combined.

"Good. Now that we have an understanding, keep those clothes on hold until they go on sale. Then call me and I'll pick them up."

She handed me her business card and blew out of the store.

I called Polly on the intercom and related the details of my latest Diva encounter.

"Oh, yes, that's another nasty trait she has. She puts things on hold and makes us hold them until they go on sale. Sometimes they're on hold for weeks."

"But, I thought we're only supposed to hold things for 24 hours?"

"Yes, but most people are not The Diva. I've received an Add-A-Note because of her, when I told Jazzy to put back one of her holds. The Diva was livid. She causes so much trouble, we just do as she tells us and stay out of her way."

Polly was obviously in no mood to fight her. She'd lost one battle and that was enough for her.

A few days later, as I was coming back from lunch, I walked past the fitting rooms. There was an attractive dark haired woman trying on a dress that made her look positively gorgeous. She was a natural beauty, with long flowing hair and olive skin. She must have been a size 0 or 2, but she obviously had some enhancements made to her bustline. *Shocker.*

As I passed, I felt she looked so beautiful, I had to comment.

"You look absolutely stunning in that dress. So many women have tried it on, but it really fits you well."

She didn't even look at me, but continued to study her reflection in the mirror.

"You don't think it makes my boobs look too big?"

Isn't that the whole idea of getting implants?

"No, not at all. You look fabulous."

I left the customer and went onto the selling floor. When I saw Jazzy, I told her what I had said to her customer.

"Oh, that bitch?"

"Why? What's wrong? Who is she?"

"Lovey, that's The Diva."

"*That's* The Diva!?!"

I was shocked. It didn't look like her at all. She generally wore her hair up in a tight bun and dressed in Armani suits. I didn't even recognize her in the dress in the fitting room.

"Well, I told her she looks great, for what it's worth."

"Lovey, she can jump off the Stratosphere for all I care. I just want her to use up her merchandise credit and get the hell out of our lives."

The Diva strode out of the fitting room looking just like The Diva.

"Nothing worked. I'll be back."

I think I'd rather see The Witch again than The Diva.

Jazzy made her way to The Diva's fitting room. I followed. Clothes were strewn everywhere. You couldn't even tell there was a chair or carpeting in the room. Hangers were on the floor, clothes were on the floor. It looked like a cyclone just hit it, and I guess one just did, this one named The Diva.

"Stupid bitch," Jazzy said as we started cleaning up the mess.

Dear Diary,

I feel as if I no longer have a voice. I'm not talking about laryngitis or desert throat. Sure, I can talk but nobody cares to listen. I'm referring to the ability to give an opinion and have someone respect it, whether they agree with it or not. Retail just doesn't allow me to do that.

As a manager and a consultant in high tech, I was paid big bucks for my opinion and my ability to implement both strategic and tactical plans. I was excited to get out of bed in the morning, knowing that I was making a difference to the bottom line of a business. Sure, people will tell me that by making my sales quota daily I'm doing the same in retail, but it just doesn't feel right. I'm so far removed from the nuts and bolts of the command center, so to speak. I feel like a nobody.

In the previous incarnation of my career, I was kind and strong, confident in my abilities. Here, I'm just expected to be nice – to the customers, to my fellow workers, to management, to The Diva – despite how rude and crude they are to me. I am a nice person, so that's not really an issue. The problem is, I want to be so much more. I don't know how long I can squelch my true voice. I feel a gurgling inside me like magma getting ready to spew!

I'm also afraid I'm losing my ability to think properly. I would sometimes get that way with a client who didn't have good marketing skills. I would follow their lead to a certain extent, then question whether or not I'd ever get back to doing things the right way. In retail, I have numerous ideas to make the business better, but no one cares. Like an emotionally battered woman, I'm constantly shut down every time I try to offer my opinion. I'm told to just show up, do my work and go home.

In the past I worked with executive management, people who could make a difference in the company, many times, people who founded it. In retail, I'm a puppet, 17 layers of management away from the place I'm meant to be. Or, in The Diva's case, just one layer away but that's not the route I want to take.

I'm not saying retail is bad. On the contrary, without retail stores, where would I shop? It's just not a good career match for me. I really have no control – over my schedule, my co-workers, management, clientele. It's not only physically difficult it's also a mental test of my well-being.

I know there's a beautiful future out there for me. I just have to find it.

More tomorrow!

All my heart,

Diana

Commission Redux

{ TWENTY-THREE }

"You took the sale on that, didn't you?"

Julie was eyeing me as I rang a return, then a purchase for Sophia. She was at lunch, so I was helping her customer.

"No, I gave the sale to Sophia. It was her customer, right? I mean, that's how we did it at Sherborne. We saved the sale for other members of our team."

That policy had been pounded into my head for nearly two years.

"Honey, you're not at Sherborne anymore. This is the way the real world of commission works. You sell it, you take the credit. Unless the customer returns the item and purchases the exact same thing, except for color or size, you get the credit."

Now she tells me. Could no one clue me in when I first started here?

I could feel every cell in my body spring to attention. What Julie was telling me was totally against everything I had learned for the short while I'd been working commission sales. While it made sense, I felt this sudden pang of guilt, that I was cheating Sophia out of her commission. But, as long as everyone followed the same rules, then I could handle it.

Since Julie seemed to be sharing for a change, probably because she's not a fan of Sophia, I thought I'd try to clarify the policy for future reference.

"So, what if I'm helping a customer who has a lot of stuff on hold, but she buys other items that I select for her?"

Julie was getting a little annoyed by my apparent stupidity.

"Then, whoever has the items on hold gets credit for those, and you get credit for the ones you choose. It's pretty straight forward."

I guess the staff here has determined that I'm not leaving, so they've decided to shed light on a few key policies. This would be an important one, and I'm glad Julie has decided to correct me.

"So, what do I do now?"

If that's the policy, I don't want to break it.

"I'll get Polly, and she'll do an exchange for you. She'll return the item to Sophia and credit it to you."

Julie was staring at me now, the same stare she used on my first day when she wanted me to clean her mess in the fitting rooms.

"Just don't do it again, honey. We don't want any goodie two shoes around here."

I have to admit this is a much fairer policy than the one at Sherborne. I hated helping other people's customers at Sherborne. I could spend hours with them, but the original salesperson was the only one who got the credit. For everything! Here, at least, I had a chance to make my own sales with that same customer. I just wish someone had told me sooner. I can't imagine how much I'd lost in commissions by following the Sherborne policy here at Positano. No wonder my sales seemed so low. But, at least, now I know better and I won't let it happen again.

I stared back at Julie. I didn't particularly like her, nor did I like anyone on staff, except for maybe Lynn. But, was it just me? I had to ask.

"Does anyone here like anyone else?"

Julie let out a smirk and shook her head.

"No."

Claire came out of the stock room and surveyed the sales floor. She noticed two casino marketing employees checking out the shoes.

"Stay away from those two. They're Jazzy's customers."

Claire was doing her signature hand-in-pocket sway as the two employees walked by. She was visibly upset at the sight of them.

"Why? Just cos they're Jazzy's customers, can't we wait on them?"

I know any logical thought I have will be met with an illogical response, but it's just my nature to ask.

Claire sneered and rolled her eyes. Julie was upset as well.

"Anything you sell them, they'll return when Jazzy is here and then they'll buy it from her, so she'll get the credit. The bitches can rot in hell."

Claire really was not happy, and was kind enough to warn me about them.

Julie angrily shared her own personal experience with the pair.

"I sold one of them a fur coat for $2,200 and she returned it the next day and Jazzy got the credit."

"And I sold the other one two belts for almost a thousand dollars, and she returned them for Jazzy to get the sale," Claire added.

"But how is that possible? Doesn't that go against some sort of policy?"

I was amazed. At a place where everyone is so vicious about getting their commissions, I would have thought that this issue would have been dealt with a long time ago.

"Have you met Jazzy?" Claire asked snidely.

I laughed.

"Yes, of course I've met her. But, why should that matter? This is crazy!"

"Just stay away from her customers. It will save you a lot of headaches. Jazzy manages to get away with everything."

"Bad accent and all?" I asked.

"Bad accent and all," Julie agreed.

We all shared a laugh, knowing that Jazzy spoke with the worst British accent we'd ever heard.

I heard some footsteps heading in my direction, so I swung around and recognized the couple walking toward me as the one I'd helped a couple of days ago. They were visiting from Australia. The wife was in the fitting room for over two hours but she finally found a swimsuit that she liked. Unfortunately, it was poorly made and she had already brought it back once yesterday. Now, she had it in her hand again.

"Hi! How can I help you today?"

"Well, Diana, I hate to be a pill, but the stitching on this suit is coming undone. I absolutely love the style, but this is the second one and it's falling apart, too."

She showed me the loose stitching on the top of the suit. Yesterday, it was the stays poking through the sides. Luckily, we had another one just like it, in the same size and style. We generally only get one in each size, but occasionally we get multiples. When I walked to the rack yesterday, I lucked out. I exchanged it and gave her the new suit, hoping that the next time I saw her, it would be for her to buy something else from me.

I couldn't believe the same customer was back holding the swimsuit in her hand once again. She seemed genuinely upset, like it was her fault, but it's not. It's our crappy merchandise that I have to pay for with my time and commission. But, at least I was here to save my own sale.

"No worries. I'm happy to help. Let me look to see if there's one more."

I thought, fat chance, but I'll give it a shot. However, she stopped me as I headed over to the suits.

"I actually have something on hold."

Noooo! That means I lose the sale!

"I noticed the problem with the suit earlier on my way to the pool, so I came in to see if there was another. Unfortunately, as much as I love this style, there aren't any more. So, I found a different one and had Sophia hold it for me."

Julie and Claire were snickering in the background. They know what it's like to lose a sale after you've spent so much time with the customer, and to lose it to Sophia was like feeding a pit bull.

"Oh, OK, let me get it for you."

Bitch! I know it's not your fault, but I waited on you now three times, and Sophia, who simply took your name and put the swimsuit on hold, gets the credit! Same size, different style. The policy's not on my side.

I wouldn't have been quite so upset, if it hadn't been one of those weeks. In just five short days, customers had returned over $3,000 worth of merchandise that I sold them, not because they changed their minds, but because it fell apart. Three pairs of sunglasses alone were nearly $2,000. That's three days' worth of work I have to make up because our vendors are sending us shoddy merchandise. With the designer brands that we carry, and the high prices, everything we sell should last a lifetime. But no, the longest any of these items lasted was two weeks. It's not our fault, but the company refuses to give us the commission. It's just part of our job.

I rang the exchange and put the new suit into a bag.

"Here you go. And, here's your new receipt. Enjoy the rest of your visit."

I handed her the bag and wished her off.

"We leave tomorrow morning, so hopefully I won't be back again. Cheers!"

My customer headed out the door, content with her new suit. Julie and Claire started counting out their registers to head home, and I made a quick trip to the restroom before they departed.

When I walked back onto the sales floor. Julie and Claire were gone and Sophia was knee-deep in paperwork. We all kept copies of our sales receipts so we had a record for our commissions, just in case the company somehow forgot to credit us for a sale.

"What are you doing?" I asked Sophia. "Did they short your check?"

Sophia was more upset than I realized.

"That fucking bitch can rot in hell."

I stepped back a bit, surprised at Sophia's reaction.

"Which bitch and why?"

You can never be sure around here. Everyone is a bitch to someone else.

"Julie. That stupid bitch stole another one of my holds. I'm looking for a copy of the receipt in her file."

"Julie! What did she do?"

It didn't seem like her. Julie, in spite of the stares, has on occasion shown a nice streak. She has heart somewhere, I was sure. She'd already left for the day so there was no direct confrontation between the two.

"Julie always rings your holds under her number so she gets the credit. And, unless you call it to her attention, she keeps the sale. When you show her the proof, she says she's sorry, she must have made a mistake, it's just habit that she punches in her own number instead of yours. That fucking shit isn't worth the breath she takes."

Wow! I'm seeing a completely different side of Julie than I knew.

"Why doesn't management deal with her? Shouldn't she be written up or something?"

I couldn't believe that this could continue to go on when everyone, including management, knew it was an issue. However, why I was concerned about the pit bull getting her commission was beyond my comprehension. After all, I just lost my commission to her on the swimsuit sale. But, every conversation in this place is one step closer to my Ph.D. in retail hell.

"That stupid bitch. When Lily tried to discipline her in HR – "

"Wait! Lily actually did something?"

"I know. Surprising, huh? Anyway, when Lily tried to discipline her in HR, nothing happened. Seems Julie has friends in high places that Lily can't match. Lily decided not to waste her time any more. Julie can do anything she wants and no one will take her to task on it. They'll never get rid of her. I wish an elephant would dump on her and crush her to bits. She's a worthless piece of shit."

Sophia kept looking through Julie's receipts as she was talking to me.

"Aha! Here it is."

She called me over to show me.

"Look. Here's my hold tag. I always write down the UPC for everything I put on hold. The expiration date is tomorrow, but it was rung yesterday, and under Julie's number. I may not be able to get her in trouble for this, but I'll at least get the commission. When she comes in tomorrow, I'll make her do an exchange. She's a fucking whore."

A commission whore, if I recall correctly.

While Sophia headed to the stockroom to put back her paperwork, I noticed a trio of women, in their late 20s, enter the store. They had the typical Las Vegas Positano shopper look on their faces. They were ready to party, but first, they needed some clothes.

"Come on, girls, let's find something to wear."

The drop-dead gorgeous leader of the trio was obviously intent on having a good time, and brought her two friends with her. She practically ran through the store, stopping here and there to momentarily calm her stiletto boots, her perfume wafting in her wake. Leader was slim, trim, and clearly worth a ton of money, which she spent to both take good care of herself and to look good. The other two girls, well, they were her friends. Pretty average looking. Probably shopped at big box stores. Both could use a facial and some good hair care. I'm sure they're nice.

"May I help you?"

I finally was able to get to the ringleader. She moved so quickly, it was hard to keep up.

"Yes, please. We just flew in on my private jet from Little Rock, and we don't have anything to wear tonight. What do you suggest?"

Honestly, we can dress *you* in just about anything in the store and you'd look amazing. The other two, well, I'm not sure we have anything that will even fit them. This situation is actually quite normal. Since only a small percentage of the world is wealthy and beautiful, the large majority are just, well, average. It's like when you find a great guy. He's the only one in the bunch that's special compared to his friends.

"Let's have a look and get a fitting room started. What do you plan to do this evening?"

There was no response as Leader and the girls flew through the store, picking up all sorts of dresses, tops, jeans and shoes. Leader never looked at a price tag, but the other two looked often, then put many items back. Again, a telltale sign of who has the money.

"I'm going in, girls," Leader said as she headed to the fitting rooms. "Just pick out what you like. Don't worry what it costs. I'm buying!"

With that, Leader disappeared into the hallway, but you could tell her friends were uncomfortable both with Leader buying their clothes, and paying the price that they were. Fortunately, we didn't have anything that worked for them, so they were saved from the guilt. Leader, on the other hand, walked out in a $1,400 outfit in 15 minutes: dress, boots and faux fur shawl. She was positively adorable, a black-haired Barbie doll with a Southern accent. With implants, of course.

It constantly amazes me how many people show up in Las Vegas without any luggage. Every weekend, folks from LA, Scottsdale, Salt Lake City, Denver and this weekend, by private jet, Little Rock, come to our store to buy something to wear, because they honestly don't have a change of clothing with them. Or, they just don't like what they brought. We love it from a commission perspective because most of the women overspend on this spontaneous purchase, and they wear it immediately, so it won't be returned unless it falls apart. Otherwise, we're good to go. It's a guaranteed sale!

Of course, there are a couple of classes of women who buy things and return them the next day. The first, of course, is hookers, of which this hotel has many. Some of them even work for the company. While management would deny it outright if anyone ever asked, the truth is, the high-priced tramps are all over the place. Either they're given the money to come and purchase an item for the night, then return it the next day for the cash. Or, the men shop with their 'friends' and charge it on their credit card. They return the items the next day, claiming their purse was stolen so they no longer have the credit card that was used for the purchase, and we give them a cash refund. You can sometimes pick them out when they walk in, but this is Las Vegas, and a lot of women dress trashy.

Then, there are the more underhanded women who knowingly buy and return. It's crazy that someone who makes more in a month than we do in a year can have so few scruples. Sophia was helping one such group of ladies.

"It's Suzie's 50th birthday. We're going to dinner tonight, then dancing at the clubs. Might as well enjoy ourselves. You're only young once."

Suzie's friend was already drinking champagne, and she, Suzie and a third friend were helping her to select an outfit for the evening. Sophia gathered up their choices, and placed the three of them in a fitting room. As Suzie tried each outfit on, the other two friends played peanut gallery and offered their rude and crude opinions.

I soon placed my own customer in an adjoining fitting room, when I realized the party girls had gotten quiet. I stopped just outside the main door, and caught a bit of what they were saying. I couldn't believe my ears!

"I love it, Andrea, but I'd never wear it back home. This is strictly a Vegas dress."

Suzie was obviously torn between spending a ton of money on a designer dress for her special occasion, or finding something more practical.

"Suzie, don't worry," Suzie's champagne-filled friend responded, "I'll take care of it for you. I have a thin slip upstairs that you can wear under it. Just leave the tags on and bring it back in the morning before we leave. It's no big deal. I do it all the time."

The three of them started snickering, and Suzie relented.

"OK, if you think it's all right to do that, then this is it. I love it! It's perfect for tonight!"

Shocked, I quickly went up to Sophia to let her know what I heard. She immediately started cussing in words I'm certain someone understood, but they never taught me in freshman Spanish.

Sophia rang the sale for Suzie, and explained in detail our return policy, that the item cannot be returned if it's been worn. Suzie blushed, but her friend hurried the three of them out of the store before Suzie could change her mind. The plot was in action, and she didn't want to stop it.

The next day, Sophia attacked Julie about the hold Julie had rung under her number instead of Sophia's. Julie was very upset. She fell to her knees, raised her hands to the heavens and started to scream.

"Satan made me do it. Lord, please protect us from all evil. Satan is among us. Bless us Lord, protect us from Satan and his evil acts."

Sophia had seen these antics before, and was unmoved.

"Get up, you stupid bitch, and transfer the sale."

Sophia stormed out onto the sales floor to prepare the store for the day.

The second the doors opened, there was Suzie, a bit worse for the wear, returning her dress. The tag was still on, it reeked of perfume and cigarettes, but she claimed she hadn't worn it and wanted a refund. Lester, in his commanding role as assistant manager, never argued with a customer. He refunded the purchase, and Sophia was out the commission on an $800 dress.

"Those fucking bitches!" she said when Lester returned Suzie's money. "Karma. Karma will get them."

Obi-Wan Kenobi. Karma is our only hope.

Dear Diary,

Oh, I can be such a ditz sometimes. Too bad the words are out of my mouth quicker than I can stop them.

Living in Las Vegas, we have visitors from all over the world. Some speak English, but many do not. Working at Positano, I always try to be courteous to our international visitors, and one of the nicest things I can do is to say Thank You in their native language. If I don't know how to say it, I ask, and they generally oblige.

Over the years, not only from my work at Positano, but also from all the traveling I did while I worked in high tech, I've developed quite a repertoire of Thank You's. At last count, I knew how to say those gracious words in 14 different languages. Not bad, right?

Yet, it seems, one country confounded me. These customers were fun, happy and spent a lot of money with me. I rang up their purchases at the register, all the while laughing and joking with them. When it came time to thank them, I absentmindedly stuck my foot in my mouth. Before I could stop myself, the words tumbled out.

"How do you say Thank You in Canadian?"

The two women nearly fell over they were laughing so hard. Fortunately, they realized I meant it from my heart, and one of them responded, "Thank you, eh."

We all shared a big laugh, and now two more Canadian women have a great story for their friends back home.

I wonder if they know the woman with the Canadian breasts.

More tomorrow!

All my heart,

Diana

Lulus

{ TWENTY-FOUR }

Aside from nightclubs, casinos and maybe sporting events, I'm not sure of any other industry that deals with the crazy public quite so much on a daily basis as does retail. In particular, my least favorite customer is the lulu.

Lulus are the ruin of retail. The venom of Vegas. The plague of Positano.

It doesn't matter whether we're busy or slow, we hate lulus. They cheerfully waste our most precious resource – time – and prevent us from our number one goal – to make money. Lots of it.

Lulus come in all shapes and sizes, colors and ages, and all income levels. I'm sure I'm a lulu on occasion. But, that's me, when I'm on the other side of the transaction. From this side, we hate lulus.

Lulu is a term Lynn coined quite accidentally. She was trying to say the word 'looky-loos' and out of her mouth popped 'lulus.' It stuck. It also gave us an opportunity to talk about lulus right next to them without them ever knowing they were the target of our wrath. Out of the mouth of babes…

Lulus often perform five basic functions, although they permeate all facets of our working lives. There are sliders, yankers, tuggers, pullers and stuffers. Each works in her own way to aggravate the shit out of us. None of them ever buys nor do they request our help. I believe they need a lot of help, just not the kind that we can give them.

The sound of sliders is like fingernails on the chalk board. They generally don't show up until you've finished straightening at least half the store. Then you hear it. Screech! At each and every rack, the lulu slides all the clothes to one side, then looks at each item, hanger by hanger, until she's destroyed everything you've just done. Finally, she walks out of the store, with a smile on her face. Occasionally, she'll thank us, but she's usually too cool for that. She just leaves.

Yankers are a bit easier to handle. They're the type who yank the clothes from the hanger, so that when you walk by, it looks like someone has her hand on her hip, and her elbow's protruding. These little triangles of perfection can easily slip right back into their original, straight, resting place. Some of our best customers are yankers, but many lulus wear the yanker crown.

Tuggers should never be let into a store. Someone should be assigned to do their shopping. They must have maids at home who pick up after them constantly. Tuggers tug so hard on the clothing that it comes off the hangers. Then, these intelligent shopping creatures have no idea what to do with the item. They never think to put it back on the hanger. No. They instead either drop it to the floor and leave it there, or they crumple up the item and throw it on top of the rack. Tuggers are sooo much fun.

Pullers are tuggers in training. Pullers pull on the clothing so that only half of the item comes off the hanger. The other half remains. Then, when we go to fix it, it completely falls off. So, with just a little bit of practice, pullers can graduate to full-fledged tuggers.

Stuffers are everywhere, not just clothing stores. They're the ones who leave the milk in the bread aisle, or conversely, the bread in the dairy section. These are shoppers who pick up an item and carry it around the store, contemplating whether to try it on or purchase it. Then, for some reason, they stuff it into a rack and run out of the store. I don't know what's so scary that they leave in such a rush, but we'll find swimsuits in with the coats, pants in the dresses, and tops in with the handbags. There must be an art to it, but to us, it's just a mess.

I'm not sure who we hate more, lulus who can afford to buy our clothes or those who can't. I think it's the former.

They aggravate us all sorts of ways. Last night we had one of the worst offenders of all. A woman in her mid-40s, quite nicely dressed in her designer duds, made her way rather methodically, rack by rack, from one end of the store to the other. Like a terribly messy child, she had to touch everything on every rack, leaving the clothes all askew, begging for help.

It didn't matter to her that it was 15 minutes till closing. It didn't matter that she had absolutely no intention of trying anything on, let alone buying. It mattered to us that it was 15 minutes to closing, and we had just completely finished straightening. The store was in perfect condition, perfect for closing the gate and perfect for opening fresh tomorrow morning. Perfect for us to actually get out of here at closing time for a change, without having to straighten up from the lulus.

Alas, tonight it would not be so. Lulu had made her mark. And, as she departed, she said she was flying out in the morning so she couldn't come back, but thank you for your time, you have beautiful stuff, wish I had stopped by earlier in my trip, have a good evening. Lulu!

That wasn't bad enough. Earlier in the day it seemed like my shift started out to be fruitful. My first customer looked reasonable, and asked to try on some comfortable but stylish shoes. Great! I just walked in and already I had an eager customer.

I brought out several pair for her to try, one at a time. Whenever I was in the stockroom looking for one of her selections, she would find another one on the floor she wanted to try. So, I wasn't able to help her select a style that might suit her. I could only pull her choices from the stockroom.

After the seventh pair, with empty boxes stacked high and shoes spread all over the carpeting, she thanked me for my time, said I was quite helpful, but she just couldn't find one that felt as comfortable as her orthotics, no matter what she tried.

Well, of course not, you idiot. Nothing will compare to the comfort of your orthotics. They're custom made to your foot! Just another lulu.

When she left, I had a group of women who were out celebrating a 50th birthday for one of them. They were desperately searching for a velour track suit. Now, I would say that most women in their 50s shouldn't be wearing velour, but these women were in pretty good shape. They tried on several different sizes and combinations, and after all of that, the birthday girl handed me the set that she liked and asked me if I could hold that until tomorrow. They had just gotten into town and this was the first store they had visited and wanted to see what else the town had to offer. She never came back. Lulu.

While I was helping them, Lynn had another customer who looked like she could actually afford what she was trying on. After a few minutes, she walked out of the fitting room and asked Lynn to hold everything for her – about 20 items – because she was late for dinner and she just couldn't decide. She never came back. Lulu.

Pamela looked like she might be lucky. She was helping a customer try on a $1,000 pair of boots. The customer pranced around as if she were in heaven. Her friend came in to offer some fashion advice.

"What do you think, Monica?" she asked.

"They're amazing, Jodi. You should get them."

Monica supported her friend. Jodi laughed.

"Monica, I'd love to, but these are an entire month's mortgage payment. I can't afford them."

Pamela looked heartbroken. Jodi was just another lulu.

Surprisingly, Jodi attempted to bargain with Pamela.

"I can't afford these, but you can give them to me, and then you'll go to heaven."

Right as she made her last ditch efforts for the boots, Polly walked by. She let out one of her trademark shrieks and responded to the customer, "Well, she might go to heaven but she won't have a job."

Jazzy had a fun group of women out on the floor, trying on a selection of shoes and boots in the shoe circle. Must have been five of them, and 30 pairs of shoes. We were all jealous, certain that she would get a big sale out of this. She served them bottled water and wine, and everyone was having a grand old time. Then they got up, said they were just having fun, thanked Jazzy and left. Lulus.

By now, it was nearly lunch time, and not one of us had sold a dime.

Not every day starts like this, and not everyone who says they're just looking is a lulu. Still, lulus drive us crazy and waste our time.

I know – er, I mean I've heard – that many books suggest that in order to set your financial and romantic sights higher, it's imperative that you learn to shop where the rich do. You need to learn the designers, the cuts, the fabrics, and most of all, how to deal with the sales staff. And, on $99 room nights, we get plenty of lulus who are pretending to live the high life.

It was a full moon the other night, and I had the lulus to prove it. The first customer who came up to me was a buyer for sure, or so I thought. She was dressed in her evening finest: a beaded dress, stilettos and a fur jacket. She was a rather elegant woman, appearing to have been raised on the right side of the tracks. She approached me as soon as she walked into the store.

"Excuse me, but I was in the shoe store across the way, and I understand that you have the pink dress that's in their window."

"Absolutely. Wait just a minute while I check to see which one it is. They change the displays all the time."

I ran across the hall to find out which dress this customer liked. Everything on display in that store was expensive, so I was sure that I might actually crack the nut today (sell over $1,000).

"It's the Carson. It's right here."

I walked the customer to the rack of dresses and pulled out the one she admired. She held the dress in her hands, and just as I was about to ask if I could put her in a fitting room, she spoke.

"Oh, how beautiful. This is absolutely lovely. Look at the fabric, the cut." She touched my arm for emphasis and said, "Isn't it nice to have money."

With that, she thanked me and walked away.

Yes, it is nice to have money. In fact, if she hadn't wasted my time and actually bought the dress, I would have had an extra $36.50 in my pocket. Or, I could have used that time to service a real paying customer. This is Positano, lady, not Discount Dan's. Dinner for two is $1,200. The dress is going to cost a bit of money.

She was followed by two girls who were poorly raised. They were obviously trying to emulate some rich bitch celebrity but in the wrong way. I'm sure Ms. Rich Bitch has respect for her clothing and her staff. These two had no idea how the really wealthy act, and, ahem, we're not their maids.

These ladies – I use the term quite loosely – went to each and every rack around the store, and completely destroyed it. They grabbed things to try on, let themselves into a fitting room, then left everything on the floor. They were just looking, they said. They would let us know if they needed any help.

On their way out the door, they were stopped by an actual customer – mine – who was buying a handbag for her daughter. She had been searching all day for just the right one, and although this wasn't exactly the one she had seen in a magazine, she liked it just the same. Her daughter was carrying her first grandchild, and she wanted to buy her something special every month until the baby's birth. She was excited and so was I. It was a $400 sale. I would finally crack the nut!

The lovely soon-to-be grandmother was a bit concerned that she was buying something that her daughter would like, so she stopped the two space cadets as they headed for the door.

"Excuse me, but I'm buying something for my daughter who is about your age, and I wanted to get your opinion. Do you think she'd like this handbag?"

The dark-haired one snarled and said, "It's cute, I guess, but it's not *my* style."

Her equally intellectually-challenged best friend added, "And the color's a bit old. Maybe it's better for you than for your daughter."

The grandmother thanked them profusely and ran out of the store, content that she would not buy something so obviously wrong for her daughter. The two space travelers were doubled over in laughter, knowing that they screwed me out of a sale. The short one even added, "Oooh, now I feel like the bad guy. Ha ha!" And they ran laughing down the hall.

They were quickly followed by a customer who needed a serious long-term membership to a gym if she planned to shop in this store. Our clothes require the thinnest clientele ever. On the bottom, she was probably a size 12, and on top, at least a size 14. I'm sorry, I'm just being honest. There really are only a few things that I can sell someone who is above a size 10: sunglasses, shoes, handbags and jewelry. Nothing else will fit, guaranteed. She was trying to be fashionable, but her black tights and low V-neck top just didn't cut it.

I greeted her nicely, but I generally don't waste a lot of time with those customers. Unless they're going to buy one of the four categories, or purchase a gift, I really can't help them. I know it's rude, I know it's crude, but in commission retail, it's just good time management.

I saw her trying on a blazer, and put it back on the hanger. "Can you get this for me in another size?" she asked.

"What size are you looking for?"

"Well, this is a size 10, so I'm thinking I'll need at least a size 14."

"I'm sorry, but if I'm lucky I might be able to find it in a 12, but that's as large as it goes."

"You're kidding me, right? Who is this designer, anyway? I want to write a letter to complain."

"To tell you the truth, most of the designers in our store don't go above a size 12. They generally stop at a size 10."

"Well, I happen to have a top in my hand that's an XL, thank you very much."

"Yeah, well an XL in designer is about a size 10."

"I don't believe you."

"Ma'am, you're welcome to try it on, but I'm guaranteeing that the designer clothing we carry runs small. Can I interest you in some new shoes?"

She proceeded to the fitting room, whereupon she emerged, convinced that I knew my merchandise, and blamed her inability to fit into the top on the fact that she had just left the buffet.

She finally did try on some sale shoes, and asked me to hold two pair. She wanted to check the Internet to see if she could find them cheaper. And away she went. She eventually called me twice from the airport, claiming she wanted me to ship the shoes to her, but alas, she never actually gave me any useful information, like her credit card number.

All in all, I think our least favorite lulus are those who work in retail themselves. It never fails. Boutique owners from some small town in Middle America will stop by just a few minutes before closing, to check out our merchandise. Rack by rack, they have to look at each and every designer, to compare it to what they carry.

If anyone should understand the desire to leave at closing time, to be prepared by having the store in great shape, it should be a boutique owner. Still, week after week, we're visited by this unique brand of lulus who entertain themselves at our expense. It's particularly difficult during the apparel trade shows in February and August, because 100,000 people involved in the clothing business from all over the world descend upon the city, and a percentage of them always manage to make their way to our boutique.

Worse than the boutique owners are the boutique owners' friends. Time after time, we'll waste precious hours servicing them, only to find out they're not buying. They're simply using us as a vendor showroom. I had one just the other day. Her friend owned a boutique, and she loved this particular dress, but she wasn't sure what size she needed. Since we had the whole size range, she tried them on to determine she needed a size 6. And off she went. She drank our wine, she wasted our time, and left. After all, why should she pay retail when her friend will sell it to her wholesale?

In the old days, lulus were akin to the airheads of today. Lynn wasn't far off with the slip of her tongue.

Dear Diary,

Work has been hell. It's so slow, I have no idea how I'm going to pay the rent, let alone eat next week. Monday night I only sold $700, and Thursday I sold a measly $226! At 10 percent commission, I'm sunk. Usually after the first week of the pay period, I have over $10,000 in sales. I'm not even at the halfway mark and I only have three more days till payday. Yikes!

Not that there isn't any traffic in the halls. The hotel is bustling with people. Unfortunately, they're not our regular crowd. This is the time of year that the hotel lowers their nightly rate to $99 so they can fill the rooms. Most people would jump at the chance to pay just $99 to stay at Positano. Unfortunately, they can't afford anything else the resort has to offer.

Over half the hotel rooms, 2,500 of them, were sucked up by a Jalapeno's Restaurant managers' convention for the whole week. I'm sorry, but those people are just not going to spend $500 on a sweater. Maybe once in their lifetimes, but not on a regular basis. We had more lulus last week than I've ever seen. My co-workers keep telling me it's going to pick up, business will get better. But I don't see it. I don't know what to do.

I thought The Shop at Positano would be the place for me. But, I thought the same thing when I joined Sherborne. I gotta get outta here.

More tomorrow!

All my heart,

Diana

Genesis Girls

{ TWENTY-FIVE }

"Hey! How's it going?" I called out to the Genesis girls when I came out onto the sales floor to start my shift.

Julie grabbed my arm and pulled me aside like a mother does to her four-year-old child, to reprimand me. I half expected her to grab me by my ear and send me to my room.

"What are you doing?"

OK, confused once again from the strangeness of this place, I asked, "What are you talking about?"

"Just who are you talking to?" Julie was whispering, but very sternly.

The look in her eyes was scary. I'd never seen her like this. She's tall, she's imposing, she's beautiful, but I've never seen her scared.

"Isn't it obvious? I'm talking to Katrina and Tracy in Genesis."

How that could be construed as harmful, I had no idea.

"I wouldn't do that if I were you. We're not supposed to talk to them."

Julie was shaking her head. She took a deep breath, looked me in the eye, then put her head down and retreated to her register.

Happy to have my arm back, I turned to her in amazement.

"What? I talk to everyone!"

And, I do. The janitors, the drunks, and even the obnoxious Diva of a casino executive whose mere mention of her name sends the staff scurrying for cover. I like to think of the good in people, so in general, I talk to everyone.

Julie wasn't convinced. She'd obviously been yelled at today and was just giving me a heads up. I suspect that meant that Lily was in a bad mood again. She's worse than a hormonal teenager.

"Well, Lily was really upset today and informed the Genesis girls that they have to stay behind their counter and we're not supposed to talk to them."

Stupidity to the forefront once again. We all work in the same store, a mere twenty feet from one another. It's just rude and inconsiderate not to acknowledge them. We send each other customers all night long. That requires talking to each other. Besides, I need my daily fix of news on kids and dogs and husbands. Something pretty major must have taken place to cause such a restriction.

"What happened?"

Julie looked around to make sure no one else was listening.

"I'm not sure, but from what I heard from the other girls, an executive was walking by this afternoon and he saw the Genesis girls and Jazzy laughing, and he didn't like it."

Julie was so serious it was as if she committed a mortal sin just thinking about it.

"Oh, so we're not supposed to laugh at work now?"

I was half-tempted to burst into a rollicking belly laugh, right at the store entrance so any executives within 100 feet could hear. Their offices were just down the hallway, so I'm pretty certain it wouldn't take much to get them in here.

"I guess not. It doesn't present a professional environment," Julie said, not thinking about the stupidity of it all but rather simply accepting it as fact. After all, we were to present a relaxed and fun place for our customers, but not for us. "And I guess Tracy has been having reactions to her meds, so she's been a little loopy lately."

"Meds! She's on meds!"

That was the first I heard of any of the Genesis girls on meds. Tracy is such a sweet, young mother with two small kids and four dogs. How could she take care of them if she was on meds?

"Oh, yeah, it seems that anyone who works there is at least on Prozac, if not something else. I don't know how it happens, but everyone they hire for that counter has some sort of deep psychological issues. They're always on meds."

Well, I'd like to see the results of their pre-employment drug tests.

Lily came out from the stock room, breezed swiftly by and left the store without acknowledging us. It looked like she was headed to executive row. I guess she's restricted from talking with us, too.

Julie relaxed for the first time tonight.

"Maybe she's going to get an Add-A-Note in her file."

We both laughed heartily, and headed over to the Genesis counter to catch up on all the rest of the gossip.

Dear Diary,

Omigod! You'll never guess who I ran into today while shopping at Bullseye. It was Gene, the general manager of Sherborne! Do you believe it!

I was looking my worst of course. I'd showered but hadn't put on any makeup. It was my day to run around, you know. Anyway, so, I'm on a mission, and I'm practically running through the store. I round the corner near menswear, and who do I literally run into – Gene! Omigod! I just couldn't believe it!

I mean, I know we all shop at Bullseye. I'm guilty of it myself. I make the trip at least once a week. But I'm not the general manager of Sherborne, buying men's clothing!

Gene was looking at the men's holiday sweatshirts. Was he looking for himself, or did he plan to give them as gifts to his husband? Didn't Sherborne pay him enough to shop in his own store? I mean, the way he goes spinning around in his Mercedes, one might think he's making good money.

Wouldn't that be a hoot if someone he gave the sweatshirt to actually tried to return it to Sherborne, only to find out it hadn't been purchased there? He'd definitely have some splainin' to do. Although, with the generous return policy that Sherborne has, I'm sure they'd take it back anyway – and give them cash!

We chatted for a few moments. He asked me how my new job was going, and I asked him how business was.

I was beet red, blushing during the entire conversation. We didn't chat for long, thank goodness. We waved our good-byes and we were on our way.

Omigod!

More tomorrow!

All the best,

Diana

Bedbugs

{ TWENTY-SIX }

One Sunday night at 11:45 p.m., I was walking through the stock room on my way back from a trip to the restroom. The Bitch was at the refrigerator pouring a couple glasses of wine.

Oh great. There must be a last minute rush. Just when I was so happy to have the day over and not have to work with her for another week.

"I have an emergency," The Bitch said.

Emergency? What kind of emergency happens on a Sunday night at 11:45 p.m. that requires two glasses of wine?

I walked out to the sales floor, and noticed a woman in a spa robe and slippers. She was rushing around the store, commenting that she needed to find something to wear for dinner tonight. Yeah, that definitely constitutes an emergency. Just out of the spa, and you decide you need something new to wear for the evening. And, isn't 11:45 p.m. a little late for dinner, even in this town?

As The Bitch went about her business helping the customer select only the most expensive items we carried, I noticed that there were quite a few other people swarming the store, too. Wearing suits. But, none of them were shopping. Polly was in the stockroom doing paperwork so I just observed. Finally, one of them approached me, speaking low as if sharing a secret.

"Bedbugs," she said.

Her nametag indicated that she was a hotel executive. I now assumed that the rest of them were as well.

"Bedbugs?" I repeated.

"Yes, bedbugs," she said. "It's really a shame how it happened. The nanny was playing with the baby on the bed when she noticed the bugs crawling over the baby. Luckily, the parents were very nice about it. But, of course, we had to upgrade them to a two-bedroom penthouse." She leaned in closer to add emphasis to the next line. "And the funny thing is, the room they were in had just been cleared for reuse from bedbug cleaning."

"Wow, that's terrible! How did that happen?"

"I don't know, but someone is definitely going to be fired over this. She had been shopping the last few days and had over $10,000 worth of new purchases from our stores alone that we had to confiscate."

Ouch! Sometimes The Shop at Positano is simply the casino executives' way to treat their high rollers. Other times, it's a life saver.

I really didn't bother helping the customer because The Bitch was. And, because the items would be comped, I didn't expect that The Bitch would receive commission on company-owned merchandise. Silly me.

When I arrived for work the next day, Polly told me that they were there until nearly 3 a.m. helping the customer. She acquired approximately $5,000 worth of clothing and – yes – The Bitch would receive full commission.

I remember a similar incident when I worked at Sherborne. Three women – a mother and two daughters – came up to the lingerie counter wearing their swimsuits saying they had to buy some underwear ASAP. Turns out they were staying at Positano, and the cleaning staff had discovered they had bedbugs while the ladies were at the pool.

Bedbugs are not something you would expect to find at an exclusive high-end resort such as Positano. But, that's now two instances I heard about this place. Positano caters extensively to international high rollers, and I guess one downfall of that is bedbugs. It must be a relatively common occurrence since they keep an exterminator on staff just for that.

The sad part of bedbugs is that everything has to be confiscated: all your clothes, your handbag, your personal possessions, everything except your money and your ID. That really sucks if you brought your favorite dress to wear for a special occasion at this special hotel, but those are the rules. Depending on your perceived stature, the hotel will reimburse you for your trouble. The ladies I met at Sherborne received $1,500 each for clothing. The lady last night would receive several thousand dollars' worth of clothing for herself, her nanny and the baby.

"Bedbugs! How disgusting. Remind me never to stay at Positano," Gizzi said when I called her to share the news about our unwelcome hotel guests.

"Well, it really can happen anywhere," I reminded her. "I've read about people buying brand new mattresses for their homes that were infested with bedbugs."

"But, the Positano! They have such a stellar reputation, five stars and all. I guess those reviewers had infestation-free rooms. I can't imagine!"

"I think it's from the $99 room nights. You never know what the riff-raff will bring in!"

Gizzi finally laughed. No, there's nothing funny about bedbugs, but there is something funny about the riff-raff rooming at Positano.

"They have an exterminator on staff, sweetie? That must be some extreme case of bedbugs!"

"That's what the casino executive told me, and they rarely lie."

We both had a good laugh over that one.

"Isn't there a way to stop it?" Gizzi asked. "I mean, I've luckily never experienced them myself, but it would seem there has to be an effective solution to this, rather than just chemicals. I'd hate to be in a room that had been recently treated. That has to be a nuclear waste site."

"I suspect we could microwave guests' luggage when they arrive. That might solve the problem! Lord knows what it will do to their hair gel!"

It was nice to have such a lighthearted talk with Gizzi. It seems lately all we talk about is how to make my life better. Sometimes, I just want to chit-chat.

"So, what's new with you, Giz?"

Now I heard it, the long inhale of tar and nicotine.

"Well, Jean-Louis says he wants to get serious."

"Jean-Louis? That's fantastic, Giz! You two must have really hit it off. You've let him hang around a long time."

"It's actually only been about six months, but he has been far more attentive and reliable than others I've dated. I just wasn't ready for the serious talk yet. I mean, I'm still young. I have a couple of years to have fun before I hear my baby clock ticking."

"Babies! Gizzi, you never talk about having babies! He must be the one!!!"

"The one. The one for now. I don't know. I usually kick them to the curb by six months, but Jean-Louis is still here. Maybe he can put up with my shit and that's enough reason to have the serious talk."

"So…how's the sex?"

Gizzi rarely shared such details, but if he was a keeper, I needed to know what was so special about him. Usually, if the sex is good, you can work through the rest of the problems.

"Well, he's French, you know, so he's either fantastic in bed or his ego is so big he convinces you otherwise. Either way, you're somehow satisfied."

Spoken like a true diplomatic salesperson.

"How's his company doing?"

Jean-Louis was the founder of a high tech startup. Gizzi had expected I would apply for the marketing director position at his company ages ago because she felt it would be something special. I just wasn't feeling it but I guess she was!

"It's actually doing very well, so well in fact, he's been turning down buyout offers. He wants the company to hit some revenue targets before he considers offers, but it's a delicate balance of taking the money while you're hot versus waiting too long and having too many players in your field. The way he handles his technology is so different, it may just be a matter of time before others latch onto his system. I keep telling him to take the money and run. Then we could have the world's most lavish wedding."

I couldn't believe what I was hearing.

"Wedding? Giz! There's so much you haven't told me!"

I kind of felt slighted. After all, we'd been the best of friends for years.

"Oh, don't get your knickers in a knot, sweetie. This is all just champagne talk. And by that I mean, these are the types of conversations we have after several glasses of champagne and it does the talking!"

"OK, fine, but promise me you'll let me know the nanosecond you get engaged."

"No worries, Diana. I'll text you a photo of the ring! But don't hold your breath. Trust me. It will be quite some time before we get to that stage."

"Well, when you do, I have a great attorney who can help you with your prenup."

Gizzi started to choke on her cigarette smoke.

"Sorry, doll. No prenup. If we marry, we're both in it all the way."

Gizzi always had this strength about her when it came to relationships, and a good head on her shoulders about life in general. Oh, how I envied her.

"Awesome! Good for you. That's what I'll do next time, too. Not that I have anything to worry about at the moment. No assets to protect here!"

"You'll get there, Diana. I know it's been rough, but things will get better. They have to!"

That's what I needed. Some kind words of encouragement from my dear friend.

"Sorry, Giz, I have to hop in the shower. Positano awaits!"

"OK, sweetie, but stay away from those nasty bedbugs!"

"Trust me, Giz. Bedbugs are the least of my worries."

"Ta!"

"Ta."

Dear Diary,

Is it really wrong for me to think of myself outside of high tech? Is it wrong to view retail as an alternative? Should I just get a job in management and go on from there? What do I really want to do with my life? I know Gizzi didn't mention it in our talk, but just having a conversation with her brings the topic to the forefront of my mind. Things are tough but they will get better. Gizzi knows that and so do I. The question is, what do I want to do with my life?

So many of my friends have left technology and moved into other industries. Several have become realtors or mortgage brokers and are quite happy. Another works in hotels. One friend designs and builds furniture. Another is a stay-at-home mom and two or three others own vineyards. Hell, even Chris is now out of tech and into restaurants.

I so felt that technology was to be my home for a very long time. The money was good, and let's face it, technology will be part of our lives from now till the end of time. It seemed like a really good field to be in. That's why I snatched up my first technology job right out of college. But, lately, the doors don't seem to be opening for me, perhaps because my heart just isn't in it anymore. Maybe it never really was. It was just a good experience that paid well and allowed me to travel the world on someone else's dime.

So, life goes on. Every day I get up, put on my uniform, and drive to work. I keep searching for that which is the real me, but it hasn't shown itself yet. Someday, I know,

I'll meet a really nice guy again. We'll marry, and build a nice home and family together. I'll move out of retail, and into my destined field, whatever that might be. Until that someday comes, my search continues.

More tomorrow!

All my heart,

Diana

Casino Shenanigans

{ TWENTY-SEVEN }

"Shit!"

Just what I don't need today – a traffic jam. Now that UpTown – the new behemoth project next to Positano, with a casino, hotel and huge shopping mall – is getting close to its grand opening, the construction traffic on the way to the Positano employee parking garage is a nightmare. And, if I hadn't spent so much time binge watching some stupid show, I wouldn't be running late. But I did, and I am, so I'd better run.

Slowly, the traffic crept forward, and finally, I found a parking space. I ran the long distance to the employee entrance, and at first hardly noticed all the police cars in front. A lot of employees were hanging around outside, too, which was unusual.

"I can't believe he got away with it for so long. What a genius!"

"Genius? What an idiot. He knew he'd get caught eventually, and now he'll be spending the rest of his life in jail. How genius is that?"

"I don't know. But you have to give him credit, he had a lot of cojones."

I overheard the comments as I made my way toward the door. Just as I approached, two police officers were escorting a young man in his late 20s away in handcuffs. A round of applause broke out. From the sound of things, I didn't know if people were happy this man was finally caught or supportive of whatever efforts he did that now made him famous. I didn't have time to find out, and strolled into the building.

I made my way down the long, long, long tunnel that takes you to the main employee area. I was just about to enter the satellite cage to get my bank when I noticed another policeman coming around the corner. Then, another. And, another. And, they had some company.

The first man was dressed in chef whites, and looked a bit familiar. Hadn't I seen him on TV? I think he has a show on cable. Hmm, he's wearing handcuffs, so that can't be good. Behind him were an older man in a suit, a younger man in a suit, a nicely dressed young woman and three cocktail waitresses, all wearing those tight silver bracelets. I'd never seen anything like this before, and unfortunately, I didn't have time to investigate.

Once I got up to the store, nothing seemed to be different. Perhaps no one knew what was taking place just two floors down. I checked with Lily and Pamela, but neither had any idea what was happening. Hazel, the resident gossip from the gift shop, happened by while I was chatting with them, and she said she'd check it out and get back with us. I had no doubt that she would. Her husband is a supervisor in baccarat and between the two of them, they pretty much could find out anything.

On cue, one hour later, Hazel came skipping into the store. "You're never gonna believe this! It's totally crazy!"

Lily was at lunch, so Pamela and I had the pleasure of Hazel's company.

"What up?" I asked. My ability to hold intelligent conversation dwindled by the day.

"Well, you know the first guy that was taken out in handcuffs? He's an employee. Or, was."

"I thought I heard he was a high roller."

"In a sense, he was. But in a very unique way."

Hazel let out one of her sneezy chuckles that we all hated but Hazel wouldn't be Hazel without it. She looked up and just missed Pamela and me rolling our eyes, and recovered our attention.

"You see, this guy, Jason, was a gambler of the legendary kind. He worked the system in a way we only wish we could."

Can you just get on with it Hazel? Otherwise, we'll be here all night just on the one prisoner. We have seven more to go.

"Jason worked in the main cashier cage. Every day on his lunch hour, he would 'borrow' $30,000 and go and play."

Pamela and I were both confused, but Pamela piped up.

"You mean he worked in the main cage and took money from there every day? He should have been caught the first day."

"Ah, but that's the beauty of his system. He played during lunch, then put the money back when his lunch hour was over."

"OK, wait a minute," I said. "He borrowed it, played, then put it back. Every day. And never got caught. And no one recognized him. And they didn't have it on camera."

Hazel was now doing one of her sneeze chortles again, with drool dripping down onto her uniform covered with remnants of today's lunch.

"That's right. That's exactly what he did."

"And how long did this go on?" I asked.

"Oh, for two and a half years," Hazel proudly declared.

Two and a half years? Impossible! We work in an industry with the most advanced security measures. Surely, someone must have had an idea what was going on long before today. And, no one recognized him? Impossible, I say.

Pamela was in as much disbelief as me.

"Hazel, that just can't be. The main cage gives money to all the table games, all the cocktail waitresses. Someone must have recognized him. And what happened when he lost?"

"That's the most intriguing thing," Hazel crooned. "He was on such a big winning streak, that he would take what he won and pocket that, then put the money he borrowed back in the till after lunch. He was listed as a high roller, and stayed in the villas many times. He got comped in one weekend more than we make in an entire year."

Well, so much for the company policy of not having a player's card.

"I still find that hard to believe," I said, "but how did he get caught?"

"Turns out, he hit a losing streak. When he couldn't put the money back in the till, he came up short and they arrested him. A very smart plan, as long as he was winning."

We were interrupted by a casino host guiding a very drunk and fragrant guest toward us. She smelled like she belonged in an old, dank alley in a very old city, not a five star resort hotel.

"Excuse me, could you help us?" the casino host said.

Pamela was brave and stepped forward. I'd never experienced anything like this before, so I wasn't sure of the protocol.

"How can I help?" Pamela, as professional as ever, approached the host.

"Thank you, Pamela. Ms. Smith has had a little accident while playing slots. Do you think you might be able to find her some new clothes?"

A little accident? She relieved herself all over herself, and then some. I think there's a trail all the way back to her chair. And, Smith, huh? I wonder whose identity we're trying to protect here. And, why the new clothes? Why can't they just take her up to her room to change?

"Ms. Smith, so nice to meet you. Please follow me to a fitting room and I'll find you a beautiful new outfit."

Pamela led the guest to a fitting room, and came out rolling her eyes and holding her nose.

Lily came out from the office. She could smell the lovely eau de Urination, and she started laughing.

"Ah, the poker tour's in town, so I guess we have another one."

"What are you talking about?" I asked Lily, never sure if she would answer or even if I should believe what she says.

"When poker players are heavy into a game, they don't want to give up their seats, so they just pee all over themselves. That's why the maintenance guys are always recovering the seat cushions downstairs. Then they come in here to buy clean clothes."

Yuk! Thank goodness we don't broadcast the tour in smell-a-vision.

The casino host was now laughing, too.

"No, Lily, Ms. Smith is just drunk."

"Are you sure?" Lily asked.

"Yep," I responded. "Just drunk. Drunk as a skunk."

"Can I please finish my story?" Hazel cried.

She needed total attention from everyone at all times. I pitied her husband. However, I did want to know what happened to the chef and the others.

"OK, so getting on with my story. That was Chef Vito you saw downstairs. And the general manager, the hostess, three cocktail waitresses and the night manager from Florenzia."

Florenzia was the most expensive restaurant in the hotel, where dinner for two starts at $1,200.

"What's the deal with them?" I asked.

"Well, turns out, they had their own little scheme going for the last year or so. They were stealing guest credit card information and had a massive identity theft ring going. There were so many whales that ate there, I can only imagine the information they stole. Now that they've been arrested, I'm sure it will cost the hotel at least hundreds of thousands of dollars in court costs. So, the next time you see Chef Vito on television, it will be from a jail cell. Maybe he could start a whole new series, Cooking for Inmates."

Another sneezing chortle, and I was about to throw up.

Pamela came rushing out from the fitting rooms and headed toward a phone. She was white as a sheet and looked like she was about to lose her lunch.

"She just created a lake back there. I have to call for someone to clean it up."

Hazel could see that she would have to fight too hard for our attention, so she sulked off to the gift shop and got back to work.

I turned to the casino host who was now chatting with Lily, trying to decide what to do with our customer.

"So, is this Ms. Smith someone we should know?" I asked.

I thought I might as well be nosy, since sitting on the sidelines doesn't seem to be getting me anywhere.

"Yes, that's Anna Edwards."

"Anna Edwards? What movies has she been in?"

Lily was a bit more up to speed than I was.

"That's Anna Edwards! Are you serious? Oh, my goodness. I wouldn't have believed it if someone else told me."

"OK, who's Anna Edwards?" I asked again, totally at a loss.

Lily and the host looked at me like I lived on another planet. Lily clarified her identity for me.

"Anna Edwards is Positano's CEO Clinton Edward's daughter."

"Oh."

I should know these things.

"Yes, that's what happens when you have a manipulative, cold-hearted, hard-nosed asshole for a father," the casino host piped in.

Pamela came back from the fitting room, looking a bit worse for the wear. She was always the picture of grace, but she definitely seemed a little worn.

A whispered, "Help!" was all she could muster.

The casino host whipped out her cell phone, and made a quick call.

"I just called for her car. Her driver will take her home. I don't want her father to see her like this."

Quicker than you can say air freshener, the host had grabbed a Positano robe from the gift shop next door, wrapped Ms. Smith in it, and guided her out of the store.

"Well, it's customers like that that keep us in business," Lily laughed as she headed back to her office.

Dear Diary,

I've been checking into business school programs. I mean, no matter what I end up doing in the future, having an MBA certainly should open doors. Nearly everyone I know has one. I have to admit, I sometimes felt inferior at client meetings just because I was the only person in the room without an MBA. It had nothing to do with being the only female in many of those executive team meetings.

I had started my studies at a great school in the Bay Area when I worked in Silicon Valley, but once I began traveling as a consultant, I quit. I just couldn't handle all the hours, the travel and trying to adjust my schedule to make it back to class, since attendance was a big part of this MBA program. Just like a good personal relationship, it wasn't meant to be for me at the time.

I could restart that program, but it would mean weekly travel to Cali to attend classes. Plus, I'd be paying out of my own pocket, and the school is just slightly below outrageous when it comes to tuition costs. Student loans? Sure, but do I want that burden right now? I have no clue how I'll utilize my degree so I'm not sure when I'll get a job. I have to know who I want to become first.

I've looked at everything from online programs to UCLA, which at least is a lot closer than San Jose though not any cheaper than my previous university. They have an amazing business school and part of the reason you attend a B-school like UCLA's Anderson is that you'll meet incredible people you'll probably keep in touch with the rest of your life.

An online program won't give me those contacts, but it is less expensive though still over $2,000/mo. I could do the course work at three in the morning if I wanted to, which is definitely an advantage. However, it will take me at least two years to complete the entire course of study, even though I can transfer credits. Where will I be in my life at that time?

Sure, there are several well-known success stories who don't even have a bachelor's degree. Bill Gates comes to mind. But, he had a plan and a vision. I'm still looking for the right map. I just hope by the time I find it, I won't need bifocals!

More tomorrow!

All my heart,

Diana

Economic Downturn

{ TWENTY-EIGHT }

"Did you read your love note?" I asked Claire when I got onto the sales floor.

"What are you talking about?" she asked. "I didn't have anything in my folder when I came in."

"Well, it's in there now."

I made my way to the front counter to bank into a register, and waited to get her reaction.

The love note, this time, was a copy of our individual productivity reports, along with handwritten comments – all negative, of course – from Lily. It's one form of the dreaded Add-A-Note. We're supposed to receive the productivity reports weekly, but we hadn't seen them in months because Lily's just been too lazy to do them. They list our weekly, month-to-date and year-to-date sales, as well as our sales per hour and units per transaction. We're expected to sell at least $100 per hour on average, and two units per transaction, which isn't hard to do when we actually have customers.

Claire left her hallowed place behind the counter to go in the stockroom and check her folder. She so rarely leaves her spot that I'm amazed she's able to make the number of sales that she does. It's as if she expects all the customers will come to her.

In a matter of moments, Claire was back on the floor. Her face was beet red, and you could tell she was upset because she slammed the stockroom door, which is hard to do. When Sophia saw how mad Claire was, she ran into the stockroom to get her own love note.

"What the hell is management thinking? I know I didn't make my sales goal. Neither did anyone else. It's been so slow for months now. And this is supposed to motivate me?"

Claire was livid. She started pacing back and forth behind the counter.

Sophia came out with the note in her hand, waving it in the air.

"This is bullshit! It's an outrage! I'm going to take this home and have my dog defecate on it. That's what I think of this!"

Sophia went off to her own corner to sulk. Luckily, or unluckily, there were no customers in the store at the time, so they weren't being exposed to our internal matters.

I could tell Claire was taking this personally.

"What am I supposed to do? It's not my fault we don't have any customers. The economy sucks! No one is shopping, at least not here."

Claire threw the love note on the counter and looked at me with her big puppy dog eyes.

"Well, knowing what I know from business, this probably wasn't Lily's idea. I suspect it was from someone above her who thinks all we're doing is standing around all day and letting the customers get away."

I didn't have much to offer, but hopefully it would calm Claire down enough until I could do my own research to find out why, all of a sudden when business is down, we're getting these nasty notes in our files.

"Lily really has no clue what goes on here, and neither do her bosses," Claire related. "Lily's hardly ever here, and certainly not on the sales floor. And her bosses haven't been in the store for more than five minutes in the last year. They have no idea how we're struggling."

It's true. Lily, who I once thought could be my mentor, plays hooky more times from this place than I can count. She goes out, gets massively drunk, and calls in sick. Or, if she manages to come into work, she wears herself out so she actually does get sick. She's hoping to get a promotion, so this note must be to kiss up to someone above her.

Sophia reappeared from her personal pacing party.

"This is bullshit. I'm going to find Lily and tell her how I feel."

Sophia went storming into the back room to find Lily. We waited to hear the shrieking but alas, all was quiet.

Sophia came back, folded up her love note, put it in her pocket, and said absolutely nothing. A lone customer walked through the door, and Sophia practically attacked her. While she was busy with the customer, Lily came out of her office, handbag on her shoulder. She was obviously going home.

"I'm outta here, gals," she smiled at us. "I planned to leave early today, so if anyone comes by looking for me, I'm out comparison shopping."

That was soooo like Lily. Not only was she leaving early. Not only was she running out of here before we could confront her about our little love notes. We had to lie for her on top of it. Yeah, great mentor.

Claire couldn't take it anymore. She started to count out her bank.

"I'm going home. If this is what the company thinks of me, of all the years that I've put in here, slaving for them, then they can shove it. I'm going to have a nice hot bubble bath and a rather large martini. I'll see you tomorrow."

And, off she went.

Lester came back from lunch, and Sophia and I decided to pick his brain a little bit about the love notes. After all, he and Lily were friends. They always talked, but mostly about what Lester hears from the employees. He tells her everything. There are no secrets with Lester.

We're not sure if it's because he doesn't like us, or because he thinks that we're beneath him. He was used to working in haute couture in New York before he moved here to be with his boyfriend, and now he's stuck with us. I think he expected more of Positano, based on its reputation, but he's been disappointed ever since he arrived.

"What's the deal with the love notes?" I asked. "Lily really knows how to demotivate the staff, doesn't she?"

Lester seemed a bit taken aback by the comment.

"Demotivate? Why, darling, it was simply meant to motivate all of you. Productivity is down, you know."

Sometimes Lester can side just a little bit too much with the boss.

"Of course we know productivity is down. It's reflected in our paychecks. You think we like what we're bringing home nowadays?"

Sophia was still upset. I had no idea what transpired between her and Lily, but she was mad to the core.

Lester was unfazed.

"We just wanted to make sure that everyone knows what their goals are. Maybe that will help to bring up sales."

We had no idea what the store sales were, to determine where we stood in comparison. Lily used to post the store goal and year-to-date sales on the white board near the time clock every day, but it's been about eight months since we've seen those numbers. We're certain the store is down significantly compared to last year, but no one except for Lily knows exactly how much.

I wasn't impressed with the excuse. I'd been in business for too long to believe this story.

"So, what is the company doing to promote the store, to bring in customers? If we had some foot traffic, we might actually have a chance at some sales."

"Well, I'm glad you brought that up. We *are* going to be making a few changes here. First of all, we'll be adding two new sales people to the staff."

"What!"

Sophia and I were in shock. True, the company doesn't pay us anything unless we sell, so it's no big deal for them to add more staff. Still, we weren't supporting ourselves as it was. Adding two more people wasn't going to make it any better. Now I know how The Witch felt. Although…it could just be a ruse to light a fire under us to work harder.

"Looking at the numbers, we just want to make sure that all the customers are being serviced."

"What customers!"

We still couldn't believe what we were hearing.

Lester seemed to relish the fact that he was breaking the news to us.

"Yes, not only are we worried that all the customers are being serviced, we thought the additional staff would make everyone more aggressive, and we'd see the numbers improve."

What a backass way of handling a bad economy. Since management is rarely on the floor, they manage by numbers and numbers alone. They don't realize that it might be hours before a customer even walks through the door. It's not our fault, but as far as management is concerned, we're responsible. It's not just at Positano; this is simply rampant in retail. Sad but true.

"What makes you think that this is an appropriate solution?"

I just had to ask, even though I knew the answer will be totally contrived.

I'd been through this once before and unfortunately, it's happening again. Previously, I was a consultant and now I work in straight commission sales. I'm in another job that has absolutely no security. And, this one has yahoos for management. Why do I do this to myself?

"I'm glad you asked. See, when we analyze what's going on at each shift, there's always one person that's selling at least three times the amount of the other people on the shift. That tells us that everyone isn't working as hard as they can. So, either your numbers improve, or you're out of here in six pay periods."

He's got to be joking.

"Lester, the reason one person has better numbers than the rest is that one person always steals all the customers. Then, she's unable to service them properly, so the rest of us are helping her customers while she's getting the credit. Management is aware of the problem but refuses to take action. In fact, management supports the situation. When the one salesperson can't service the customers, she calls management in to help while we're just standing around. If she can't take care of her customers, then she should relinquish them to us. But, management doesn't seem to care."

We knew who we were talking about, so there was no need to mention Jazzy or The Bitch's name.

"Diana, dear, if you were aggressive enough, you wouldn't lose the customers to another salesperson. You really should re-think your sales strategy. And, management feels that since this is a competitive work environment that you girls should be able to resolve these issues on your own. It's not up to Lily, Polly or me to settle these disputes."

"So, Positano believes that it's OK for two or three salespeople to chase after a customer. That's the type of image the company wants to portray?"

I just couldn't believe what I was hearing.

"Hey, whatever works. As long as the customer is serviced and the numbers go up."

Since I had Lester's ear, and I knew everything I said would go straight to Lily, I figured I might as well just let it all out.

"You know, I have other issues with this whole love note thing. I've been here nearly a year, and not once has management spoken with me to ask if there's anything they can do to help make me a better salesperson. Nor have they asked for any ideas to help improve the store, the inventory mix, or business in general. There are no store meetings except for those provided by vendors which are few and far between, and absolutely no communication from management to us unless it's negative, and even then, just like the love notes, it's written down and put in our folder without any warning. What kind of shit is that?"

"As long as you work here, that's the kind of shit you'll get. You're hired to be retail salespeople, not CEO's, Diana. Deal with it."

And with that, Lester headed to his office.

Dear Diary,

I wonder if I should freeze my eggs.

Having children has never been a top priority in my life,
but so many things are happening that I must give it
some thought, and I want to do so before my eggs have
shriveled and died.

First off, I'm not the same person I was just a few years
ago. I have to admit, if I met the right guy, I would consider having children. Then they could grow up with
Aunti Helen and Uncle Gabe and their cousins, Grace
and Justin. Now that I'm around my niece and nephew
more often, it makes me wonder what my own children
would be like.

Then, there's Gizzi and Wonderman. I call him that because it's a wonder Gizzi has let him hang around for as
long as she has. Even she mentioned having kids! If it's
on Gizzi's mind, then it's definitely something I should
be thinking about.

But, the icing on the cake was an e-vite I received to Tarek
and Krissie's baby shower. I don't know if it was their
10th anniversary celebration a couple of years ago that ig-
nited the spark, or all of us just getting older, but after so
many years of just enjoying each other's company, even
they decided to take the plunge.

Now, of course I'm not going. First of all, I can't believe
I was even invited! Somehow, someone forgot to cull the
list. Secondly, I can't afford it. Hell, I can't even afford a
gift for their new offspring. But, worst of all, this baby

shower will be a lot like a class reunion, and we all know that you only attend if you have something to brag about.

I'm not convinced I'll ever have children. I don't even know if I enjoy the thought of being pregnant. I just don't want to have any regrets. From what I can determine, it's at least as expensive as B-school to freeze my eggs, so I have a tough choice to make here. If only I could take out a student loan for that.

More tomorrow!

All my heart,

Diana

The Bitch is Gone

{ TWENTY-NINE }

It was another Sunday night. Another exciting shift with my favorite co-worker. I made my way out onto the sales floor and banked into a register. I looked around, but I didn't see her. The Bitch usually arrived early for her shift, so I was surprised that she wasn't there.

"Is The Bitch here?" I asked no one in particular.

"She was but she left," said Pamela.

That was odd.

"She left? What happened?"

"I don't know. She was in the stockroom ready to clock in when Lily said she had to tell her something important in private. The next thing we knew, she ran out of here in tears. Hopefully, her Mom is OK. That would be terrible if something happened to her Mom. She's going home next week for a month to see her."

Pamela actually spoke with The Bitch, so she had all the trivial details of her personal life. From my perspective, she was going to be gone for a month and I was elated.

"So, am I closing alone or is someone coming in?"

Right then, Polly arrived and said it was just her and me on the floor tonight. She seemed a bit shook-up, but it doesn't take much to rattle her nerves. She was BFFs with The Bitch, so if something happened to her family, I'm sure Polly would be concerned.

The day crew went home, and I have to admit, it was one of the most peaceful Sunday evenings I'd had in months. It only took one beer to fall asleep instead of two.

The next day when I arrived at work, the atmosphere was a bit different. I could tell that the normal and abnormal cliques were conversing in corners of the store, but The Bitch still wasn't around and no one could tell me what was going on with her. I mean, I'm really sorry if something happened to a member of her family. I'm not that cruel of a person. Still, working with her has been hell. And, she hasn't always been known to follow policy when she helped her customers.

A week went by, then two weeks, and no new schedules materialized. We wanted to see if her name was taken off the schedule. That might indicate that she was terminated. Or, if she was on an LOA, the schedule would indicate such. Since she was already planning to be away for five weeks, her shifts were covered. No responses from management, no new schedules. Nothing.

The entire staff was speculating about what had happened. Only management had the answers we sought but no one was talking. We weren't taking up a collection as we normally do when someone has a death in the family, so that was a good sign. However, things were just too quiet regarding The Bitch. Polly certainly had the 411 but she wasn't sharing.

Finally, after about six weeks, bits and pieces of info started to trickle out. We finally got new schedules, and her name was gone. It still didn't mean she was terminated. She might have quit to be with her family.

Then, Pamela received a phone call from a very angry male customer. Polly was on her lunch break, and all the other managers were gone for the day, so Pamela took down the information and promised to give it to Polly. When she hung up the phone, she looked like the Cheshire cat. What she didn't know was that this was only the tip of the iceberg.

The caller was the boyfriend of one of The Bitch's regular customers. She'd been in the store just a few days before The Bitch's odd disappearance. The boyfriend purchased a number of expensive items for his girlfriend, which was a common occurrence. They were in town on average once a month, so his girlfriend had quite a fabulous wardrobe from our store.

However, this visit was different. The day after he made the purchase, his girlfriend came back to Positano. She had a bag of returns with her, and The Bitch didn't seem to be too upset. After all, she'd lose the commission on the sale. The girlfriend started looking around the store, and before you know it, she was in the fitting room trying on more clothes.

I was on the sales floor by myself, helping other customers, so I didn't really pay attention to what she was doing. I did notice that she had spent quite a bit of time in the fitting room speaking with the customer, but since she was here every month, I'm certain they developed some sort of weird friendship. The two of them finally came up to the register, and The Bitch rang the return as one transaction, with the new purchases on another. I thought nothing of this, again, since I assumed that the return would credit the boyfriend's card and the new purchase would go on hers.

Silly me. The returns were credited to his card, but the purchases were also charged to his account. Gee, that sounds like credit card fraud to me. Turns out, she'd done this a number of times in the past, and he didn't seem to mind. However, this time the girlfriend purchased over $12,000 of new items! And, golly gee, they were breaking up.

All returns had to be signed by a manager, so The Bitch was covering her butt. When Polly signed the return, that's all she saw. There was no indication of the additional purchases because it was rung on a separate ticket. Very ingenious.

The Bitch had quite a little business going with women from her home country. They'd come in with their boyfriends, and she would add one or two things to each sale. Rarely did the boyfriends complain. In fact, until this particular one blew up in her face, The Bitch had been trouble-free in this regard. Now, it finally caught up with her.

But that wasn't the only activity The Bitch participated in. Hear tell, she also had a number of escorts as her customers. When the men would purchase outfits for the ladies of the evening, The Bitch would throw in an extra item or two without charge. She also tried to get the men to pay in cash. Then, the day after the escort's activities were complete, she would bring the clothing back and return it. We'd refund the purchase, body-odored, perfumed, cigarette smelling and all. When the escorts got their money, they would split it half with The Bitch. So, her sideline income was nearly as good as her legitimate take.

However, the icing on the cake was Cami. Cami was a cocktail waitress whose long legs and long blonde hair attracted the eyes of many a high roller. Cami was often called in by the marketing department to entertain the troops, so to speak. There were a handful of super high rollers who demanded Cami's presence whenever they were in town.

Cami always made sure her name was on the room to purchase food and beverages. However, the register screen in our store didn't indicate that she was limited to those categories. Whenever she was called into duty, she made her way to the store to get a new outfit. Since the casino was utilizing her talents, they overlooked the charge on the customer's bill and comped the purchase.

One day, Cami got really upset at one of her guests. She'd been used and abused by him for a number of visits, and she finally had enough. She told him she was going shopping while he played poker, and shop she did. She made her rounds through all the designer boutiques, then settled into the Shop at Positano.

While she looked somewhat familiar to us, we just couldn't place her. The Bitch, on the other hand, knew exactly who she was. She'd helped her several times in the past. The Bitch had one of the biggest sales of her life - $15,000. She checked with the front desk, and Cami's name was on the room for purchasing, so management approved the sale.

Cami had all the packages delivered to the bell desk, and when her shopping spree was complete, she hired a limo to take her and her goodies away. On the way home, she stopped by the post office and shipped all her packages to Italy, to a friend. She then went home to change, headed for the airport, and took a late night flight to Rome.

The next day, the proverbial shit hit the fan. The high roller was upset, not only that she had purchased over $70,000 worth of clothing, but that she had also taken money from his room. She was gone, the clothes were gone, and no one knew where she was. And, since there was no way to track the packages from the post office, she was free and clear, roaming the countryside in Italy. While Cami will probably never be allowed back into this country, it's amazing that The Bitch wasn't deported for her part in all the activities.

Polly said security had been watching The Bitch for several months, but everything she did appeared to be legitimate, so they didn't have anything to pin on her. However, once the first guy complained, a barrage of complaints filled the store, and The Bitch's file was as thick as the U.S. tax code.

Dear Diary,

Well, at least someone is moving on with her life. How nice to be young and free and have zero financial responsibilities!

In the middle of our shift last night, after all of our co-workers had gone home and Polly was doing paper-work in the office, Lynn told me she just accepted a new position with another company. She starts in two months when they finish the buildout for their new store. She'd been complaining for some time now about how she was throwing her life away at Positano and that there was a brighter future for her, she just had to find it.

Well, she did.

"I have a college degree, you know," Lynn would tell me – nearly every shift we worked together. "Why would I waste it in such a shithole like Positano? I was promised certain things with this company that prompted me to move to Las Vegas, but they'll never happen. I want to be a buyer but Positano doesn't see it that way. I've spoken with the buyers. They've each been here over 20 years, in sales for most of that time. I'm not about to wait for 15 years before I can fulfill my dream. I'm outta here!"

Well, more power to ya, Lynn. I would remind her I, too, have a college degree, coupled with some irreplaceable experience marketing in the consumer electronics indus-try, and extensive worldwide travel, but her only reaction was, "Then what the hell are you doing here? Get your ass out there and put all that experience to work."

From the mouth of babes…

Don't get me wrong. I'm happy for Lynn, though I can't express it as I've been sworn to secrecy until her day of departure. She's pretty sure Lily won't let her work her entire notice so she's going to tell her the day before she leaves. Lily won't care.

But it's that assertiveness, that devil-may-care attitude that Lynn has that I'm so jealous of. I used to be like that. That's how I got to California in the first place! I graduated and packed my bags, heading for parts hitherto unknown to me. But now…

Why is it that when we get older, we stifle that naiveté that allows us to do things like Lynn – jump ship without regard to the consequences? Sure, I could probably do that, too, if I was willing to sleep on a floor in an apartment with seven other roommates. But I can't. I've matured.

I, too, have a college degree. I, too, have dreams of a better future. I, too, cannot wait to leave Positano behind for greener pastures – and I'm referring to the almighty dollar here – that await me. (I can't believe how much I focus on money nowadays.) I know there's a divine plan at work. It's my destiny. We each have our own. I just hope mine drops in my lap pretty soon because my brain is not doing a very good job of locating it!

Ah, more mature and more philosophical, too!

More tomorrow!

All my heart,

Diana

What a Pleasant Surprise!

{ THIRTY }

"My, what a beautiful ring you have. What type of stone is it?"

I approached the customer because I couldn't believe the size and beauty of her engagement ring. It was the perfect yellow color, with a bit of champagne tinge. A large pear shape, surrounded by small diamonds, on a diamond band. Amazing! I do see some spectacular jewelry in this store, but this was over the top beautiful.

"Why, thank you. It's a Canary diamond. I just love it!"

"A Canary diamond! I thought that's what it might be, but I've been wrong a few times in the past and I didn't want to embarrass myself. The more I see the colored diamonds the more I love them. I'd like to have a pink or purple one when I marry."

Finish the thought, Diana. When you marry a wonderful man who treats you like the queen that you deserve to be, after that last wretch of a man you were with.

"My, what would you know about diamonds? Although, I totally agree."

Great. Another condescending little bitch, just like the rest of the customers.

"For the longest time, I was insistent upon a white diamond, but my husband really likes the colored stones, so he convinced me. He's from Europe and he likes to be different. I'm so glad he persuaded me to go with this diamond. I couldn't be happier!"

Inside, I rolled my eyes. Some of these women think that just because their men are from Europe that they are more cultured and are purveyors of finer goods than Americans. I beg to differ, especially after my own personal odyssey with Chris. Whatever.

"So, what can I help you with?" I asked, biting my tongue.

I followed the customer around the store, holding her selections. She was quick to choose, so she was either in a hurry or knew what she was looking for. We went through all the racks of every high-end designer. Tops, pants, skirts – she selected it all. I prayed she was not a lulu wasting my time and actually planned to buy something.

Before long, we had a fitting room filled to the brim with nearly every designer piece of clothing we had in her size. She was tall and slender, not quite model thin, but certainly shapely. A size 2 or 4 overall, although she did have enhancements, like that's a shock to see in this town. Her auburn hair was a striking contrast to her deep green eyes, and she had an absolutely perfect complexion for someone in her early 30s. Yep, she was full of money. Money kept her looking good. I'd love to meet her European husband. Maybe he has a brother for me.

"Where are you visiting from?"

"Oh, we live here. We just finished a meeting with the developers of UpTown to talk about the space we're leasing."

"Are you a retailer?"

"No, I'm in real estate. I was helping to broker a deal."

"Some exciting new designer store coming to town?"

Like this city needs another designer boutique as badly as it needs another poker room.

"I really can't say. It will open when the development opens, but until then, mums the word. Sorry!"

She seemed to be in a hurry, rushing through the clothes, so I didn't pursue the line of questioning. I'd like to know if there are more options for me so I can get out of this prison, but she didn't seem like the type that I could push for more details.

"My husband should be here shortly. We're running late for dinner. If you see a handsome man out there looking a bit lost, send him in, please!"

I left the customer to her business for a bit, and put some of her rejects back on the racks. I knocked on her fitting room door and asked if she needed anything else. She opened the door and let me in. She was nearly dressed and ready to go.

"Sorry to leave you such a mess, but I really must get ready for dinner."

There were clothes everywhere – on the floor, on the chair, hanging from the doorknob – everywhere but on a hanger.

"I'll take all of these, but the rest just didn't work out."

She piled about 20 items in my hands. Hmm, a pretty good sale. Maybe I'll be able to pay my rent this month.

"Hey, baby, are you ready?" the voice boomed from outside the door.

It was an unmistakable voice, a very distinct accent, but it really wasn't possible. I must be dreaming, right?

"We don't want to be late for dinner. This is an important meeting for me, you know."

Omigod. Omigod. It's him. Chris. It can't be. But it is. What am I supposed to do? This is obviously slut wife, the real estate agent he left me for. And, I can't let him see me like this, slave to the obnoxious rich, in my attractive wine-colored polyester uniform. Maybe I can find one of the other girls to ring for me, as long as he doesn't hang out near the fitting rooms. That's it. I'll slip into the stockroom and someone else can ring.

"Honey, I'm just getting dressed. I'll send the girl out with my things. Can you pay for me? It will save time."

Girl. Girl! GIRL! She'll send the GIRL out with her things! I'm the GIRL! How rude is that! I'll take the sale, but the two of them can shove their black credit cards up their asses!

"OK, I'll wait here."

Shit! Well, this is one nightmare I never thought of before, but now I'll be certain to dream it every night for the next five years. I grabbed her selections, turned around, opened the door, and fifty shades of red later, took a deep breath so I could face the music.

"Diana."

Slut wife was behind me.

"You know her, honey?"

"Yes, I do."

Slut wife was a bit bewildered why her husband would know the sales GIRL at the women's boutique at Positano.

"Oh, did" – she turned to read the name on my badge – "Diana interview for you at the restaurant? I don't recall her."

"No, dear. Diana and I were married for a short time. You remember, don't you?"

Slut wife gave a nerve-rattling chuckle that I felt to my bones.

"Why, yes, how could I forget the name? Your parents have a dog named Diana. Chris, she's positively darling. I'll bet she loved to dress you. I, on the other hand, prefer to undress you."

She put her arm around Chris's shoulders, flashing her enormous Canary diamond in my face, giving him a little nibble on the neck. War on, bitch, but you can have him.

"Diana, I had no idea you were working as a sales girl. You really must get your life together."

"I actually quite enjoy the boutique. I'm thinking of opening one of my own, and I thought the experience would do me good. Besides, I love the discount."

Just then Jazzy walked by. Never one to keep her nose out of someone else's business, she piped in, "Oh, Diana, lovey, you know we don't get any discount here. This company's so damn cheap, we're lucky we have toilet paper."

Thanks for that visual, Jazzy. Just keep embarrassing me, why don't you.

And, embarrass she did. In typical Jazzy fashion, she grabbed slut wife's arm and started pawing it as she spoke.

"Don't mind Diana. She's a little crazy since her husband dumped her for some hot realtor. She's been a bit delusional ever since."

Just then. Just as I was about to crawl into the woodwork. Just when I couldn't turn any more shades of red. Just when I lost all potential for regaining my composure and saving myself from this situation, an angel of mercy swept through the stockroom door. I could swear the heavens above opened and shone their glorious light upon me. Pamela, dear, dear Pamela, gracefully as ever glided past slut wife, arms outstretched, and took the merchandise from me.

"I'll ring these for you, hon. You have a call in back."

And, just like that, I was saved. How she knew I needed help. How she knew Jazzy was humiliating me beyond recognition, I have no idea. I was just grateful for her intervention.

"Oh, thanks, Pamela. Excuse me."

And just as gracefully as Pamela exited the stockroom door, I entered. I knew Pamela would control Jazzy and quickly dispense with my customers. Once I knew I was a safe distance from the door and they couldn't hear me, I collapsed against a shoe shelf and sobbed. My body quaked in anger and frustration, but I knew Chris was right. I really needed to get my life together. This just isn't right for me. I'm better than this. I hate when he's right.

Funny thing is, I really did have a phone call.

Dear Diary,

I can't believe how much my life – no, I've – changed over the last few years. I went from living a single, happy, prosperous life in California, to being a divorced retail salesperson living paycheck to paycheck. I thought life was supposed to get better as we got older. However, I think there are a lot more people in my current predicament than in my dream life, if it's any consolation.

I've set a goal – September 15. By that date, I will have a better job. Maybe even the start of a career. I chose that date because that is my anniversary date at Positano, which means I'm entitled to one week's vacation. Whoop-de-doo! At this stage of the game, you take what you can get. If I plan it right, I'll have one week to finalize the start of my new life, albeit at minimum wage. But, if I don't need to take the time off, I'll at least be entitled to one week of additional pay when I leave.

So, that begs the question. What am I leaving to? I've decided time and again to live in Las Vegas so I can be with my family. Like Suze Orman says, people first. I live in a city that caters to tourists so my career options are very different than what I had in Silicon Valley. Of course, there's a whole city here that needs far more than cocktail waitresses and valet parkers. I just have to figure out where I fit into this glorious town.

I might have had an easier time with all of this if I had a detailed plan for post-college graduation. I fell into the find-a-job syndrome, taking my business degree with me to the first company that offered a decent salary in a warm locale. I was very lucky – no, blessed – in that I fell into one opportunity after another that afforded me an amazing lifestyle and worldwide travel at others' expense. Although I was never drawn to the technology industry in the first place, I just assumed those good times would continue. I mean, look at Gizzi! But, she's doing what she loves and had a plan from the start.

I, on the other hand, am lost and confused. I want a job where I can control my environment and use my creativity and management skills. Can someone please tell me what that is? Helen keeps suggesting I take on teaching. With a bit of schooling, I can have my teaching certificate and my summers off, far less costly than B-school. Plus, the school district is so short of teachers right now, they'll actually pay for me to get my teaching certificate. And, they have a pretty good pension plan. Retirement! Yikes! Now I sound like my Dad! Not a bad option, but I think teaching needs to be a passion, not a job. Of course, I've never tried it and I did enjoy holding forth at training sessions as a consultant, so I'll keep it on the list.

There's always retail management, or at least a job at a higher volume store for the time being, but it's still not what I consider my future. I'll check into my options after a nap. I think I've had enough to deal with for one day.

More tomorrow!

All my heart,

Diana

Where Do I Go from Here?

{ THIRTY-ONE }

"Diana, we've talked about this before. Why don't you just move back to California?"

My dear friend, Gizzi, was in town on an unexpected business trip. She was my mystery caller when Pamela angelically saved me from Chris and slut wife. If ever I needed a good friend and a martini, tonight was the night. It was a chance for me to get away from the drama at Positano, and a chance for a little social outing.

However, it seemed odd she would suddenly appear in Vegas without some notice. I checked her left hand. Still no sparkler even though I know Jean-Louis is still in the picture. I thought, perhaps, she wanted to share her good news with me in person. Perhaps not.

"At least you'd have your friends around and there are a lot more opportunities to consult in California than there are in Sin City."

I took a long, slow sip of my martini.

"I can't tell you how much I miss California, Giz, but it's just not feasible. And, honestly, I haven't been in touch with hardly anyone in California aside from you, ever since the whole Tarek debacle. But I have family here. After living away from them for so many years, it's really great to spend time with Helen and Gabe and their kids. They grow so fast!"

Gizzi looked at me understandingly and nodded in agreement.

"Well, it is nice to have family around, sweetie. Especially once you get remarried and have kids. I grew up in San Jose and I couldn't imagine leaving. My whole family is there."

Gizzi took a sip of her martini topped off with a drag off her cigarette.

"So what are your career options here? You can't keep doing what you're doing."

We'd discussed this topic over and over. Hadn't Gizzi heard the saying, beating a dead horse?

"I don't know. I've been stumped since Chris and I broke up. I really want to be near my family, but I still have to make a living. I guess I could cocktail waitress if I got a boob job, but I wouldn't really be using my skills and education."

"Silicon. Silicone. What's the difference? Men can't tell!"

Gizzi and I laughed. That was a running joke in our industry. Guaranteed, some female somewhere said it at least once a day.

"I thought about maybe going back for my MBA. UCLA has a great program, and if I found a job in L.A., maybe I could split my time between SoCal and here. But in reality, it's just wishful thinking. I'd be so busy, I'd rarely come back so that blows the whole family situation. Then, there's the money thing."

"What money thing?"

"Uh, like the fact that I don't have any?"

"And whose fault is that, Diana? I know you. You're a risk taker. It's so unlike you to succumb to your situation like you have."

I felt a little put off by Gizzi's comments. Here I am struggling and she's acting more like a parent than a friend.

"This coming from Ms. VP of Sales! Things worked out for you so far, Giz, and I'm really happy for you, but…"

Gizzi glared at me.

"What do you mean 'so far'?"

I glared right back at her and we both burst out laughing. Gizzi realized she needed to try a different approach. It was the salesperson inside her. What did she have to do to make the sale?

"Well, you could take out a student loan or borrow from your parents. They want you to succeed, don't they?"

"I could do that but B-school is so expensive. If I told my Mom how much money I needed, she would have me on a plane back to Detroit in no time. I have to figure out how to do this on my own, and I can't imagine taking on such huge student loans at this point in my life."

"But B-school would be great for you, Diana. An MBA is practically a requirement nowadays for any management position."

"I know, and it doesn't really matter what industry. A bachelor's degree just doesn't cut it anymore."

"I understand, sweetie. I'm so glad I got mine when I started my first job. I couldn't imagine going back to school now. First of all, I have no time and secondly, I'd have no patience for it. If you can do it, more power to you."

"You know, I've thought exactly the same thing. Will it really pay off for me? Will I ever recoup what I invest in the schooling?"

"Unfortunately, that's an unknown but going to a great school like UCLA should give you an advantage. Before you do that, what about researching local companies? I heard there's a burgeoning high tech community here downtown. Have you checked into that, maybe talk to some of the companies? That would get you out of retail and back on a normal career path."

I looked at Gizzi, not exactly sure how she would react when I answered.

"Yes, I've heard about it and there are some really cool companies. But, it's been so long I don't even know how to approach any of the founders any more. I seem to have lost my edge for that. And, the bigger issue is, I'm not sure that I'm even interested in technology at all. I feel like I'm destined to do something else. Fashion is fun but retail sucks. Maybe there's another avenue I could take."

"Fashion!" Gizzi gasped.

"Yes, fashion. It's just an option. I haven't really put a lot of thought into it."

"Diana, sweetie, you should have taken the job with Jean-Louis's company when it was available. You'd be in a much better place right now."

"Shoulda, woulda, coulda. I know it was a great opportunity but I'm just not feeling it. I'd have more money but I wouldn't be with my family. Besides, I kinda like it here."

Gizzi took a long drag from her cigarette, then turned and stared me down.

"I'm worried about you, kid. You don't look good."

I knew this was coming. Much as I tried to convince myself I hadn't changed, years of living in hell had changed me. I definitely couldn't hide it from Gizzi.

"Of course I don't look good, Giz. I'm exhausted. My entire body hurts. I can't afford the same lifestyle that I had in California. I just don't make that kind of money anymore. I'm too tired to work out and I can't afford a personal trainer. Hell, I can't even afford a gym membership! And, I'm getting older, too."

I knew my next comment would really hit home.

"I honestly can't remember the last time I had a facial, a wax or a massage. I get my hair done at a discount beauty salon. And, I don't shop at Whole Foods anymore. I buy whatever is on sale at the local grocer and I use a coupon. Yes, Gizzi, I've become a clipper."

I honestly thought that Gizzi was going to pass out from the shock. However, good friend that she is, she recovered quickly.

"Well, that's it then. You have to come back. Please come back to California where you can have a life. I just can't stand to see you this way. If you move I'm certain you'll be able to recharge your consultancy. I'll check with Jean-Louis. I'm sure he has friends who could use your help."

"Gizzi, let's be realistic about this. I've been trying to get new clients for years now and budgets still haven't opened up. You know yourself that people are keeping more and more in-house. The accounts aren't there like they used to be."

"OK, you don't have to consult. You could work in corporate. You have the experience."

"Sorry, Giz, but I feel like we have this exact conversation every few months. You know yourself that technology changes so fast that three or four years is a couple of lifetimes, and that's how long it's been since I've had any worthwhile experience. Besides, I'd have to have time and money to fly back to interview."

Gizzi let out a heavy sigh.

"Diana, honestly, I'm sick and tired of you complaining about the money thing. Where there's a will there's a way."

If Gizzi really wanted me to move back to California so badly, she could offer to front me the money and stay at her place, but I hadn't heard those words coming out of her mouth.

"You're tired of it! *I'm* tired of it! Try living it. I've been so cash-poor I've even contemplated becoming a phone sex actress just to make rent! You want me to move back to California but it cost me nearly $2,000 just to move across town, not including hooking up my utilities. I can't imagine what it would cost to move back to San Jose. Plus rent, plus surviving until someone finally hires me. It's just not feasible. I've been thinking about this for a long time, and I just don't have any answers."

"Fine. Then what about finding a job in PR or marketing here in Las Vegas."

"I've talked to several companies. I don't have any consumer experience, so they don't want me. If the economy was better, they might consider it. For the time being, they'd rather get a 22-year-old really cheap and train her right out of school. I have my own work habits and they won't necessarily mesh with the agency's culture. It's easier to train someone new."

I could see Gizzi was getting tired of my complaints but she pressed on.

"What about transferring into marketing with Positano? At least you would get some current experience. Then you could transfer to an agency or another company or even build a B2C consultancy here in a whole different industry. Or, you might surprise yourself, like it and stay. At least you'd be making more money."

"I've checked into that as well. I could start as a coordinator, which pays about $25,000 a year, less than I'm making now. Plus, they work crazy hours for an intense sleazebag. The only way I'd move up is to kill my boss."

Gizzi rolled her eyes and sighed.

"It sounds like you're just making excuses. I don't know how to help you. I feel like I'm wasting my breath."

"It might sound like excuses, but until I figure out what I want to do, I can't make any plans and I can't move forward. I have to admit, now that I've been away from technology for a while, I don't even think about it. And, the only stress I truly have at my job is making a decent paycheck, since it's all commission based. As long as I'm selling, my boss is sweet as can be. I don't bring work home. I don't work on projects at two in the morning. I'm not on a plane six months out of the year. It's kind of a relief.

"As for working in casino marketing, now that I've seen what goes on behind the scenes just in our little corner of the world, I wouldn't feel good promoting any casino, Positano or otherwise. Sure, I'm grateful for the tourists who visit our fine city, but I really need to get out of the casino and into something I can truly believe in. I want to help people in some way. I want to use my time more intelligently. I just don't know how."

Gizzi sat back, defeated.

I took a deep breath, then I hit Gizzi with the big one.

"I saw Chris today."

"You what?"

She shot up to full attention in her chair. I thought she might spill her martini but that would be sacrilege.

"I seem to have waited on his wife without knowing it. He came in to meet her." I started to cry. "It was so embarrassing."

"You waited on slut wife? Oh, you poor thing. And for him to see you like this! The ex always wants to be better off, not worse."

"Well, actually, I am better off. At least I have an income now. Last time I saw him I was unemployed and draining my retirement account."

We both managed a chuckle, though it was a poor attempt at one.

"It sounds like he's finally implementing his plan to open a restaurant here in town. Slut wife mentioned they were interviewing for staff. I haven't heard anything about it but she did mention something about UpTown."

Now it was Gizzi's turn for a deep breath.

"You're not hoping to hook back up with Chris, are you? I mean, that's not why you're staying here, is it?"

"No, of course not. I hadn't thought of him in ages. He's slime and I don't want anything to do with him. I do plan to spend the commission from the sale, however! I'm here for my family, and for some other unknown reason. Whatever it is, I know I'll find out in due time."

Gizzi took one last drag from her cigarette, snuffed it out, gulped the remnants of her martini and paid the check. I hate when people do that nowadays because they do it out of pity, not out of love. Unfortunately, I can't afford to argue right now, so I graciously accept their hospitality.

"I gotta go, sweetie. I have an early morning meeting. Let me know if you need my help, or if you just want someone to talk to. I'm here for you. You just need to tell me how I can help."

With that, she got up, gave me a hug, and ran off.

I sat at the table, nursing the last of my martini. It had been so long since I'd been out on a social basis, I just wanted to soak up the atmosphere a bit longer, and think about what just transpired.

I felt angry at the way Gizzi treated me, but deep down inside, I knew that the person I was angry with was myself. How long was I going to let this wonderful human being named Diana stay swallowed up in a cocoon – no, jail? I had to take some action, but I was too tired to think about it tonight.

I enjoyed the long, slow walk back to my car, taking in the Las Vegas Strip at night. So many casino resorts reminded me of the many places I've visited all around the world, and they're all within walking distance! The architecture, the lights, the energy – what a beautiful town this is. A little crazy for me sometimes, but still a lot of fun. People come to Las Vegas to fulfill their dreams every day. And, many of them make a very good living. I just have to discover my dream.

Dear Diary,

Sometimes you just don't know why someone is brought into your life at any given time. Take Pamela, for instance. She's a sweet gal but never in my wildest dreams could I imagine she'd save my life. And the smooth way she did it. I honestly don't know how I'll ever thank her.

Then there's Jazzy. Well…no words can describe how much I hate her for butting into my sale the way she did. Chris or no Chris, she should never have said a word. I don't insert myself into her conversations with customers. But, that's Jazzy.

And, Chris and slut wife. Why are they here? And, why now? What a horrible encounter. That look on Chris's face will forever be seared in my mind.

I had no details about their nuptials – nor would I want them – but they actually seemed happy together. In love. Well, la-de-da. I wonder what her prenup looks like, or how Magnus feels about her. At the very least, he spent far more on her ring than he did on mine. Although, she did mention that he talked her into it. He must have gotten it at a good price. That's soooo Chris.

But Gizzi. There's a special friend. She's been my absolute rock through these last few years. Sure, Helen is there for me, too, but in a different way. Gizzi understands how I want to change business minds on a worldwide stage. Helen is passionate about enticing second graders to read in order to change minds at a much earlier age, one on one. Each has her place in this world, but my inner guidance is more in alignment with Gizzi.

How intriguing that she would call right at the moment of my darkest despair. How did she know I needed to be rescued, and that Pamela, an angel of mercy, was there to help? Maybe it's that sales radar of hers. No wonder she's so successful.

As Helen always tells me, you're exactly where you're supposed to be at any given time. My only question is – why? What did this chance encounter with Chris and slut wife mean? Or, am I just tying up emotional loose ends?

Only time will tell.

More tomorrow!

All my heart,

Diana

UpTown

{ THIRTY-TWO }

As I walked in through the employee entrance, I was accosted by a bank of computers manned by employees wearing t-shirts that read, "Move on up to UpTown." I didn't think they were trying to sell condos to the employees, so I thought I'd stop and find out what all the excitement was about.

"Excuse me, but what's going on?" I asked.

The gal behind the counter looked at me like I was stupid.

"This? This is only the most exciting hiring event of the decade. We're taking applications from existing employees who want to work at UpTown. It opens in three months, you know."

Oh. I didn't realize just how soon it was, even after my slut wife encounter. I had thought about it as a potential on my 'Where do I go from here' list, but I'd been reading the paper and checking the job postings on the employee kiosks and I didn't see anything. So, I really had no idea what types of openings they had.

"That's awesome! What do you have available?"

It seemed like this could be a sign from the universe, so I might as well explore the possibilities.

"What department are you in?" she asked.

"I'm currently in retail, but I'd like to know about all the opportunities."

I mean, why limit myself to retail.

"I'm sorry, but we're only doing direct transfers right now. If there are any openings available afterwards, then we'll put them in the general postings."

Great. That means I'd still be stuck in retail.

"Well, then, what positions do you have in retail management?"

"Are you a manager now?"

No, I'm not. Please don't make me stay in sales.

"I'm not currently, but I have several years' experience. I'd like to be considered."

"Well, you can apply, but if you really want to transfer, I suggest you stay in sales."

What to do, what to do. I can stay where I am, but I know that the minute UpTown opens, Positano is going to be empty probably for the first year. That's just the way it works on The Strip. Tourists always want to go to the new resort. So, if I stay put, I'm sure my income will drop significantly.

I could make a lateral transfer to sales at UpTown, and it would probably be quite lucrative, but then I'm still in the same position as I am now. I'm a glorified cashier making a living with sore feet and an even sorer persona. I can try for management, but if I'm not accepted, then I've lost the opportunity to transfer altogether, and since UpTown is the latest and greatest, chances are a lot of managers are applying for those positions. OK, I'll go for sales.

"All right, you've convinced me. I'll try for a sales position."

UpTown will have 30 retail boutiques, so I had a lot of options. I decided to go for a position at Slick, a contemporary boutique that will carry nearly 200 designer brands. Sounds like fun to me!

I submitted my application, ran down the employee tunnel to get my bank, then up to the store.

When I arrived at The Shop at Positano, Lily was sitting at her desk. She gave me a nasty look when I came in, then returned to reading her email. I put my handbag away, then searched Lily's desk for her ID card so I could clock in. Lily handed me her card without looking at me, just staring straight ahead at her computer.

"So, you want to go to UpTown, do you?" she asked.

How could she know? I hadn't submitted my application but ten minutes ago. They don't tell your boss, do they? She must know someone down in HR.

"Uh, well, I hadn't really thought about it until I saw the job fair downstairs," I lied. "But, I think it might be fun."

Lily continued to stare at her screen.

"I would have been happy to recommend you if you hadn't gone behind my back, but since you did, I'm not sure what I'll do."

Everything here is about drama. Can't someone just step back and support a co-worker? Is it always about them? Lily is generally a bit weird, but even in her drunk-induced stupor she would agree that moving to UpTown was in my best interest. I guess when she feels betrayed, she shows her true colors. I don't feel I betrayed her, I was just looking out for my own future.

"Sorry, Lily, I just thought it might be fun to open a new property."

Lily turned around in her chair to look at me as she spoke.

"Of course it is."

Then, she went back to reading her emails.

I clocked in, put Lily's ID card back on the desk, and ran out onto the sales floor. I didn't know what Lily's problem was today. When she's having a bad day, she's really obnoxious to everyone, so they leave her alone. How mature is that. Teaching is sounding better and better. At least there I don't have to deal with management that has such mood swings. Education administrators are certainly more stable than Lily.

When I looked around the sales floor, everyone seemed to be in a bad mood. I didn't know who to approach first. Claire was in her usual spot, Julie was up near the front of the store, Sophia was in the back of the store near the lingerie, Jazzy was checking herself out in a mirror, and Lynn was cleaning the counter. Claire usually has the biggest mouth, so I thought I'd check in with her first. Plus, she's the closest.

"What's wrong with Lily? She's in a terrible mood," I said as I brushed past her to check into a register.

Claire looked at me with her signature glare, as if I should know what's going on.

"Didn't you hear? Lily requested a promotion to UpTown, and she was turned down. The slime assistant at the gift shop got it instead. Lily's devastated. She was planning to take all of us with her, but now we're stuck here."

OK, so I wish someone would have said something to me beforehand. Regardless, why are we all stuck here? If we have an opportunity to move to UpTown, why can't we pursue it?

"I don't understand the reasoning with that. Why do we have to stay at Positano, just because Lily didn't get the promotion?"

I'm sure that there's some stupid reason, but I need to know. In the meantime, the rest of the staff came around to participate in the conversation. No one invited them, but like bees to honey, or zombies to live flesh, they have to sink their own two cents into the conversation.

"Oh, lovey, you're so naïve," Jazzy started. "Lily is very strong about loyalty. She doesn't allow any dissension. I certainly hope you didn't apply at UpTown without her knowing or your days here are numbered."

"You really think so?"

I was stunned. She couldn't legally do that to someone on her staff, could she?

Sophia pushed Jazzy aside.

"Jazzy's just being melodramatic, Diana. Don't pay attention to her."

"I honestly don't know how she'll react if anyone decides to apply for a transfer. I guess we'll just have to wait and see. She's usually OK if you talk to her about it first. However, I'm not going to be the one to test the water."

Claire was never one to be risky, so her stance didn't surprise me.

I decided to spill.

"Well, actually, I already applied. Downstairs. When I came in. I didn't think it was such a big deal."

After their initial in-unison gasp, all the girls crept slowly away from me, clearly making the point that I had somehow done something wrong.

"You traitor," Jazzy said.

Traitor? Jazzy's calling *me* a traitor? Those are harsh words coming from someone who quit the company when the last megaresort opened, then came crawling back to Lily after she got fired. Gee, some managers are smart enough to clear the chaff from the wheat, but not this one.

I can't believe this. I'm working with the Seven Dysfunctional Dwarfs: Mopey, Bitchy, Sleazy, Ditzy, Skanky, Creepy and Loopy.

I ignored Jazzy's affront and asked, to no one in particular, how Lily could have known so quickly about my request for a transfer. Julie piped in.

"Oh, that's easy. As soon as you apply, an email is sent to your current boss. If she doesn't authorize the transfer or provide a positive recommendation, you're denied."

Oh great. My future lies in the hands of a hormonal ditz.

"But, that's stupid. You never want your boss to know that you're looking. I understand if they ask for a recommendation once you get an interview, but to notify them right off is nonsense."

Sophia shook her head.

"You're not telling me anything I don't know. I've been trying to transfer for months, but the system is so stupid, I'll be here forever."

Being naïve when it comes to this business, I had to ask, "What's so stupid about it? It seems pretty straightforward. The kiosks list available positions in the company, then you apply, you get an interview and you transfer, right?"

Everyone started laughing. Now I felt like the ditz.

"You haven't been here very long, lovey, so I don't expect you to understand," Jazzy said. "But look around you. Think about all the people you've met since you've been here. How many have been in their positions for years? Probably everyone. When was the last time you heard of anyone being transferred? Probably never."

"I don't understand. Why do they have these postings if no one gets transferred?"

It seems to me that your current employees would be your best bet for future openings. Promote from within, right? Maintain the culture, right? I just don't understand this whole system.

Julie tried to clarify it for me.

"Diana, once you've been hired, you might as well kiss your freedom of choice good-bye. When you apply for a posted position, you are stuck in a hell hole of technology. You can only apply for one position at a time, and unless the position is filled, the hiring manager releases your name or you're turned down, you can never apply for another position."

"And just try to get an interview!" smirked Sophia. "By the time you even find the hiring manager to try to talk to them in person, the position is filled. When they closed one of the boutiques at another hotel, the executives couldn't even get returned emails when they were trying to place the sales staff. It's useless. Once you're hired into a position, you are there for life."

"But I have a lot of experience besides retail, and I'd like to see about transferring to another position, or even to work in retail management."

Again, the dwarfs were roaring.

"Give it up, lovey," Jazzy said. "You're stuck with us forever."

Dear Diary,

It never ceases to amaze me how screwed up this multi-billion dollar company I work for is, yet somehow they continue to grow year over year. Certainly, longevity with a company is a benefit for the employees and provides stability for an organization, but when there is so much dysfunction and drama, something is wrong. The company culture is all screwed up but for some reason, the employees just accept it.

Maybe I'd worked in a small company/startup environment for so long, I don't really know what happens when companies reach those great heights of billion dollar revenues. Most companies I'd worked with were between the $5 million and $50 million mark, a far cry from Positano's parent company. Perhaps that's why I'm here, to learn how big business works. Or, to realize that I much prefer the small fry.

In actuality, I don't believe it's either of those. I think I'm just supposed to bide my time, let my brain rest, until my destiny reveals itself. That might not seem like I'm moving forward to some people, but I've grown to accept it. I want to be passionate about my next career move, so that might mean I'll have to try on several hats until I find the one that fits just right.

Change is all around me. Chris has moved on with slut wife, and will undoubtedly have a successful restaurant concept. I still admire how his mind works, even though, on a personal level, I didn't reap the benefits like slut wife obviously is.

Then, there's Helen and Gabe who picked up their family and moved out here to Vegas for new opportunities. They're both very happy with their decision and so am I. We're very different people, but we're family and I couldn't love them more.

Even Gizzi is moving forward with her life. She's not engaged yet, but I wouldn't be surprised to get a text any day now with the good news. She's vice president of sales and will certainly form a business with Jean-Louis sometime in the future, after they've wed. Yep, she's doing just fine.

I honestly have no idea what's happening with my former co-workers at Isabella's or Sherborne. Once I left, it was as if a door closed on those chapters of my life. I don't want to look backward, only forward.

Now, here I am at Positano, working with some of the rudest, meanest women I've ever met in my life. Sure, Lynn is cool but she'll off to her future soon, and Pamela is nice but she's been friends with Jazzy for so long, I have to question her sanity. I know there's no future for me with this company. I see that Positano door closing, ready to end another chapter of my life, knowing that I really won't care what happens to these women once I leave here. I hate to be so harsh but I'm just trying to be honest.

I'm excited to discover what the next chapter in my life holds. I feel as though someone above me has hands to keyboard, planning and plotting my next move, but I know better. It's up to me to take that next step. Baby steps, baby steps. I'll be enjoying my future soon enough!

More tomorrow!

All my heart,

Diana

Lotto Ladies

{ THIRTY-THREE }

"Are you watching that new television show about those folks who won the lottery?"

Oh, it's gonna be one of those nights. My skin crawled, my stomach was nauseous and I just wanted to hurl in her direction. I hated the nights I had to close with Jazzy, especially after the way she ruined me in front of Chris and slut wife. Life is hell enough as it is without dealing with Jazzy. And, now, she wants to make idle conversation. Can't she just go to her corner and pretend she has a timeout?

"Actually, I have seen the first few episodes. Pretty interesting, huh?"

I had to reply. Much as I hate her, it's just like working with the rest of this dysfunctional family. You despise them. You talk about them behind their backs. But, to their face, when it's just the two of you, you pretend that all is well.

"Excellent," Jazzy said, in her obnoxious fake British accent. "I have an idea."

Lord, please. Not one of Jazzy's ideas. No matter what she does, it annoys the hell out of me. Like when she gives you air kisses when she's leaving early. It's not that she's being gracious. She's really covering up for the fact that she left three fitting rooms full of clothes that need to be put away, and a stack of unsorted shoes. An idea from Jazzy is like being pegged by the Don, or tagged by Judas, a nightmare waiting to happen. My ears are burning already.

I started puttering around one of the displays, trying to signal to her that I was removing myself from the conversation without being rude. After all, we still had six more hours until the store closed and I was in no mood to argue with her or have her stress me out. But I could see Jazzy was not to be silenced tonight. She had a stick up her butt, and an amazing amount of energy. I relented.

"Oh, what idea is that?" I finally asked.

If only I could get my life together, like Chris suggested, I wouldn't have to spend countless hours with people like Jazzy.

"What do you think about starting a lottery club here?" she finally asked. "It will be like our own private investment club."

Well, I had to admit, a lottery club wasn't such a totally idiotic idea. I wouldn't use it as my first course of action regarding my future, but as a backup, it might just work. I don't want to be greedy. A cool $20 million or so would be sufficient. But, I could see how twisted Jazzy's mind was simply by thinking buying tickets would be an investment. There's no return unless we win.

I hated myself. Now I was sucked in. I have that problem. I'll work on it in my diaries.

"Sure, I might consider that. What are your thoughts?" I asked, hoping the conversation would really go nowhere but trying to be pleasant. I didn't want to have another work situation like I had with The Witch. I like to talk with my co-workers, particularly when there are no customers and the shift can drag oh-so-slowly.

Our discussion was momentarily delayed while a group of Japanese tourists made their way through the store. Positano has very strong ties to Japanese high rollers, and I suspected these were their spouses who shopped while their husbands played. The ladies purchased quite a few items from us, which made us very shiawase-na. We knew they wouldn't be returned tomorrow. They were going home tonight on a private jet. We had made our sales goal for the day, and it was still early. That took a lot of pressure off and lightened our moods significantly.

Once the customers left, I retreated to a corner of the store, rethinking my enthusiasm about the lottery group. I thought if I started straightening in this area, Jazzy might get the idea to start on the opposite side like we normally do. Tonight, however, she seemed to have an agenda, and was at my side in a matter of moments.

"Lovey, don't you want to hear the rest of my idea?"

Honestly, no, but what the hell.

"Sure. What do you have in mind?" I finally conceded.

Jazzy grabbed my arm like only Jazzy could, and led me to the back counter. She used her hands in an excited way as she spoke, and acted like she was selling me the world.

"Just think about it, dahling. Millions, just for us." Jazzy was really getting into this. "So many groups of people have won. We could be one of them!"

"Yes, yes we could," I agreed, pulling my arm away.

Just get on with it Jazzy. I have a store to straighten.

"We'll get the whole night crew together. Well, at least eight of us. If we each give five dollars a week, we can take advantage of the power of numbers. That gives us 40 chances a week to win!"

But, is that enough? I wondered. I'd heard of people who purchased hundreds of tickets and still lost. Plus, we had to drive to California or Arizona to get the tickets since Nevada doesn't participate in the lottery. Now, who was going to do that?

"Have you thought about who will buy the tickets?" I asked.

Maybe if I make it seem like it's really hard, she'll back off her idea.

"Oh, please, lovey, it's only 40 miles to the border. There's a store right on the state line that sells tickets. If there are eight of us, certainly someone should be off each week so we can take turns. It's really rather simple, lovey. It'll work."

That's true. It is only 40 miles to the border. However, in all the time I've lived here, I've never made that trip unless I was passing through on my way to LA. And I could probably count on one hand the number of times the other members of the night shift went there, too. It sounded so simple but you know there are obstacles to her plan.

"So, who do you think should be part of the group?"

Jazzy thought for a minute.

"Well, we would only allow people who can keep their mouth shut. We don't want anyone to know – at least not until we win! That automatically eliminates a few people."

Jazzy paused for a moment, grabbed my arm again, and with twinkling dollar signs in her eyes, said, "Just think, lovey. Think of that feeling. How great will it be for us to walk in as a group and say, 'I quit!' Can you imagine the joy, the happiness? Think about it, lovey. It's a perfect master plan. We deserve it. We all want out."

I had to admit it would be a great feeling. However, I now had ideas of my own.

"I really think it would be more fun to say that we just bought the store and all of you are fired."

Jazzy let out a shriek of laughter that I thought would bring security in from the hall.

"That's a fabulous idea, lovey. Let's do it!"

My, oh my, what am I getting myself into?

"OK, but I'm not so sure about this weekly thing. First of all, I don't think we'll be able to find someone to go to California every week to buy tickets. Plus, I think we need to have a larger dollar amount when we purchase. It just gives us more chances to win."

"Fine, lovey, fine. What do you suggest? Every other week? Monthly? I'm open. I just want to win. You're the business person here."

Well, Jazzy did have a point there, even if I had forgotten that on a daily basis for the last few years. Still, she has this subtle way of manipulating people and I was her current victim. I wondered what she really wanted me to do.

"I'll have to ponder this for a bit, but I think once a month should be fine. That gives us 160 chances each time. Those odds are better depending on the jackpot. But, we'll have a lot of things to figure out. Like, what do we do when we win just a few dollars? And, what if someone wants out of the group? Do we let the computer select the numbers or do we play the same sets of numbers every time? There are so many things we haven't discussed."

"Diana, you just type something up and we'll sign it. You probably have more experience with things like this than we do. We're just sales associates."

Bingo, there I am, totally sucked in. Before you know it, I'll be in charge of the whole affair, driving to buy the tickets each time. How does she do it, and why do I fall for it? But here we are, she's the master and I'm the slave. I really must find someone who can help me with this problem. Perhaps the company benefits cover therapy. The way this place operates, it should be a lifetime gift.

"Who are the eight people you're thinking about?"

"I've put a lot of thought into this. It would be you, me, Pamela, Tracey, Katrina and Emily from Genesis, Lynn and Polly. I think that would make a great group. Once we win, we'll be tied together for life."

Well, obviously Jazzy didn't know about Lynn's future plans and I wasn't about to break my oath. Surprise, surprise, considering how much Lynn adored Jazzy at one point. But that comment about being tied together for life, oy! I don't want to work with these people another day! How am I to spend the rest of my life as part of this winning group?

Well, Pamela and Lynn are sweet, but I can't believe that I'll stay in touch with them once I leave Positano, particularly since Lynn is already on her way out the door. Our friendships are just stops on the highway of life. And, I suspect, once we win, we really wouldn't have to see each other all that much. Or, at all for that matter. We'd have enough money to stay away from one another. Right now, however, I'm so desperate, it's a risk I'm willing to take. My how my life has changed.

Maybe I'm over-thinking here. Perhaps it won't be that bad.

"Do you really think that Polly would be interested? I mean, she is after all, the night manager. She's not even supposed to eat lunch with us."

"Ah, but that's the beauty of the plan, lovey. If she's involved, she can't tell us not to do it. And, what a tremendous hurt Lily will be in not only when we leave, but her trusted night manager as well. It's positively brilliant!"

Jazzy was really getting into this. She seemed to have it all worked out. I still had a lot of questions, and a bit of anxiety about the whole thing, but I didn't have much time to dwell on it.

Jazzy ran behind the counter and pulled out an empty white business size envelope. She reached in her pocket, pulled out a five dollar bill, and put it inside. She signed her name on top followed by $5 and the date, and with that scheming devilish smile, she handed it to me.

Now it was my turn. Is this how people get started on drugs? It seemed so sinister, yet offered a ray of hope. I had a choice to make. Join in and reap the potential rewards. Or, watch from the sidelines as everyone else in this hellhole celebrates while I keep hoping for a decent paycheck. I had so many reservations, but there wasn't time to think. This could prove to be a monumental decision of a lifetime.

I reluctantly pulled money from my pocket, placed it in the envelope, and signed my name under Jazzy's. That was it. Decision made. We were now the Lotto Ladies.

I kicked off my shoes, threw the breakfast burritos and hash brown sticks on the counter, cracked open a beer and took a long, cold gulp.

What has my life come to?

In the last few years, I'd gone from being a highly-paid high tech marketing consultant, married to the man I loved, moved to a town where I knew no one and expected to build a long and loving life with my husband to this mismatch of a life I now live.

Today, as I sit on my sofa, a sofa I purchased with the proceeds from the sale of the previous sofa that once held court in Chris's living room, I felt like a broken woman.

Am I really throwing my future to the lotto gods, potentially sharing the winnings with the likes of Jazzy?

I took another long gulp, reflecting on all those times Gizzi would take a drag from her cigarette, allowing her to think before she spoke.

I got up and went to my dresser. In the top drawer, buried under my unused special occasion lingerie was the little blue box that held my wedding ring. I opened the lid and the sparkling diamond hadn't lost its luster.

I could pawn it and perhaps use the proceeds to start over. Certainly it must be worth something.

I put it on my ring finger and admired it for a long time, recalling how I felt when the messenger brought the ring to my apartment in San Jose, how thrilled I was to know that Chris had a change of heart and finally wanted me. Me! Those feelings were now long gone.

I looked to the ceiling, blinking back tears, took off the ring, restoring it to its velvet chambers, closed the lid and put the box back in its burrow. I wasn't yet ready to accept the absolute end of that relationship, no matter how badly he hurt me. I'd feel like a failure.

I should have pawned the ring right after the divorce. Now, I struggle to find the inner strength to forgive myself and end that chapter of my life.

I changed into the comfiest pajamas I could find, went back into the living room, grabbed a notebook and pen and sat down with my beer.

I will not let the circumstances of my current situation get me down. I'm better than that.

I began to make a list of everything I was grateful for, promising myself I would read it daily and hopefully, add to it, until once again, I was living the life of my dreams.

1. *I am alive.*
2. *I am healthy.*
3. *I am a good person with a loving heart.*
4. *I have a nice, safe place to live in a city I've grown to love.*
5. *My family and friends are loving and supportive.*
6. *Helen, Gabe and the kids are now living nearby.*
7. *I am gainfully employed during some of the worst economic conditions in decades.*
8. *I am now smarter about my finances.*
9. *I rid myself of a toxic marriage to free myself to find the true love of my life.*
10. *My mind is strong, providing the foundation for creating new ideas for my future business success.*

As I finished jotting down the last item on my list, I fell asleep, content that I had already begun the journey to reclaim my life.

My favorite midnight snack went to waste, but it didn't matter. My life won't be wasted and that's more important to me than anything.

About the Author

Cindi R. Maciolek is entering the fiction world with the release of her first novel, **Destiny Drop**, part of **The Diana Diaries** series. The first three books in the series complete the initial story arc, with more books in the series to follow.

Divatiel: Reflections of a bird's companion, is a loving tribute to her fine feathered companion. Through the book, she reaches out to bird and animal lovers about the loving place pets have in our lives and the lessons they teach us.

Poetry and lyrics are a mainstay in Cindi's writing life. She loves to tell a story through rhyme. Her collection of poems published under the title, **Java Jems: 5 Minute Inspirations for Busy People**, both in book form and audio CD/mp3.

Cindi's first foray into the publishing world was the release of **The Basics of Buying Art**. It sold out its printing and is currently unavailable pending an update.

Cindi was a contributing writer to *Luxury Las Vegas Magazine* and *The Robb Report* for many years. She's also had articles published by *Delta Sky Magazine*, the *Old Farmer's Almanac* and syndicated by *The New York Times*.

Cindi was born and raised in Detroit, Michigan, an MSU Spartan for life – Go Green! She worked in high tech marketing and public relations in Silicon Valley and currently resides in Las Vegas, Nevada.

Her travels have taken her to 23 countries in North America, Europe and Asia and most of the United States.

Keep up-to-date with Cindi on her website at www.cindimaciolek.com. Book club questions are also available.

Acknowledgments

I am so very grateful for all the love and support I received during the development of **Destiny Drop**, far more than anyone realizes.

First off, I'm grateful to my family who dealt with my quite-often updates and lack of sleep as I plowed into the wee hours of the night to get this book done.

I'm so very thankful to my friends who took the time to read an earlier version and provide useful comments and opinions. I love you dearly, but you shall remain nameless lest you be interrogated by anxious fans to get the scoop on future releases.

Warmest thanks to Chuck, who nailed the cover on the first try and continues to impart his knowledge on a nearly daily basis, teaching and sharing with me over a vast array of subjects. You are amazing, Chuck, and I totally appreciate all the time and effort you put into everything you do.

Thank you to Glenn who took on the challenge of proofreading and for your many insightful comments and corrections. It was a joy!

Now, to my readers. There is a reason I was inspired to write these words, whether to entertain you or to guide you or just to acknowledge that these types of situations happen in real life and now others can feel your pain. Thank you for taking the time to follow Diana's journey.

www.ingramcontent.com/pod-product-compliance
Lightning Source LLC
Chambersburg PA
CBHW070204260626
47160CB00002B/441